'Look!' cried Scruff. 'Th

Ahead of the   gledy-
piggledy

When t   ped
out into th   s a
foreign vo   ad
wanted to k   ad legs and
hissed, revea   ooking fangs in its
open mouth.   or three bounds it was
on Maudlin, gripping him by the shoulders,
the head dipping to sink those sharp fangs
into the artery in his throat.

'Get it off! Get it off!' shrieked a hysterical
Maudlin . . .

GARRY KILWORTH

VAMPIRE VOLES
A WELKIN WEASELS ADVENTURE

CORGI BOOKS

VAMPIRE VOLES
A CORGI BOOK : 0 552 547050

First publication in Great Britain

PRINTING HISTORY
Corgi edition published 2002

1 3 5 7 9 10 8 6 4 2

Set in 11/12pt Palatino by
Phoenix Typesetting, Ilkley, West Yorkshire

Corgi Books are published by Transworld Publishers,
61–63 Uxbridge Road, London W5 5SA,
a division of The Random House Group Ltd,
in Australia by Random House Australia (Pty) Ltd,
20 Alfred Street, Milsons Point, Sydney, NSW 2061, Australia,
in New Zealand by Random House New Zealand Ltd,
18 Poland Road, Glenfield, Auckland 10, New Zealand
and in South Africa by Random House (Pty) Ltd,
Endulini, 5a Jubilee Road, Parktown 2193, South Africa

Made and printed in Great Britain by
Cox & Wyman Ltd, Reading, Berkshire

For Ellen

These are troubled times. But when have those words not been true? Most, if not all, times have their troubles. I know my weasel ancestor Bryony, who was an outlaw in the medieval era of my country of Welkin, thought her own century had its problems. In those olden days the stoats ruled absolute, with Prince Poynt at their head. Monty's ancestor, Sylver, and his band of weasels were hunted throughout the land, though later they became respected aristocrats, opposing the stoats through democratic means. Now at least we mustelids are all supposedly equal – and the humans run one side of the city of Muggidrear, while we mammals have our side to ourselves. Mayor Jeremy Poynt, having given up his royal status unlike his sister Sybil, carries on stoat traditions by making things as difficult for the weasels as possible, but we cope.

Ringing Roger, our beloved clocktower (blown up by Monty's anarchist cousin, Spindrick) is being rebuilt. It should soon be sending its chimes over the city of Muggidrear once more. Queen Varicose of Welkin, our human monarch (just six years of age) will be amused once that happens. It is said she misses the sound of Ringing Roger like anything. Maudlin will be pleased too. His good friend Scruff never carries a watch and relies on the great clock as his timepiece and is forever late for appointments these days.

Spindrick is out of jail now, a shortened sentence for good behaviour. He will be up to his old tricks again, I'm sure. Monty – that's Montegu Sylver, to give him his full name, my neighbour who loves nothing more than solving mysteries – saved the city last time, with the help of the sewer rats, but can he always out-wit his misguided cousin? Mayor Poynt is still running his Police Chief, Zacharias Falshed, ragged. It's my belief that Falshed has a 'thing' for the mayor's sister, Sybil. I could be wrong, but I don't think so. If the mayor ever suspects then our poor stoat chief of police will probably end up in debtor's prison after being sacked and made destitute.

Well, dear Journal, that's all for the time being. I'm tired after such a long day patching up mustelids in my surgery. Time to close my eyes.

CHAPTER ONE

A horrible scream rent the midnight air.

A well-dressed weasel, the Right Honourable Monty Sylver no less, stopped in his tracks and peered into the mist. He had been wandering along the embankment of the river Bronn, on the mammal side of Muggidrear city, after he and his friend had been to see the progress that had been made rebuilding Ringing Roger. The clocktower was now on its way back up to heaven, pointing like a stern stone claw towards the place in which celestial forests were waiting for all good weasels and stoats when they died.

'What was that?' cried Monty's companion, Bryony Bludd. 'It sounded like the cry of a stoat.'

Indeed, a moment later, out of the shadows of

a cobbled gaslit alley, staggered a jack stoat, clutching his throat. Neither Monty nor Bryony were fond of stoats, but they both immediately went to this creature's assistance.

By now the stoat had fallen into the gutter. He lay there groaning. When Monty turned him over, Bryony pulled the stoat's claws away to reveal his wounds. Underneath she found two monstrous, puffy-edged holes in the poor fellow's neck. His eyes bulged with terror. He clutched at Monty's collar, pulling him closer, before uttering one word: 'Vole!' he croaked. Then his head flopped back. He was dead.

'Vole?' repeated Monty, a puzzled expression on his furry brow. 'Surely this jack hasn't been attacked by a vole? They're such passive, simple creatures.'

'Let's get him to my surgery.'

'We'll need transport,' said Monty. 'He's too heavy for us to carry.'

At that moment a pawsom cab came out of the mist. The mouse between the shafts was an elderly, weary-looking creature in heavy blinkers. In contrast the driver was a sharp-faced individual in a cloth cap too large for his narrow head and a cloak with several folds. It seemed as if he were not going to stop, despite Monty's signal, so Bryony stepped out into the road. The mouse shied away from her. It came to a halt, even though the driver flicked the reins.

'What?' asked the driver, in a surly fashion. 'I'm on my way home.'

'You still have your flag up,' Monty pointed out.

'Forgot to take it in.'

'No you didn't,' argued Bryony. 'You just want to get to the stoat gentlemammals' clubs where you're likely to get a bigger tip. You're not interested in ordinary fares, are you? Well, let me tell you, weasel, the mayor is a good friend of mine. If you want to keep your pawsom cab licence, you'd better start obeying the rules.'

The weasel blew down his nose in contempt, but seemed ready to accept them as a fare now. However, when he saw them lift the stoat's body out of the shadows, he became obstructive again. 'Hey, you're not bringing that stiff into *my* cab. I don't want no stinkin' bodies in there. You find some other mug—'

'It's weasels like you,' fumed Bryony, 'who give other weasels a bad name.'

But by now they had the door open and had bundled the stoat inside. There was little the driver could do but wait until they had boarded themselves and then set off. He seemed to disappear inside his own hat, muttering about midnight weasels dragging corpses through the streets. Instead of heading for the address Bryony had given him, however, he took them to the nearest police station. It so happened that the chief of police, Zacharias Falshed, had called in that night to see how his minions were faring.

Once outside the building with the blue gas lamp burning, the weasel cab-driver jumped

11

down and ran inside. Falshed was standing by the sergeant's desk when the driver gasped, 'Got a couple of body-snatchers in me cab. Caught 'em red-pawed, I did. They was down by the river. Fair frightened the life out of me, coming out of the mist like that wiv the corpse of a rotten ol' stoat.'

Falshed stared at the becapped weasel sternly. 'You be careful who you call "rotten".' Then he ordered three constables to go outside and arrest the body-snatchers.

Monty and Bryony allowed themselves to be dragged into the police station. In front of Chief Falshed, however, Bryony gave way to her spleen. 'What's the meaning of this?' she demanded. 'Falshed! I might have guessed it would be you. What, has the mayor promised you some shiny new buttons if you arrest your quota of innocent victims this week? Get away from me, you oaf . . .' The last remark was addressed to a stoat constable who was trying to put pawcuffs on her forelimbs.

'Let them alone,' muttered Falshed. 'I'll deal with this. Now, Sylver, Bludd, how do you explain this?' He pointed dramatically at the body of the dead stoat, which had been lugged into the police station by the other two constables. They let it fall to the floor with a *flop*. The head hung to one side, the tongue poking out between two white fangs.

'We found it,' said Bryony, who was more used to dead bodies than others in the room.

'Oh, you just found it lying in the street. A likely story.'

'He died,' murmured Monty, more sensible that this had not so long since been a living, breathing mammal, 'right in front of our eyes.'

'So! You admit it! You killed him.'

'I didn't say we killed him, I said he died.'

'Of a heart attack, I suppose,' sneered Falshed.

'We don't know how he died,' replied Bryony. 'We were just taking the body back to my surgery to find that out. I need instruments to perform an autopsy. There are two puncture marks on his throat. Perhaps the cause of death has something to do with them. Just looking at the eyes, the pale tongue and the shrunken appearance of the pelt, I would say this stoat has been drained of blood.'

Falshed, the pawsom cab-driver and several policemammals let out a shocked gasp, stepping back and staring at the body.

'Well,' said Falshed, the wind taken out of his sails, 'I think we can deal with this, Jis Bludd. We have our own very good stoat vet. We'll let her decide whether he's been – been drained of blood or not. That's all. I suggest you go home now. We may, or may not,' he added in a sinister tone, 'be in contact with you. Don't leave the country. If we need a statement – which we shall – I'll send one of my constables round to obtain it.'

'Not at three o'clock in the morning, this time,' said Monty wearily. 'When I found that fountain pen beside a park bench I was roused from my sleep in the middle of the night to give a statement.'

'The law never sleeps,' said Falshed. 'We must use our time as we see fit.'

The cab-driver gave a little cough and shifted his cap on his head. 'Is there any reward?' he asked.

'For what?' cried Falshed, spinning round to face him.

'For turnin' these two in.'

'Get lost.'

The cab-driver looked indignant. 'Well, there's gratitude for you. You does your duty, and what do they say? *Get lost.* Last time I bring two body-snatchers in.' He stormed out of the police station.

Monty and Bryony made their way home to Breadoven Street. 'Where have you been?' said their landjill, Jis McFail, when they let themselves in the front door. 'It's past midnight.'

'Just for a walk along the river,' replied Monty. 'Please, Jis McFail, you shouldn't wait up for us. We're quite capable mammals, you know.'

'The river? There's all sorts of bad humours and vapours comin' up from the river at this time of night. It's a wonder you haven't both caught your deaths. Off you go, up to your rooms. I've put hot-water bottles in your beds.'

'Well, that really wasn't necessary—' began Bryony.

'Of course it was. Freezing out there.'

The pair of them climbed the stairs in a sub-dued mood. Monty said, 'I suppose we should talk about this in the morning.'

14

'I suppose we should,' replied Bryony. 'I – I just can't seem to get that horrible scream out of my head. Do you think he was stabbed in the throat? By a stiletto blade?'

'A double one, or twice?'

'Twice, I suppose.'

'It's possible. But it's not possible that he lost all that blood in the time it took to stagger out of the alley towards us. There'd be buckets of it.'

'*Vole* – what do you think he meant by that?'

'His attacker, I suppose,' said Monty. 'But as I said before, voles are such docile creatures. I just don't understand what's going on here. Perhaps the light of the day will help. Goodnight, Bryony.'

'Goodnight, Monty.'

They left the landing to go to their separate flats.

Once Monty was inside he picked up his chibouque – a long-stemmed pipe – and began sucking on the stem thoughtfully. He then reached into the pocket of his waistcoat and removed what looked like a few wisps of hair. These he had taken from the dead stoat's claws, without Bryony noticing. Turning up the flame of the gas lamp, he studied them and frowned. Then, getting up, he picked up his magnifying glass from the Queen Ogg writing desk. Again, he peered at the spray of hair. 'Not *Welkin* vole,' he murmured to himself. 'Foreign of some sort.'

He went to his bookshelves and, after a cursory glance, reached up and took down a large volume entitled, *Voles, Mice and Cattle*. He turned to an index entitled, 'Common and Rare Breeds'. Finally, he flicked to a page which was headed, 'Slattland Herds: the Transylvladia Saddleback'.

'Transylvladia . . .' Weasels are not fond of the written word and have great difficulty with reading, but Monty was one of those who worked hard at it. He found what he suspected. 'There you are, my beauty,' he murmured, looking at the picture and description of a Transylvladia Saddleback Vole. 'So that's where you come from.'

Satisfied, he put the hairs into a clean envelope, turned out the lamp, and went to bed.

Chapter Two

After a good breakfast of mouse-blood sausage and larks' eggs, Monty sat back in his chair to plough laboriously through *The Chimes*. He looked through the obituary column to see if anyone he knew had died recently. There was always the vague hope that he would see Mayor Poynt's name in that column; then he chastised himself for being uncharitable. Villain though the ermine mayor was, he did not deserve to make his way into the obituary column at his age.

It was while he was scanning the other pages for any mention of the strange death he had seen the previous evening that he heard a knock on his door. He got up and opened it to see his stoat friend Lord Hannover Haukin in a County Elleswhere Cricket Club blazer.

'Hello, what's-his-name,' said the young lord, stepping inside. 'Come to pay you a visit.'

'Good morning, my lord,' said Monty. 'Do come in.'

Lord Haukin let his monocle drop into his right paw, before answering in a faraway voice, 'Already in, old thing. Surprised you didn't notice that.' The stoat walked over to the breakfast tray and picked up a cold piece of toast and jam. He crunched into it. 'Got any tea? The crumbs get stuck in my throat otherwise.'

Monty poured out a cup of tea in the spare cup which Jis McFail always left for breakfast visitors. If it wasn't Lord Haukin, it would be Monty's valet, Scruff. Or Maudlin, his close companion. Or even Bryony, if she wasn't working at the surgery. (This morning she was, so Monty hadn't had a chance to discuss last night's events with her.)

'What are you doing in that awful blazer, my lord?' asked Monty.

'This?' Lord Haukin looked down at himself. 'Oh, *this*. Well, I've just been visiting that silly ermine—' by this he meant Mayor Jeremy Poynt, who never changed out of his white fur coat – 'and you know how he goes on about Fearsomeshire CC. I thought to forestall him with my County Elleswhere badge. I used to keep wicket for them, you know, until I broke my wrist.' He flexed the body part in question. 'Too

18

stiff now, for professional cricket. There you go. Any more toast?'

Monty rang a small bell and Jis McFail came huffing and puffing up the stairs with a fresh pot of tea and more toast.

'I say, you have got her well trained,' said Lord Haukin, after she had left them.

'I've been trying to train her *out* of it,' replied Monty, 'but she won't listen. Now I'm trying to be as much of a nuisance as possible, so that she gets fed up with coming and going. It's not working very well.'

'These old landjills, they think they've been put in this world to look after mammals. Mine is just as bad, really. Always knitting me mittens and tail-warmers and things. The other day she presented me with a knitted model of Whistleminster Palace. I ask you. Now I've got the thing on display in my library and it looks ghas'ly, I can tell you. Where were we? Oh, yes, thingamyjig and whodyamaflip. Can they help at all?'

'Help you what? Who?' asked Monty, as usual at a loss when in conversation with the young lord.

'Crates. You know, the lamplighter chappie and his friend, the watchmammal.'

'Scruff and Maudlin?'

'Those are the fellows. Good stout weasels, eh? Muscles of iron and heads of wood. Jolly willing types, eh, what?' Lord Haukin slammed his monocle into his other eye with a great flourish.

Now that they had established *who* it was just a matter of *what*. 'Crates?'

'Yes. Got some goods coming in from Slattland. Cricket pads. Tons of 'em. Hoping to make a killing in the import business. You know our pads are inferior – the ones we make – but Slattland has this special bark from the cork trees. Jolly spongy stuff. Takes the sting out of the ball, you know. Need someone to shift the crates from the docks. Thought your workweasel friends might just be right for it.'

'Well, I'm sure they won't mind.'

'Good. There's a shillin' or two in it for 'em.'

At that moment Scruff entered the room carrying a bundle of clothes. It might have been a pile of washing, except that it wasn't – it was the clothes that Monty was to wear that day. Monty winced, wondering, not for the first time, if he had been right to employ Scruff as his valet. The well-meaning (but often very dirty and untidy) Scruff had no idea how to treat a gentlemammal's wardrobe. He dumped the bundle at Monty's feet and said, 'Let's 'ave that dressing-gown off you, Jal Sylver. Up and at 'em.'

'I think I'll go to my bedroom to change,' said Monty stiffly. 'Er, Scruff, Lord Haukin has something to ask you.' He took the crumpled heap of clothes and went to dress in private before joining the other two again.

Scruff was beaming. 'Yep, your lordship, me 'n' Maudlin will sort out those crates for you, no worries. We'll get on to it right away. Ah, here's Jal Sylver back again.'

'If you're going down to Docklands this morning,' Monty said, 'I might join you for the

20

walk. I need some good air in my lungs. The city seems to be full of yellow smoke these days.'

'I'm off to bell-ringing practice,' said Lord Haukin. 'St Pompom's has got these new bells, you know. Steam-driven. Invented by Wm. Jott, of course. Instead of pulling on the ropes, which have been hung for humans rather than us mustelids, you jerk levers just like in a railway signal box. Much easier to ring the changes. We did a bob major the other day in just two hours, instead of the usual four. Not bad, eh?'

'Not bad at all, my lord,' said Scruff, not having the least idea what the stoat was on about. ''Spect you'll do even better today.'

'One can but hope.'

Scruff left just after Lord Haukin and immediately went round to Maudlin's lodgings, telling his friend to hire a wagon and a team of two yellow-necked mice. He then came back to the flat for Monty and the pair of them strode out towards Docklands, where Scruff enquired of the harbour-master the whereabouts of a ship called the *Mosquito*, which had a picture of the insect painted on her prow.

'The *Mosquito*?' muttered the harbour-master, a grey squirrel with a sorry-looking tail. He lifted his cap and scratched his head. 'I remember her all right. Yesterday. Came cruisin' up the river as smooth as you please – then crashed into the first wharf. When we boarded her there wasn't a solitary mammal to be found. Spooky it was. Just this cargo of crates in the hold. We towed her off the wharf – she was a wee bit damaged but not

21

enough to cause a leak. Now she's moored, seventh along from the end—'

'You mean she had no pilot?' asked Monty.

'Never asked for one. Had no captain, neither. Nor crew, nor passengers, nor visitors on board. Nobody. Place was as empty as a graveyard at midnight. Very strange. Can't get my dockers to go anywhere near it now. Can't blame 'em, can you?'

'So that's why Lord Haukin wanted us?' said Scruff cheerfully. 'Ah, here comes Maud with the mice-'n'-cart.'

Monty and Scruff climbed up on the cart and Maudlin flicked the reins. The two mice responded obediently, drawing the wagon along the edge of the dock until it came to the *Mosquito*.

Maudlin jumped down and looked at the ship in a puzzled way. 'Where is everyone?' he asked. 'Hasn't it been unloaded yet?'

'Ah, there's the thing, Maud,' replied Scruff, 'the ship's haunted, so no-one but us'll unload her.'

'Haunted?' Maudlin's head fur stood on end, making him look remarkably like a toilet brush without a handle. 'What do you mean, haunted?'

'It's a ghost ship,' replied Scruff with great satisfaction. 'No-one on board. Came glidin' up here all of its own accord, no-one steerin' it, no-one chuckin' out anchors. Lucky for us, otherwise we wouldn't have the work, would we? I mean, Lord Haukin wouldn't have had no need for us, if it weren't hexed.'

'I'm – I'm staying here,' stammered Maudlin. 'I'm loading the cart from here.'

"Course you're not. You got to help me,' As ever Scruff could not believe his friend was scared. 'Come on buddy,' he continued, grabbing Maudlin's upper limb. 'Let's get to it.'

Maudlin looked about him fearfully when Scruff ordered him to help with the hatch. 'Now the lid's off,' cried Scruff, 'you can see nuffink's down there but boxes. Long boxes.'

'They l-look l-like coffins,' muttered Maudlin.

'Cricket pads, his lordship said. That's what they are.' Scruff jumped down into the hold. 'Come on, give us a paw, Maud.'

It was clear that Maudlin was not going down into a dark hold at any price, so Monty put down his gloves and cane and joined Scruff. They each took an end of one of the oblong boxes and heaved it up onto the deck. Then Maudlin dragged it across to a clockwork derrick invented by Thos. Tempus Fugit, where he looped ropes around the crate and swung it up and over the side, and then down onto the wagon. The two yellow-necked mice waited patiently in the shafts, knowing that their job was to stand still for the moment.

'Flippin' heavy for cricket pads,' muttered a sweating Scruff, after a dozen crates had been shifted.

'I agree,' said Monty. Then he called to Maudlin, 'That's the last. Be careful with it—'

Just at that moment the clockwork motor on the derrick started to whirr at an alarming rate.

Maudlin had swung the crate up and out over the dockside, but now he jumped back, letting go of the control lever. There was a loud *twang* and the sound of a spring snapping. The line suddenly went slack and the last crate crashed down onto the dock, splitting open and spilling its contents all over the stone slabs.

The yellow-necked mice twitched and almost bolted, but Monty leapt down from the ship and soothed them with a calming voice. Then he stared at the mess. 'Earth,' he said. 'Plain earth.'

'Not cricket pads at all,' cried Maudlin. 'We've got the wrong crates.'

'There's only these down there,' said Scruff. He jumped down onto the dockside and pinched a bit of the earth between his claws, sniffing it. 'Grave earth,' he said. 'Comes from somebody's tomb, over there in Slattland. I know. I used to be a sexton. Dug most of the graves in Lowgate Cemetery, I have. I know the scent of grave earth when I sniff it. Got a sort of musty, corpsey smell to it. Sort of rotten-fleshy, dead-meaty odour—'

'All right, all right, we get the picture,' said Maudlin. 'Let's have a look at the others.'

They jimmied open the rest of the crates. Every one of them was filled with soil. Grave earth, Scruff insisted. It was a strange business, they all agreed. Why would anyone want to transport earth from tombs in Slattland, all the way to Welkin, which had its own? It didn't make sense. And where were Lord Haukin's cricket pads?

Just at that moment the bells of St Pompom's started ringing the changes. They started out fine,

24

but halfway through a peel they began getting faster and faster. There came the familiar sound of steam escaping from a fissure in an engine: a sort of hissing scream. Then a muffled explosion, a terrible clanking, and finally the three watchers witnessed a bell flying from a belfry and landing in the river, narrowly missing the rowing-boat of one Jaffer Silke, an otter who earned his living on the Bronn.

Jaffer looked up indignantly at several heads now poking out of the belltower of St Pompom's. He shook his paw at them. ''Ere,' he yelled, 'you watch where you're throwin' them bells. Go an' play ducks 'n' drakes somewheres else. Flippin' pranksters, I don't know what Muggidrear's comin' to these days . . .'

CHAPTER THREE

Mayor Jeremy Poynt was visiting the work-house. He was required by law to visit once every six months. He hated it. But Queen Varicose was said to take a very keen interest in workhouses. As stoats like the mayor knew, females of tender years always get bees in their bonnets about poor mammals, poor people, poor bees even. Poynt had to show himself or suffer the queen's wrath whenever he went to tea across the river. He enjoyed going to tea, eating cakes and drinking ale with humans. It made him feel important, and it was important to feel important.

The workhouse was a Varicosian institution.

As every poor weasel knew, it was the penultimate port of call, when you were down on your luck. The next and final port was the grave. If you were so poor you had to seek assistance from the parish council, you were forced by law to enter the workhouse. These places were dreaded by mammal paupers, who believed that if you went into one, you never came out. There was a graveyard attached, filled with hundreds of nameless pauper graves. And the daily routine within the workhouse was dreadful.

Roused from their straw mattresses at four o'clock in the morning, the paupers were made to clean out the grates and fireplaces, and then scrub the whole place from top to bottom. At 5.30 they got their breakfast: thin porridge which had been allowed to go cold. A cup of water and a stale crust of bread completed the meal. The paupers then went to their workstations, where they sewed, or sawed, or did whatever task had been allocated them, until lunch-time, when they received a bowl of gruel and a further few crusts of bread.

'Everybody happy?' cried the mayor as he entered the great hall, where lunch was in progress.

There was a long table running down the centre of the hall. On either side, close against the walls, were wooden benches. Mammals – mostly stringy-looking, patchy weasels, with one or two stoats, pine martens, polecats and others – were sitting on these benches supping from shallow wooden bowls. In reply to the mayor's question a collective moan went rippling down the two lines. One weasel actually stood up and raised his forelimb.

'Yes?' growled the mayor irritably. 'You have a question?'

'I was just going to say . . .' began the weasel timidly.

'Yes, yes, speak up. We all want to hear. We're all interested in this complaint of yours, however time-wasting and petty it is. We're all interested in drivel, aren't we?'

'It's – it's not a *complaint* exactly.'

'Praise, then?' said the mayor, brightening visibly. 'You wish to thank your mayor for the largesse you receive from the parish?'

'Not – not that, either.'

'What then? Come on, weasel, spit it out.' Poynt's white tail brushed the dirty floor behind him impatiently, becoming also very dirty in the process.

'Well, when the Princess Sybil was here last, she promised us some meat with our gruel.'

'*Meat?*' Poynt's face screwed into a mask of disbelief. He turned to the fat stoat cook, ladling out the gruel. 'Meat?'

The cook nodded slowly, as if to say, Yes, it's true, Mayor, even though it sounds like a great big fib.

The mayor gave a great big sigh. 'Ah, did she now? My sweet sister? The trouble is, her heart is bigger than my purse. You see, Princess Sybil is such a kind stoat that she can't bear to see

28

others in want. But the truth is, we can't afford it. Now *me* – I too would like to see meat on the tables, but then I'm an accountant. I have certificates to prove it. There's one hanging in my study at home. I know it's impossible, you see. There's – oh, I don't know – *seven* workhouses in Muggidrear alone, not counting the provinces. How could we ever afford to provide meat for all those establishments. You do understand?' The mayor smiled silkily. He was getting a little cold. Being in ermine all year round he was forever cold, and his fur was always getting dusty in places like this.

'Well,' said the weasel, who didn't really understand, 'I heard that mouse-meat was down in price. It said in *The Chimes* yesterday that even paupers could afford it now . . .'

'What are you doing reading the newspaper?' snapped Mayor Poynt. 'How can you afford newspapers?'

'I found one – it was left behind by a visitor.'

'*Stole* one, you mean? Beadle? Beadle?'

A stoat even fatter than the cook or Jeremy Poynt shuffled out of the shadows. 'Yes, Mayor?'

'I think there's someone who deserves to go without supper here, don't you? Someone who steals other mammals' property.'

'It was left behind – thrown away,' cried another weasel sitting nearby. 'They should be prosecuted for littering. My friend here should be rewarded for picking it up. Fat slugs like you should be thankful there's civic-minded weasels like him clearing up after them. Not giving us

29

abuse and talking about punishing us by with-holding our rights. It doesn't come out of *your* pocket. It's the parish that pays for us in here. I'll know who to vote for next time there's an election, won't I? Not for you, that's certain.'

The mayor almost exploded. 'Fat slugs like – who *is* this creature? How dare he speak to me like that?'

The beadle shuffled a few more steps forward. 'Name's Spindrick, yer honour.'

Mayor Poynt's eyes narrowed. 'Spindrick! I might have guessed. The bomber. The arsonist. The anarchist. Cousin of that brute weasel, Montegu Sylver. All the same, you weasels. Never grateful. Always whining about your lot. What are you doing in here, anyway? I thought I'd sent you to prison for blowing up Ringing Roger.'

'Out on probation,' smirked Spindrick. 'Working for a radical newspaper now. The *Daily Toiler*. Undercover work. Seeing what really goes on in the paupers' workhouses.'

'The *Daily Toilet*, more like,' thundered the mayor, suddenly very pleased with his wit. 'Well, it's rags like that which give our country a bad name. Did you know there's a deputation from Slattland here today, from Transylvladia, no less, who read in your so-called newspaper that foreign lemmings in their region are exploiting their workers? How do you think that reads? How do you think that fosters foreign trade?'

'Foreign trade! That just lines the pockets of

rich stoats like you! It doesn't do anything for us poor weasels.'

There was a murmur sweeping the benches. Mayor Poynt gave a sidelong glance at the thin, ragged weasels sitting there. Things could get ugly with someone like Spindrick stirring it up. The mayor began backing towards the doorway. 'You just watch your step, Spindrick Sylver. Just because the judge let you out on probation doesn't mean you can go around making up lies to print in your rag about mammals like me, your benefactor, your patron. You just watch—'

The mayor came to a sudden halt, just as he was about to bolt, bumping into someone who had crept up behind him. He spun round and raised his claw, ready to strike his attacker, only to find it was a very respected jill. 'Jis Bryony Bludd,' he gasped. 'What are you doing impeding my retreat?'

'Impeding your retreat?' said Bryony, for it was indeed she. 'I'm doing nothing of the sort. I just walked through the door and you backed into me.'

'What are you doing here anyway?'

'I do a free surgery here every other Wednesday,' she said. 'I'm with a team of vets who cover all the workhouses in the city.'

'You charge *nothing* for this service?' gasped the mayor.

'I do what I can to help.'

'Oh – while I'm here then,' said the mayor, 'I wonder if you'd look at my gout. Left hind paw. It's killing me.'

31

Bryony raised her eyes to heaven. 'I am here to help the *poor*,' she said. 'And as for your gout, if you'd stop drinking so much rich honey dew and eating red vole-meat, you'd be a lot healthier. Now, if you'll excuse me, Mayor, I have a lot of patients to see.'

She walked into the hall to find her patients in angry mood. However, when they saw it was the 'jill with the light', as they called her – because she always insisted on the hall gas mantles being turned up high while she was there, inspecting their sores and injuries – they calmed down instantly. 'It's Jis Bludd,' the word went along the benches.

The mayor beat a hasty exit, almost running down the steps outside the workhouse, and into his coach. The driver whipped the mice and soon he was rumbling away from that dreadful place that smelled of overcooked cabbage and urine. He settled back in his seat, still a little ruffled but calming down by the minute. The party from Transylvladia were meeting him at Jumping Jacks, the gentlemammals' club near Cobbled Garden. Mayor Poynt had ordered wild vole cooked overnight in woodland herbs and he was looking forward to his lunch.

When he arrived at the club the three lemmings – two jacks and a jill – were waiting for him. Removing his cloak and giving it to the weasel cloakroom jill, he apologized for being late. 'Seeing to the poor, you know,' he murmured. 'One has to do one's duty.'

The three approving lemmings nodded in unison.

'By the way,' asked the mayor, as they were shown to their table by the stoat headwaiter, 'how is my old friend Prince Miska?'

'Prince Miska?' said the jill lemming, in a sharp and heavy accent. 'You mean *President* Miska. We do not have very much to do with him. Our region, in the far south of Slattland, is quite out of the way of his efforts to reform the country. We are our own people, you understand. We do things our own way.'

So much the better, thought the mayor. Better he was out of the picture. This trade agreement between Welkin and Transylvladia was important to the mayor. Timber. Timber for building wooden houses and ships. Timber from the dense dark forests of southern Slattland. Such materials would help Welkin grow in population, swelling its workforce. The mayor would, of course, take a small percentage of any sum paid to the Transylvladians for their wood. That was natural. That was in the course of things. Heaven helps those who—

'Water or honey dew?' His train of thought was interrupted by the waiter, a rather scruffy individual whose fleas were visible on his ragged coat and running all over the white towel folded over his forelimb.

'Honey dew, of course,' snapped the mayor. 'Why would we be drinking water?'

'Better for you,' replied the waiter, who was

not supposed to answer back, but just nod and do as he was bid. 'Honey dew rots yer liver. Gives yer the trots too. Only one toilet in 'ere, y'know. You often get long queues with the fidgets. That's the trouble with these gentlemammals' clubs. Nice an' matey, but the buildin's old an' the plumbin's older. Straight out of the ark, it is. My advice is, drink water. Nothin' like a glass of clear stream water to set you straight.'

The mayor's eyes bulged in fury. 'When I want your advice, I'll pull your chain,' he snapped. 'Just bring a jug of honey dew.'

'Suit yerself, squire. Not my liver. What about you gentlemammals? You goin' to be so foolish as to follow this 'un into an early grave?'

The lemming contingent looked helplessly at the mayor.

'What's your name?' thundered the mayor. 'I want your name. I'll have you sacked, so help me.'

'Don't think so, squire,' smirked the weasel. 'Only here temporary. They got me in 'cause there's a shortage, due to the bout of weasel flu what's sweepin' through the country. You can try, though. Can't blame you for that. One jug of honey dew comin' up. Now, what about dinner? How about some nice salad? Do you good, greens will. Puts iron in yer blood. No? All right then, don't do yer hearts a favour.'

He sauntered away from the table, whistling under his breath, winking at the nearest dowager stoat and causing the veins in her eyes to turn purple. At the door to the kitchens he turned and

34

yelled across the dining room, 'Oh, yes, name's Scruff. That's what you wanted to know, ain't it? Scruff by name and scruff by nature. Enjoy your meal.'

With that he was gone into the steaming interior.

CHAPTER FOUR

The harbour-master rang Monty to tell him that another shipload of grave earth had arrived in Muggidrear's port. Once again the ship was unmammaled. 'Not a soul on board,' he said. 'It just drifted in on the tide and whacked another one of my quays.'

'Thank you, harbour-master,' replied Monty. He replaced the phone on its cradle and sat down to suck on his chibouque. Bryony was sitting by the window, staring into the fog outside. Occasionally a patch cleared, revealing buildings like the National Gallery – full of paintings of stoats, of course, painted by stoats, the only weasel picture being 'Peasants' Dance' by Bugle.

Monty suddenly lurched forward and whipped the pipe from his mouth. Any other mammal might have thought he was having a heart attack, but Bryony knew him better than that. This was Monty's classic 'Eureka!' pose.

'Eureka!' he cried. 'I've found the answer. What we're dealing with here is *vampires*.'

'Vampires?' said Bryony in hushed tones. 'What – you mean coming over from Slattland?'

'Yes – from the Transylvladia region. It's the traditional home of the vampire. Someone's flooding Welkin with vampires. It all makes sense now. The poor stoat drained of blood the other night. The coffins full of grave earth. Pass me that book on the shelf by your side. No, not that one, the thick volume bound in black leather. Yes, that's it. Oh, dear, I do find reading difficult, but it's got to be done. We have to inform ourselves.'

He read carefully for about an hour, then slammed the book shut. 'Well, it seems it all depends on what *kind* of vampires they are. Vampire bats are the worst. Not likely, though they could fly across the Cobalt Sea. It could be vampire lemmings, in which case we're still in deep trouble, because they're fairly intelligent. That, too, is fortunately unlikely, since there would be a ruckus over there in Transylvladia if half their citizens were leaving in coffins. It would be noticed.

'However, it could be that they're vampire mice or vampire voles, stupid creatures which stumble around grabbing at anything. A herd of mice or voles wouldn't be missed. Someone, or some group, over in Transylvladia is sending voles over here. Give me the phone again, Bryony, I want to call Chief Falshed.' He dialled.

"Ello, 'ello, 'ello, Sergeant Plum, 'ere.'

'Could I speak to Chief Falshed?'

'Who wants to know?'

'The Right Honourable Montegu Sylver.'

There was a long pause with whispering in the background. Then the sound of a mustelid clearing his throat. 'Zacharias Falshed, Chief of Police.'

'Ah, Chief. Can you tell me what happened to that body Jis Bludd and I brought in the other night – the stoat with the puncture holes in his throat?'

'*That* stoat?' cried Falshed, suddenly losing his composure on the other end of the line. 'That stoat came to life again. At about a quarter to one his eyes flew open and he leapt from the cold mortuary slab and tried to sink his teeth into my neck.'

'You – er – didn't let him?'

'Of course I didn't let him. We struggled while three constables tried to pull him off me. Finally they succeeded and fought with him all the way out into the street. The sun was just coming up when they managed to throw him down the steps. Before he reached the bottom he crumbled to dust, right before our eyes. Most extraordinary. Most remarkable. Ashes to ashes, dust to dust.' There was another pause, while the chief apparently contemplated this strange phenomenon, then he added, 'Why, what do you know about this, Sylver?'

'I believe he had been turned into a vampire that very evening. You had a lucky escape, Chief. You could have turned into one of the living dead if he had bitten you.'

'A vampire?' There was a gulping sound at the end of the phone. 'He – he didn't bite me much. Just the tip of my tail.'

'Did he sink his fangs into a vein.'

'D-d-don't think so.'

'Well, Chief, you may be lucky. If you get these cravings for blood, try to resist them. Nothing yet, I take it? No sudden urges?'

'I – I *really* wanted blood sausage for breakfast.'

'Could be the first signs.' There was a whimper at the other end and Monty began to feel sorry for the policemammal. 'On the other paw,' he added, 'I think it would have affected you by now. Thanks, anyway, Chief.'

Monty told Bryony all that had happened. 'Look, I've just remembered that there's a delegation of Transylvladian businessmammals in town. They're visiting the mayor. Something about timber, I believe . . .'

'I hope they're not chopping down all the trees.'

'Well, so do I. Anyway, the mayor's taking them to see the queen this morning. I think I'll pay Whistleminster Palace a visit. The queen said I could come any time I wanted, last time we met.'

'She had her face buried in a cream puff at the time.'

'Yes, well, that doesn't make the invitation any less genuine. Do you want to come?'

'Most certainly. I'll get my best wrap.'

The two weasels made their way across Whistleminster Bridge. The fog was lifting, but there was still much of it clinging to barges in the water. A weak, pallid sun was trying to force its way through the misty air but not having much luck. Smoke curled from tall chimneys on the edge of the city and a yellowish sky was creeping in from the coast. In the distance the tower of Ringing Roger was almost finished. Bryony and Monty could see a new bell for chiming the hours being hoisted aloft, ready to go into its chamber. It seemed rather a large one for the task, but they had had a whip-round for a new bell, and the response had been rather good.

The bridge was relatively free of traffic. There were one or two humans crossing to the mustelid side, and vice versa, but in the main the two species kept apart. One was too big and clumsy and the other was too small and slinky. It just did not suit them to mix.

After the formalities had been completed, Monty and Bryony were admitted to the palace. The queen was expecting them, they were told. But they were warned that she was giving audience to some lemmings from abroad.

All this was quite new, since the queen had only been 'on show' for a few months. Until quite recently everyone had thought she was the middle-aged biddy sitting at the palace window and waving at the traffic going by, but that had turned out to be an automaton. Her uncle had now decided that although only six she was old enough to be shown to the public and to receive visitors – foreign ambassadors and the like.

As usual, apart from her visitors, the queen was surrounded by cats, who came to 'look'. 'Hello, weasely things,' she said brightly, peering down at the weasels. 'We're having a tea party. Would you like to join us?'

'Happy to, Your Majesty,' replied Monty and Bryony together.

The pair sat down on the wooden floor next to a sour-faced Mayor Poynt, who was holding a china cup and saucer in his paws. Three lemmings were all doing likewise. There was a doll's house not far away, full of furniture and with one or two dolls leaning against it.

The queen gravely poured an imaginary cup of tea from her doll's teapot into a doll's teacup and handed it down to Monty. He pretended to sip it. Bryony did the same: 'Wonderful,' she said, smacking her lips.

Monty added, 'Delicious tea, Your Majesty. From the Chino-Indus continent, I presume.'

The queen clapped her hands delightedly. 'Oh yes, from there, of course,' she said in her best dowager duchess voice. 'From that place, yes. So glad you came. These stoaty and lemming things won't drink their tea. They just keep looking at it.' She frowned darkly at Jeremy Poynt, who then proceeded to pretend to sip his

41

too. The lemmings obviously had no idea what was going on and seemed thoroughly bewildered by it all. They kept blinking and looking in their empty cups as if expecting liquid to appear magically.

'Your Majesty, I wonder if I might have a word with the mayor?' asked Monty.

'Oh yes, you can do that.'

Monty turned to the mayor. 'Mayor Poynt, could you ask your guests if they know of any reason why vampires should be coming from Transylvladia to Welkin?'

The mayor looked annoyed, but the change in the expressions on the faces of his guests was astonishing. They looked utterly horrified.

'Wampires!' cried the child-queen. 'Nasty, nasty wampires!'

On hearing the queen the cats began to wail. There must have been at least a hundred of them in the room, keeping a respectful distance but staring hard at the queen all the while. The noise was so loud it brought the queen's uncle from his study. He wanted to know what was going on. Monty told him his suspicions about vampire mice or voles.

The queen's uncle didn't seem to think humans had much to worry about, mice and voles being such small creatures. 'But I can see it would concern you mustelids,' he said. 'Well, what have these Slattlanders got to say about it?'

'No vampires in Slattland,' said one.

'No – no vampires in Transylvladia,' said another.

'No, no, no,' said the third.

Monty stared at them. It seemed clear he and Bryony were going to get nowhere with this crowd. 'Vampires congregate at churchyards,' he muttered. 'I shall go to Lowgate Cemetery tonight and see what I can find. I shall be armed with a hammer and several stakes.'

The mayor looked alarmed. 'You can't go driving stakes into the hearts of tourists,' he cried. 'I'm in the middle of an important trade agreement. What will they say in Slattland if we start puncturing their citizens? It won't do, Sylver. I'll have the chief of police on to you. You leave well enough alone.'

'You don't seem to realize, Mayor. It's catching. Anyone bitten by one of these creatures becomes one of the living dead themselves. And they're hardly tourists – they're cattle. What if one of them were to attack you, or your sister, Sybil? We must stop these creatures before they bite any more Muggidrear citizens, never mind what they're going to think in Slattland.'

'Over my dead body.'

'Over your living dead body,' Bryony said. 'Anyway, stakes and hammers might not be necessary. First we've got to find these short-leggedy beasties. Anyone got any ideas?'

'I could lend you a few cats,' said the queen sweetly. 'They'd soon catch any mice or voles.'

All the mustelids in the room shivered involuntarily at the thought of cats running wild on their side of the river.

'Any more tea, anyone?' asked the queen, in

43

her dowager voice. 'Cream cakes? Anyone want a cream cake?'

The cats, on hearing the magic word 'cream', suddenly broke their silence with loud whines of 'Me, me, me, me, me.'

CHAPTER FIVE

It was close to midnight. Four weasels approached Lowgate Cemetery, one of them reluctantly. They were all carrying sheaves of wooden stakes and hammers in their paws. Those who have not seen Muggidrear's Lowgate Cemetery will not know that it has a very ghostly atmosphere. Situated on a hill in the middle of the city, it is a tumbledown place, with gravestones and large tombs scattered randomly amongst tufted knolls and dips filled with twisted elders and stunted oaks. It is crowded with dead stoats and weasels, their graves shrouded in moss.

The weasel rebel, Carl Musk, is buried there, with a simple rude block for his headstone. On the other paw, the stoat poetess Kristobel

Rosepetal has an elaborate tomb as large as a house, with wrought-iron decorations and a marble faceplate inscribed 'TO HER SPLENDID JILL-HOOD'. There was a rumour that her brother exhumed her body to retrieve some poems that had been buried with her, only to find that her fur had continued to grow after death and filled the coffin with long wavy curls.

'I don't like this place,' whispered Maudlin. 'It's spooky.'

'Don't think about it,' advised Bryony. 'Just imagine it's a sunny day and we're going to have a picnic.'

Ringing Roger chose that moment to strike for the first time since its restoration. The sound was deafening. When the twelfth note had died away, leaving a ghastly silence, the weasels shook their heads to clear their ears of the muzzy feeling.

'Too big,' murmured Monty.

'What's too big?' asked Bryony.

'The new bell they installed. I suppose they wanted a grander and posher striking bell, but that was a monster. I expect it's woken just about every mustelid in Muggidrear.'

'Including the vampires?' asked Maudlin in tremulous tones.

Scruff shook his head. 'They're already awake. Must've bin awake for hours. They've got to be up with the crack of evening to be first at the throats. Since there's so many of 'em, all wantin' to suck blood, and not so many mammals out in the streets when this fog's about, I expect it's first come, first served.'

Maudlin groaned. 'How can you talk like that?'

'Look!' cried Scruff by way of reply. 'There's one!'

Ahead of them, lurking amongst the higgledy-piggledy gravestones, was a dark figure.

When they approached the creature, it stepped out into the moonlight. They could see it was a foreign vole, which told Monty what he had wanted to know. It rose up on its hind legs and hissed, revealing two sharp-looking fangs in its open mouth. In two or three bounds it was on Maudlin, gripping him by the shoulders, the head dipping to sink those sharp fangs into the artery in his throat.

'Get it off! Get it off!' shrieked a hysterical Maudlin. 'Scruff! Scruff!'

Scruff grabbed the creature by the part of the body bearing the same name as himself, and wrenched the vampire vole away from his friend. The vole was immensely strong. It whipped round to face its attacker and slashed out with its claws, narrowly missing Scruff's eyes. Bryony then grabbed it by its right ear, while Monty took it by its left. In this way they were able to control the beast – for beast it was, with its gnashing, foaming mouth and wild eyes – and keep its head from lunging forward at Scruff. It clearly wanted to bury its teeth in a weasel – any weasel. Thus they struggled with the vole for several minutes, before it broke away and headed off into the night.

They were all left shaken and panting. 'Very strong,' said Monty. 'Immense power in those limbs. Nothing like a normal vole.'

'You're telling me!' cried an excited Maudlin. 'Did you see the way I grabbed its leg? It just flicked out and I went sprawling.'

'I saw it, Maud,' replied Scruff gravely. 'You did well there – very brave move on your part, I thought. Captain Courageous.'

Peering into the darkness, Monty was able to see several other vole-shaped creatures ambling about amongst the graves. As he had thought, this was a gathering-ground for the invasion of vampires. From here they would go out into the town to seek their victims in dark alleys, even climbing up drainpipes to enter bedrooms. If the four friends did not do something soon, the whole of Muggidrear would be on its way to becoming a vampire colony.

He looked down at the hammer and stakes. 'This is not the way to do it,' he murmured. 'I was quite wrong. What we must do is find out where these creatures sleep and come upon them in the daytime. Then we can drive stakes into their hearts, or drag them out into the sunlight, where they will crumble to dust.'

'Shall we go home now, then?' asked Maudlin. 'We – we can come back in the morning.'

'I think that's the best idea,' replied Bryony. 'We can't do anything against these vampires at night. They're far too powerful in their own environment.'

'I'll stay here,' Monty said, 'while you all go home. I want to see which tombs they use to sleep in. I'll be all right. Don't you worry about me.'

48

'I'll remain with you,' replied Bryony promptly.

'An' me,' said Scruff.

Maudlin said nothing.

They remained hidden behind the grave of Carl Musk.

In the early hours there was a commotion by a large, elaborate tomb. A badger staggered forth with vampire voles clinging to either side of him, trying to climb up his body to reach his throat. Badgers are large creatures and quite fierce if roused. This one was roused all right. It was downright furious. It roared and thrashed, calling for assistance. Another badger came out of the darkness wielding a spade. The second badger gave each of the voles a whack, sending them flying into a bunch of thistles. The vampires screeched in pain.

'What was them?' cried one badger.

'Mad voles, by the look,' replied the other.

Monty stepped out of hiding. 'Vampire voles, actually.'

The two badgers jumped and the one with the spade raised the implement to strike Monty. He only stayed his paw when three other weasels emerged. 'Wha— what's the idea of scarin' honest folk?' he said defensively. 'Honest folk, just – just out for a stroll?'

'Herk and Bare,' said Bryony. 'I might have known. You two are out body-snatching again, aren't you? Well, you could be in trouble this time. Lowgate Cemetery is crawling with vampires. Have you been bitten, Herk? I saw two of them on you.'

Herk felt around his throat with feverish claws. 'No – no – none of them got me. I'm clean. I swear.'

'One of 'em bit my spade,' said Bare, staring at it. 'Look at them dents in it!'

'You're very lucky, the pair of you. What's that smell?' Monty sniffed. 'Ah-ha, a corpse. You've dragged a corpse from that tomb, haven't you? Look, I can see it lying on the ground in front of that marble slab. It's not even fresh. Vets won't want a body that old.'

'Nothin' to do with us,' said Bare. 'We're just out for a short walk, we are.'

Herk said, 'We don't mind helpin' to clear up someone else's mess, though.' He walked back and grabbed the leg of the corpse and started to drag it towards the open tomb. The limb came away in his hands. 'Ooops,' he said. 'A bit high, this one, eh? You're right, Jal Sylver. A touch on the ripe side. Bare, give us a paw, will you? Do I have to do everythin'? That's it, you take the shoulders an' I'll take the pelvis. There we go. Lug it up the steps, chuck it in, shut the iron grill. All nice an' snug now. Nothin' to see.' He went back and picked up the leg, tossing it into the dark vault along with the body. 'All right and proper.'

'If Falshed catches you two,' said Bryony, 'you'll be back in prison again, you know.'

'Just doin' the veterinary profession a service,' replied Bare.

Monty said, 'Well, the law doesn't approve of such services.'

The two badgers melted into the dawn, which was just tracing the edge of the sky with its grey fingers.

Now, in the gloom of the early morning, the vampires came back into the graveyard and began to enter the tombs. There seemed so many of them. One or two weasels and stoats came with them, obviously victims who were now themselves of the living dead. By the time the sun had spread over the cemetery, all the vampires were safely in the dark, keeping company with the dead.

'Time to knock in a few stakes,' Scruff said. 'Time to puncture a few evil hearts.'

'I don't like this idea,' muttered Maudlin.

'I agree with Maudlin,' Bryony said, surprising Monty. 'I think the idea of driving stakes into hearts is grotesque. I've got an idea. Maudlin, would you run to my surgery and fetch my instruments?'

Maudlin was off like a shot, only too happy to be out of the graveyard and far away from the vampires.

Monty asked Bryony, 'What do you intend doing?'

'I'm going to pull a few teeth. Fangs, in fact. If they haven't got their hollow fangs, they can't suck blood, can they? They'll be sleeping under a natural – or I should say, a *super*natural? – chloroform, so they'll be perfect patients.'

'Why didn't I think of that?' marvelled Monty.

'Basic, my dear Monty, very basic. You're not a vet – and anyway, you're not the only one to have ideas,' replied Bryony.

After they had waited quite a time, with Scruff wandering about amongst the tombs, a funeral cortège appeared. Two stoats in black top hats with black silk ribbons hanging from them led a glass-sided hearse pulled by two stately mice with black plumes. Behind the hearse came a crowd of mourners. Following the usual ritual, the dead stoat was being buried with his pocket watch and chain. In the world of the dead time was important. There were celestial appointments to keep. Words spoken over the coffin before it was lowered into the ground were usually chosen from old mustelid sayings, such as 'You can't take it with you, when you go,' or 'It's no good being the richest stoat in the graveyard.'

Just as the ceremony was reaching its most poignant part, with the relatives throwing the first handful of earth on the dead stoat, Maudlin arrived back, breathless, with Bryony's brown leather bag.

The weasels then proceeded to race through the cemetery, opening the grills and gates of tombs, rushing inside, and drawing teeth right and left, but not centre. The stoats mourning their grandfather were horrified by this unseemly business and threatened to call the mayor and the chief of police and report the behaviour of these uncouth weasels.

'One over here!' Scruff would shout, and into

the tomb would go Bryony, steel pincers in paw. Then there would be muffled orders of 'Hold his head while I get a grip – that's it. That's one –' *clink* – 'and the other – coo, that was a tough one –' *clink*. Maudlin would then emerge with a metal dish rattling with pulled fangs.

'Disgusting,' said a matronly stoat, standing at the graveside. 'I expect they're stealing gold fillings. You know what these weasels are like. Horrible creatures. I shall report them to the mayor.'

On hearing this, Monty became aware of the seeming recklessness of their manners. He went across to the group of stiff and starchy stoats and bowed low, before saying, 'I do beg your pardon. We must get this task finished before the setting of the sun, or the whole of Muggidrear will become a shambling, shuffling capital of monsters. Do forgive our seeming lack of respect for the departed . . .' He stared down into the grave and his eyes widened. 'One just gone into the ground!' he shouted. 'Quick, Bryony!'

Bryony raced over. To the horror of the stoats in their sober black funeral garments she jumped down into the open grave and proceeded to force open a jaw locked in rigor mortis with a jemmy. Then she wrenched out two of the corpse's teeth with her pincers, holding them up proudly for all to see.

The matronly stoat fainted dead away and had to be revived with smelling salts.

CHAPTER SIX

Spindrick had been up late studying by gaslight.
There were rings around his eyes. He lived in a
top-storey room in a lodging house. Just below
him lived an actress (no-one was *quite* sure what
kind of mammal she was under all that make-up)
who engaged him in conversation every morning on the way down to breakfast. Although
Spindrick did not dislike females as much as male
mustelids, he did like a little peace and quiet early
on in the day. No such luck: this morning the jill
was asking him whether he played a musical
instrument.

'No,' replied Spindrick, 'I have no talent for
music.'

'I have,' said the stoat salesmammal from the

next flat down, joining them as they went past his door. He was snappily dressed, with white toe-caps to his brown shoes and a sharp seam in his trousers. 'I can play most things. You put a tuba into my paws and I'll have you dancing till dawn. I'm a party animal, I am. I can be as outrageous as a human, once I've had a drink.'

Spindrick gritted his teeth. 'A traveller in jills' underwear – I don't think so.'

'I wasn't always in jills' underwear,' said the salesmammal, looking affronted. 'I used to sell collar studs at one time.'

'Well, that makes a difference,' Spindrick said sarcastically. 'Put him in Daggerwobble's *Hambone*, for goodness' sake.'

The salesmammal decided to ignore Spindrick and talk to the actress instead.

On the next landing they were joined by a retired stoat colonel, with grey whiskers and a habit of clearing his throat in company. 'Mornin', mornin',' he gruffed. '*Harrrrkkkhhhaaa*. Bugle call gone out for breakfast, has it? Heard you lot comin' from a hundred metres. Never make stalkers, would you, eh? *Eeecchhhrrrrrkkkk*. Artillery, perhaps, but couldn't send you out on a dawn raid. Enemy would hear you comin' before you'd started out.'

'We're going down to breakfast, Colonel,' muttered Spindrick coldly, 'not attacking a rat watchtower. And I might add, hawking in that fashion would not allow you to get within a mile of any enemy.'

'Quite. Quite.'

On the next floor they gathered up two elderly sisters, weasel schoolteachers, also retired. They twittered like birds, but were wholly inoffensive and Spindrick quite liked them. He did *not* like the last creature they gathered into their fold, a badger with big bushy eyebrows who was a bank clerk. His name was Lob Kritchit and he always spoke of himself in the plural: 'We are a bank clerk!'

There were very few badgers in the city and he was proud of having a well-paid job and felt he represented other badgers in that post. He sat at his high desk with a swallow-quill and laboriously copied figures from one big ledger into another big ledger in the neatest paw a body had ever seen. His 5s and 7s were a wonder to behold. They had thick top bits and narrow, sweeping downstrokes and he had often been complimented on them by his superiors. As for his 3s – well, there was no other bank clerk to equal them. It was true the even numbers were not quite as powerful and striking as the odds, but that was because he had been born one of an uneven litter, the third cub in a thriving sett. He was fonder of odds than evens and this was reflected in his work.

'How are *we* this morning, bank clerks?' asked Spindrick, in a cutting voice. 'Ready to storm the accounts section in our hundreds, are we?'

'Go and blow spit bubbles,' said the badger. 'At least we've got a white-collar job, not like a dead-beat weasel I know.'

Spindrick was affronted. 'I'm a very intelligent

weasel. Any work I do has to utilize my very extensive talents!'

'Tell that to the sewer rats,' replied the badger scornfully.

They all sat down to breakfast.

Spindrick made a mental note: when the revolution came, and those on the bottom were at last on top, this badger would have to be taught a lesson. I've got you in my little black book, he thought, as he watched the badger butter his toast. Come the revolution, we shall no longer be a bank clerk. We shall be a cleaner of Muggidrear drains, if this weasel has any say in the matter!

'And you can stop looking at us like that,' said the badger, grabbing a boiled wren's egg from under Spindrick's nose. 'We know what you're thinking, but you'll never be in a position to do us any harm. We have a very good name at the bank. We are very well thought of. Our copying is second to none.'

'Yes,' replied Spindrick wearily, 'you were born to copy the work of others. How talented you are, Jal Kritchit.'

'Yesterday,' said the encouraged Kritchit, with great pride in his voice, 'the manager, Jal Scrunge, let us put another piece of coal on the fire without even asking permission from the owner of the bank. That's how well we are thought of.'

'Oh, how delightful,' said one of the sisters.

'How nice!' murmured the other.

'*Errccccchhhhheeech*,' came the hawked reply from the stoat colonel. '*Huuccchhhaaaarrrggck-swutt*.'

57

Charming, thought Spindrick. Come the revolution I might even break my own rule of not killing anyone on purpose, just for this lot. I think I'll send the tanks to raze this building to the ground *before* any evacuation can take place. They're worse than sewer rats and I was quite prepared to do away with a couple of those if they upset my plans, when I blew up the heating device installed by the mayor.

You see, he told himself brightly, you *can* be ruthless if you really put your mind to it. You're not just a political animal, you're a revolutionary one too. It all depends on how badly you want to reach your goal.

Now, the actress, for example. He'd like to see her on the cart, heading towards the guillotine. What an image that conjured up! Her pretty bewhiskered head ready to drop into a basket after the blade . . . what? What was her mouth opening and closing for? Why did she look so cross?

'Sugar?' asked the actress. 'Please, Jal Sylver, I've asked you twice now. You seem to be in some sort of reverie.'

'Eh? Oh.' The distracted Spindrick pushed the sugar bowl towards her. 'Sorry, I was dreaming.'

'It says here,' said the bank badger, who actually *enjoyed* reading *The Chimes*, 'that two explorers have discovered a rare kind of soil in the jungles of Tarawak which makes things grow at twice the normal rate.'

'Really?' said Spindrick, quite uninterested.

'The only trouble is, it says, when any plant

58

grown in it blooms it gives off sleeping fumes. Sends creatures to sleep for ten years. Well, that's not much good, is it? You pot your primrose, it grows, flowers, and the next moment you drop off for a decade.'

'How do they know?' asked the colonel.

'Eh? What?' The badger ruffled the newspaper. 'What do you mean?'

'Well, if these explorer chappies found the flower and it gave off these fumes, they'd be asleep, wouldn't they? – *harrgggcchhhphut*.'

'Not necessarily,' said Spindrick, leaning forward, now very interested in this news. 'Perhaps they found the plant *after* it had bloomed and died, and discovered sleeping creatures around it. What's their names? The explorers? Who are they?'

'Two professors doing research. The elderly Speckle Jyde and the young and ravishing Margery Spred. Jack and jill. Both gerbils. Academic types, those gerbils. They're still out there, in the jungle. The newspaper heard the story from the captain of a yacht which made landfall at Tarawak in order to take on provisions. He, the captain, heard it from some native mongooses – shouldn't that be mon*geese*? – who came across the pair when they were canoeing down the Klangalang river.'

'Who was canoeing?' asked the actress.

'The mongooses – mongeese. They were snake-hunting and they met the pair when portaging around a waterfall.'

'I bet it doesn't say the *ravishing* Margery

Spred,' muttered the colonel. 'You made that up.'

'Guilty,' clicked the badger, 'but you've got to spice these stories up a bit, otherwise they'd be as dull as—'

'Bank clerks,' said Spindrick, and received a dark look from the badger.

'What's portaging when it's at home?' asked the actress. 'It doesn't sound like a real word.'

'Carrying one's canoe between two unnavigable points on the river,' explained the colonel.

'Oh,' replied the actress. 'Why can't they just say *carrying*?'

'It goes on to say,' continued the badger, 'that they want a correspondent to go into the heart of darkness, into Tarawak, and find the pair.'

'What, the mongeese – mongooses?' asked the colonel.

'No, the professors. They're offering a thousand guineas to the mammal that meets up with them. They say they'll sponsor any serious expeditions as well as paying the prize money. *The Chimes*, that is.'

'What's wrong with their own reporters?' asked the actress, curling her whiskers with her claws. 'Why don't they go?'

The badger lowered the paper. 'My dear, the Tarawak jungles. Why, hardly any foreign mammal comes out of them alive. Malaria, sleeping sickness – hey, that's funny – black-water fever. There have been one or two, of course, who escaped being bitten to death by mosquitoes and sucked dry by leeches, but only one or two. Mustelid's Grave, they call that large island in the

60

Specific Ocean. There are more weasel, stoat and badger bones there than in Lowgate Cemetery.'

'I think I shall go,' muttered Spindrick. 'I think I shall.'

'You?' cried the actress, the mystery mustelid.

'You, sir? *Hrrrccchhhggch*,' hawked the stoat colonel.

'Not you,' said the stoat salesmammal, who had remained silent throughout the whole meal.

'I can't see it,' came in the badger, last as usual. 'You'd be eaten alive by insects. Look at you. Pale and wan creature that you are, from too many late nights, burning the candle at both ends, never going out into the fresh air and sunlight. Even us, who work in a bank from morning till night, we get out at weekends and get *some* fresh air.'

Spindrick rose and threw his napkin on the table with a great flourish. 'Yes, me. Me. You'll see.'

'He will do it,' said one of the sisters.

'He always does what he says he's going to do,' chimed in the other.

He left them with the actress saying, 'Well, I hope he knows what he's doing.'

Spindrick knew what he was doing all right. He was going to get that special soil. If he could put the whole city to sleep for ten years he could wreak all sorts of havoc while they were dozing. This plant food was an anarchist's dream. When everyone woke up there would be no governments, no monarchies, no authority or law of any kind. They would wake up to a world free from oppression and rules. 'That's the kind of world I

61

want,' muttered Spindrick. 'A world in which everyone is free to do what they want.'

Spindrick vacated the building and made his way to Swift Street, where the newspaper offices were situated. When he got there he entered the building dedicated to *The Chimes*, the most respected newspaper on the mammal side of Muggidrear. He left the building an hour later with a spring in his step. He had been accepted as the most promising candidate for finding the two lost professors. Spindrick had been given leave to purchase equipment and clothing, steamer and rail tickets, pith helmet and guides through the jungle (be they mongeese or mongooses), canoe, paddle and anti-insect cream. In fact the newspaper had been very generous and he intended to go on a weekend jaunt to the seaside town of Kidneypool before he set off for Tarawak.

Might as well look at the lights of Kidney before setting off for the heart of darkness, he told himself.

CHAPTER SEVEN

They were gathered in the mayor's office –
Jeremy Poynt, Zacharias Falshed, Montegu
Sylver and Bryony Bludd.

'That was the funeral of my cousin's cousin,'
the mayor was ranting. 'How *dare* you desecrate
my cousin's cousin's grave.'

'One cousin will do,' murmured Bryony.

'What?' yelled the mayor.

'You don't have to keep saying, "my cousin's
cousin" – just call him your cousin and leave it at
that.'

Monty tried to explain again. 'Your cousin had
been bitten by a vampire vole. That's why he died.
However, he would have risen that night from his
own freshly dug grave. Having been bitten, he

63

was now a vampire himself. Jis Bludd was merely removing his fangs so that when night came, he wouldn't be able to roam around the city sucking blood from innocent strollers. Without being able to suck blood, he'll soon waste away, and be able to be put to rest for eternity.'

'Pah!' cried the mayor. 'This living-dead thing won't work with me. You were stealing teeth. I expect you sell them to dentists, don't you? I know you weasels . . .'

Falshed cleared his throat and the mayor rounded on him in his fury. 'What? It'd better be good, Chief.'

'Jal Mayor, I don't like to go against you, you know that.'

'No – otherwise I'd sack you,' said the mayor with narrowed eyes.

'Well, be that as it may, I have to this time. I'm afraid I was in the station when the body of a stoat was brought in by these two. It was definitely dead. Dead as a stone mouse. Yet it got up and smashed up the station just a few hours later. When it was forced outside into the sunlight, it crumbled to dust. I was as sceptical as you, Mayor, but I went to the library and looked it up. I think that stoat was a vampire.'

The mayor shivered in his white fur and purple rings formed around his eyes. He seemed about to explode when his sister walked into the office. In her paws she carried a rather bedraggled bunch of wild flowers, grasses and herbs. 'Oh, hello, brother,' she murmured dreamily. 'Company?'

Jeremy Poynt stared at his sister thoughtfully. Now Sybil was not a dreamy stoat, not normally. Usually she was rushing around, doing this and that, organizing charity benefits: sightseeing tours for blind stoats, country walks for lame weasels (or was it the other way around? – he admitted he was never very good at understanding how one went about helping other mammals). Yet for the last few hours she had been dripping about the place like a stoat with the flu, not of this world and hardly in it. Even now her eyes looked glazed and listless. She definitely seemed ill. She also looked soaking wet, as if she'd just been bathing.

Now if there was one mammal in the world who had power to rule Jeremy's heart, it was his sister. He did not like her briskness, nor her criticisms of him (which were often forthcoming) but his fondness for her overruled these shortcomings. She was all the direct family he had left in the world and, though she disapproved of a lot he did, she still acknowledged him as a brother.

'Jis Bludd,' said Jeremy, 'would you mind having a look at my sister while you're here? She doesn't seem to be herself.'

Bryony glanced across the room and saw two blood spots on the fur of Sybil's throat. She knew immediately what was wrong with her. However, she did get up and examine Sybil, just to make sure, before she gave Mayor Poynt the bad news. 'I believe she's been bitten by a vampire.'

Jeremy started forward, trembling. 'What? Not my little sister? Will she live?'

65

'Yes, but for ever unfortunately, and not as a real mammal.'

'Garlic!' cried Falshed, leaping from his chair and looking about him wildly. 'We need garlic.'

'It's a bit late for that,' Monty said.

'Oh, my poor Sybil!' moaned Falshed.

The mayor looked at him. '*Your* poor Sybil? Falshed, you're getting a bit above yourself. She's my sister. If you think my sister, the *princess*, is interested in *you* . . .'

'Please,' interrupted Monty, 'let's not argue. Look, she's distressed enough as it is. No, Falshed, the garlic won't work.'

Bryony asked Sybil, 'Where have you been?'

'Floating on my back in the fish pond,' whispered Sybil. 'Floating amongst the lily pads with these wild flowers and herbs.'

'Do you have wild garlic there?' asked Falshed hopefully.

'Garlic? That's for long life,' murmured Sybil in a dreamy voice. 'Here's rhubarb – that's for distemper – pray you, brother – and there's dock leaves, for garden stings. There's watercress – we call it herb o' stickleback – and mustard. Here's ragwort, you must wear it on your bib for luck, and bladderwrack, which gives you wind . . .'

'What's the matter with her?' cried Jeremy, clearly distraught. 'Sib? Sib? Do something for her, please, Jis Bludd. I'll pay you anything. Look how wet she is. She's dripping on the floor.'

'You just need to pay me my normal fee,' said Bryony, rising. 'But actually I don't think there's very much we can do for her.'

66

Monty went over to Princess Sybil and took her paw. 'When were you bitten, Princess? Last night?'

'Last night I left my bedroom window open and a dark prince wafted in on a zephyr,' she murmured. 'How I love those evening zephyrs. But just as he took me in his arms, Ringing Roger struck midnight, and the sound frightened him away. He will be back, my prince, when the darkness falls in long purple lanes over Muggidrear. He will return. He told me so.'

'It sounds as if the vampire was interrupted,' said Bryony, now inspecting the puncture wounds. 'Perhaps the hold of the living dead is not so secure on Princess Sybil.'

'Maybe we *should* feed her with garlic?' cried Falshed. 'Maybe we should squeeze the juice out of the cloves and rub it on her lips?'

'No, no—' began Monty, but Bryony cried, 'Wait. He's got an idea there. But not garlic juice – *holy water*. We mustelids don't have churches, but the humans do. Why don't we borrow some holy water from St Pompom's font and administer it to Sybil? It's only water. It can't do any harm, after all. And it might work. I know that vampires are terrified by religious artefacts and symbols. It wouldn't hurt to try.'

A runner was sent for and despatched to St Pompom's Cathedral post haste. In the meantime Sybil was taken to her bedroom and tucked up in bed by Bryony with a hot-water bottle. Monty was left with the mayor and his chief to talk things over.

'I think this vampire business is getting out of paw,' said Major Poynt. 'For once, weasel, we are on the same side. That which threatens the life of my sister threatens Muggidrear. Any thoughts on the matter will be carefully considered before being dismissed, reassembled in my own mind, and repeated by me to tremendous acclaim.'

Falshed said, 'I don't think . . .'

'I was joking,' muttered the mayor, enjoying this chummy atmosphere for once in his life. It was not often that he felt close to anyone besides Sybil, let alone weasels. Yet here he was, making plans, being matey and pally with his most hated enemy.

'There's someone over in Transylvladia who is trying to flood our country with vampire voles,' said Monty. 'I propose to take some good weasels and go to that region to find out who it is and why they are doing it, and to ensure they *stop* doing it.'

'Good idea,' growled the mayor, incensed by this unknown perpetrator of heinous crimes. 'Would you like a twiglet, Sylver? My house-keeper brought them back from somewhere foreign. They're sort of biscuits.' The mayor held up a cigar box full of long, thin, crispy-looking things.

Monty took one dubiously and inspected it in the light. 'Where did you get these?'

'From my housekeeper. Been on holiday. Brought them back from Uskalland.'

'They're not biscuits,' said Monty; 'they look remarkably like petrified garden slugs to me.'

The mayor frowned hard and picked one out

himself, looking at it very closely. 'Really?' he said. Then he bit it in half and chewed it thoughtfully. 'You're quite right. They *are* slugs. Very nice too.' He chomped on the other half with great relish.

Bryony came back into the office looking washed out. 'Well, we got it into her. She screamed blue murder, saying it was burning her mouth . . .'

'If you've hurt my sister . . .' cried the mayor.

'. . . but she eventually calmed down,' finished Bryony, glaring at Jeremy Poynt. 'Now she's sleeping peacefully.'

'Can I go up to her?' asked Falshed. 'May I see her?'

'Certainly not,' snorted the mayor. 'Who do you think you are, Falshed?'

'I wasn't talking to you,' growled Falshed. 'I was speaking to the vet. Sybil is old enough to receive visitors without needing to refer to her brother. In fact I'm going up now.' He left the room even as Jeremy Poynt's jaw was dropping.

'That stoat is getting far too uppity!' snarled the mayor. 'I won't have it. My sister, indeed. I'll trim his waxed whiskers. I'll have his tail docked. I'll have his ears clipped. My sister? Why, she's far too good for the likes of a common police-mammal.'

Bryony said, 'Surely she should be the one to make up her mind on that score. I think the chief is genuinely very fond of your sister, and if he's a mind to do something about it, Mayor, I doubt you can stop him.'

'I can snip his pay in half at a moment's notice.'

'Not legally,' Monty said quietly, reminding the mayor that he was not alone with his cronies, but with two honest citizens.

Jeremy Poynt glanced at the detective. 'No – no – not legally. But that's my sister we're talking about. I'd break every law in the book for her.'

Falshed returned after a few minutes, just as Ringing Roger struck three. His mouth opened and closed as he tried to tell the others something, but no-one could hear a word. Chairs, desk, showcases rattled across the floor with the vibrations. The mayor held onto the corner of the desk, looking grim as he was dragged halfway across the room. 'What did you say?' he asked, as the note died.

'I said, she's sleeping peacefully now.'

'Jis Bludd said *that*,' snorted the mayor. 'And don't think this will be an excuse to stay here all night, mooning over Sybil. I can take care of things.'

'I'm going to sit outside her door,' replied Falshed stubbornly.

Monty stood up. 'I think it's time we were going. Tomorrow my friends and I set out for Slattland. I think we've got to go to the root of the problem. There's some Prince of Darkness out there, some Lord of Vampires, creating these monsters and exporting them to Welkin, as if we hadn't enough supernatural problems of our own. I shall find that someone and put him or her out of business.'

'Do so,' said the mayor, nodding, 'and – and I'll

recommend you for a position in the newly formed post office. We're bringing out a stamp, you know, for putting on letters. The Penny White, it's called, because I'm on the front – my ermine coat, you know – and – well – I could make you the new postmaster-general, Sylver. How would you like that?'

'Well, I'd have to think about it, Mayor.'

'Of course. See you when you get back then. Goodbye.'

'Goodbye.'

Monty and Bryony left the office.

Chief Falshed turned to the mayor. 'You're really recommending him for the position of postmaster-general?'

'Don't be daft, Falshed. If that weasel even gets promoted to dustcart-driver-general it'll be over my dead body.'

Outside, Bryony was looking at Monty. 'You're really going to accept the position of postmaster-general from the mayor?'

'Don't be daft, Bryony. If I ever get made lord high chancellor, it'll be over my dead body.'

Chapter Eight

Scruff was, typically, very excited about going abroad. 'I've never bin further than Sluggsborough,' he said, speaking of the seaside town he had once visited as a youth, 'so I'm really lookin' forward to this.'

Maudlin, equally typically, was not so happy. 'Don't they have different food over there? What about beds? Do they sleep in beds? I won't understand the money. I hear that they throw you in jail if you cross the street without touching your forelock at the policemammal on duty. Is that true?'

Bryony said, 'There's lots of myths and misconceptions about overseas countries. The trouble is, we're an island species and we get a bit silly about all this. Actually, Slattland is not all that different to this country. The local dish in Transylvladia, for example, is suckling mouse. You've had suckling mouse before, haven't you?'

'Only at Wexantide,' replied Maudlin piously, 'and we always have greens with it.'

So the two friends, the ex-lamplighter and the ex-watchmammal, had their own feelings on the subject. Bryony and Monty had been before – Monty with a poorly maiden aunt who wanted to take the waters in central Slattland, Bryony on several occasions to a vets' conference in Worms, a prestigious gathering-place for vets of all species.

Bryony actually spoke a little Slattlandish, but it would probably be unnecessary, since most continentals could speak Welkin. As an island with a large sailing fleet Welkin had once ruled the seas and traded with all species and nations. Its inhabitants had imposed their language on those who had fought and lost against them, or wished to trade with them. Bryony did not consider this a good thing but it had happened – one could not go back and change the clock.

Monty booked their passage on a new steamship, a monster of a craft built by Wm. Jott's uncle, Isobars Kingpin Frunnel, called the *Great Steamship* (Jal Frunnel was an engineer and not noted for his imagination). They had luxurious cabins in first class, even though Scruff had insisted that he and Maudlin would rather travel steerage. It was a grand way to cross the Cobalt Sea and very exhilarating.

The four friends stood on the deck of the *Great*

Steamship and watched the quayside slip away. They waved, as others waved, to the mammals standing on the dock, fluttering pawkerchiefs in their claws, saying goodbye to relatives and friends, some emigrating to distant lands in the hope of finding a better life. It was a very emotional affair. Then Scruff took Maudlin to the prow and they stood on the sharp bit while the wind whistled through their tawny locks and up their noses.

'What about a game of hollyhockers in the saloon?' suggested Scruff. 'It's gettin' dark out here. You can't see nuffink now the harbour-lights is faint. Dinner ain't until eight o'clock.'

'Eight?' cried Maudlin. 'I'll be famished by then.'

Monty and Bryony declined, saying they wanted to stay out on deck. Scruff realized they wanted to talk in private and ushered his pal into the saloon, where they found some hollyhock seeds and a shaker and soon proceeded to attract a crowd with their skill at the game. Some mammals started making wagers on one or the other of them, but since both weasels were equally talented the outcome was chancy.

Bryony and Monty leaned over the rail and looked at the dark water washing by. They were not much interested in the stars, which were regarded not for their beauty but as good navigational aids. Weasels rarely look at the heavens for inspiration.

'Well, where do you think we ought to start, once we reach port?' asked Bryony.

'I suggest we proceed by mouse-coach to the southern city of Krunchen, before proceeding to the eastern region of Transylvladia—'

Monty's speech was interrupted by another steamship, this time a vast one full of humans, passing by to port. It was a lovely sight, encrusted with lights. The sound of orchestra music drifted over and there was laughter and gaiety coming from various parts of the vessel. In the bows were two humans – a youth and a girl – who were standing dangerously on the rail, holding onto some stays just like Scruff had been doing, letting the wind rush through their clothes, letting it lift their hair. The human ship was heading north towards a much colder ocean.

'The *Colossus*,' murmured Monty. 'They say she is unsinkable. Now, where were we? Oh, yes, in southern Slattland. Not too far south, you understand. On the continent the humans have all vacated the northern regions and chased the sun south. Most of them live below the Jagged Mountain Range, in warmer climes.'

'It's because of their lack of fur,' Bryony said, nodding. 'They have trouble keeping warm.'

As they were talking, two lemmings came strolling along the deck. Bryony and Monty bid them good evening. The pair stopped, smiling at them, and returned the greeting.

'Good evening,' said the first. 'I am the fat one. I am the singer.' He was indeed quite corpulent.

'And another good evening,' said the second. 'I am the thin one. I am the dancer.' She was indeed very slim.

They stood there, grinning, waiting for a response.

Monty cleared his throat, 'Are you – are you on your way home, back to your own country?'

'We are indeed,' said the fat one. 'We have been touring your wonderful country of Welkin, singing and dancing. It has been very good experience, but tell me, why do mammals throw litter in street? In our country of Slattland we are not allowed to do that.'

'It's a bad habit we've picked up from our humans,' explained Bryony, 'though one shouldn't blame another species for one's faults.'

'And why,' said the thin one, 'do you always queue for omnibus? We never queue for anything. Half the fun is pushing mammals out of the way and scrambling for the best seat.'

'Well, that's one of the *good* habits we've copied,' replied Monty. 'That and not spitting in company.'

'Oh, that too,' said the fat one, still grinning. 'A very quaint custom, not spitting in company.'

'Tell us,' added the thin one, 'when you get to *our* country, where will you be going? Will you visit our great cities? Or do you wish to go up into mountains for some clean air? Or perhaps you have friends over there? I am Florette, by the way, and this is Boombach. Perhaps we could travel together in our land?'

'Well, there are four of us altogether,' explained Monty, 'but if we should be going in the same direction, perhaps we could dine together one evening? I am looking forward to your local

76

food – and to the drink, pear dew? – and you would no doubt tell us where to get the best meal.'

'Indubitably.'

'Our pleasure.'

The two lemmings passed on, forelimb in forelimb, heading towards the bows. Bryony heard one say to the other in Slattlandish, 'Let's stand on the front rail and permit the wind to run its claws through our fur . . .'

'Nice couple,' said Monty.

'Yes,' replied Bryony, with a sidelong glance at her friend. She was silent for a while, before saying, 'Have you thought that – that we might run into the evil lemming Sveltlana over there? It is her country, after all.'

Sveltlana. Monty remembered her well – the lemming assassin who had tried to murder the prince of her own country for selfish political reasons. She was an evil creature – yet – yet Monty was fascinated by her. He said, as casually as he could, 'The thought had crossed my mind.'

'You – you used to think her quite beautiful.'

'Oh, in a sort of academic way,' replied Monty, with a little cough at the end of the sentence. 'You know, these foreigners with their dark eyes.'

'How do you mean, *academic*?'

He swished his tail on the deck, a sure sign that his spirit was in a disturbed state. 'Well, if I were a painter, which I'm not, of course, I would view her as a good subject, I think. Or perhaps a poet? That sort of thing. Her soul, of course, is dark with sin, but viewed in a good light, her – her physical

77

appearance can be quite – eye-catching?'

'I see.'

'Yes, well – there you are.'

Bryony could not leave the subject alone. 'So, do you find all lemming jills so entrancing? Or is it just *her*. I mean, what is it about her that makes her stand out?'

'Who can define beauty? Or its worth?'

She said, a little crisply now, 'You're not answering my question, Monty. Is it her species you find beautiful, or is she beautiful even amongst her own kith and kin?'

'See the way the phosphorescence sparkles on the water!'

'Monty?'

'Look,' he said, turning to face her, 'I really don't feel like going into this right now. I don't see the importance of it, nor do I see the relevance to our mission. Sveltlana is not a vampire.'

'How do you know?'

'Well, if she is, I'm sure you'll pull her teeth at the earliest opportunity, Bryony.'

'Scratch her eyes out, more like,' muttered Bryony, in a louder voice than she intended.

At that moment both weasels were saved from further embarrassment by the sound of the deck bell, announcing that dinner was being served. Monty offered his forelimb and Bryony – it seemed a little reluctantly – took it lightly in her paw. They then proceeded to the dining-room, where Scruff and Maudlin were already tucking in with the gusto of mammals from poor backgrounds.

After dinner there was entertainment in the form of a dancer and a singer, one slim, the other almost circular in shape. They were, of course, Florette and Boombach. The act was rather good and by the time it was over the green-eyed monster had fled from Bryony's soul. She felt warm and good in the company of her best friend and for the moment the evil Sveltlana was forgotten.

In the middle of the night, when everyone else was asleep in their cabins, Monty was pacing the deck. He was going over in his mind what actions they should take when they reached Slattland. As he passed the bridge he heard a commotion. The crew were in quite a state, arguing with one another. It was all settled by the captain, who stated bluntly, 'We are not deviating from our present course! Maintain direction – and that's an order.' He was a pine marten and was used to being in authority. Those members of his crew who did not agree with him obeyed such a command without question.

A deck-paw, another pine marten, came out of the bridge looking a little aggrieved.

'Might I enquire what is the matter?' asked Monty.

'Oh, some human ship has got into trouble. Hit a bit of ice, according to the telegraph message. Good bit of salvage there, for the right crew. Someone will get rich . . .'

'Are we going to rescue them?'

'No, captain thinks they're too far away. Other

ships are going, but not us. They'll be all right.'

So that was it. Monty hoped they *would* be all right. But there was not much he could do to influence a sea captain. They were gods on their own ships. He decided to go to bed. He would get up early and take a turn around the deck. His mind would be clearer then.

CHAPTER NINE

There were lemmings just about everywhere.

'I've never seen such a crowded place,' said Maudlin, as the ship came into dock at Nanbuchet. 'Look at them! They're everywhere.'

'Slattland has highest population in world,' Boombach told him. 'It makes us do suicide – or would do, but there is law here stating that for one week of every year we must lock ourselves in house and post the key out through letter-box. A badger comes along all garden paths and collects these keys in big bag. 'Uncle Clink' the lemming kittens call him. All the keys are carefully labelled and when week is over, the badgers – there are many, though kittens think there is only one – go round and post keys back through the letter-boxes in the right houses. Of course, Uncle Clink always includes some sweets for the kittens, with the keys, which is why he is such big favourite with them.'

'Wow, I never heard of that,' Maudlin said, impressed. 'I suppose the week they have to be locked up is the suicide season when everyone would run amok and kill themselves.'

Boombach nodded gravely. 'If houses were not prisons, you would find flood of lemmings pouring out of cities, towns and villages, heading towards high cliffs on the coast. There they would fling themselves from the high ramparts of the coast, dashing their bodies on sharp rocks beneath, or ending their lives in roaring foam of the sea.'

When Maudlin went to tell his friend Scruff what he had learned about Uncle Clink, he found himself being clicked at.

'You don't want to believe all those old jills' tales about lemmings jumpin' over cliffs, Maud,' clicked Scruff. 'It's a load of old tom's droppings, that is.'

Maudlin went looking for Boombach to give him a piece of his mind, but the wise fat lemming had taken himself off.

Once on the quay, Bryony and Florette went off to book rooms at the inn, while Monty and Boombach went to hire a coach and twelve. They were going to cross some of the wildest country, probably at night, when savage creatures would be on the prowl.

'We will need guard with pistols,' Boombach

advised. 'You know there are highway wolves hereabouts, who attack coaches and kill all the occupants?'

Monty nodded. 'This is the Right Honourable Montegu Sylver you're talking to here, Boombach, not Maudlin the watchmammal. I happen to know the last wolf left Transylvladia fifty years ago, heading for the northern wastelands.'

Boombach was upset. 'Oh, it's such a nice story. I like to frighten visitors. Why don't you play along, Monty?'

'Sorry to disappoint you, Boombach.'

While the others were away, Maudlin and Scruff looked after the luggage, which was piled on the quay. They gathered it together and took it to a nearby tavern, where they had their first taste of pear dew. Scruff thought it was delicious, but Maudlin said it wasn't a patch on honey dew. There was a game of hollyhockers going on between a group of lemmings. Maudlin had to get involved, of course, but was soon in trouble.

'Hurdy-gurdy!' he cried after a shake of the leather cup and a throw of the hollyhock seeds. 'I win.'

'No, no,' said a lemming with a patch over his eye. 'You no win. *We* win. Is a jabbyknocker, no a hurdy-gurdy.'

'What rubbish!' cried Maudlin. 'You're trying to cheat me.'

'Cheat?' murmured the eye-patch lemming, with an ugly look on his face. 'I don't think we like that word.'

'Whoa! Whoa!' cried Scruff, intervening. 'See, what my friend here don't understand is that the rules is different in Slattland. Maud, me ol' candle-snuffer, this is not our country. They got different rules over here. You got to respect another mammal's culture.'

'Different rules? The rules are the same everywhere.'

'Have you *bin* everywhere?'

'No – I've never left the shores of Welkin – you know that.'

'Then,' replied Scruff, 'how do you know?'

'But this is hollyhockers. I've been playing this since I was two years old.'

'So 'ave these lemmin's, an' they play it *different*.' Scruff tapped his temple. 'You got to change yer thinkin', Maud. This ain't Welkin, it's Slattland. These ain't Welkin weasels, they're lemmin's. New ways, see, new light on things. Can't let yer mind clog up. Got to start lookin' beyond what you know and learn some new things.'

'All right,' said Maud, in a very strained but reasonable voice. 'I'll remember.'

He went and sat down with the fuming lemmings and once more the game started. Within a minute Maudlin was on his feet and yelling again. The lemmings began to harangue the irate weasel. Scruff called for peace and calm, but Maudlin took the hollyhocker table and tipped it over, sending leather cup and seeds scattering all over the floor.

'You know what we make hollyhocker cup

from over here?' cried the eye-patch lemming. 'Weasel skin. And I make one now.'

He waded in, catching Maudlin with a heavy claw on the snout. Scruff was only against his friend until the fighting started; then he went windmilling into the fray, knocking lemmings right, left and centre. The tavern owner and the waiters came out from behind their barrels of pear dew and began wielding socks filled with potatoes. Jills screamed and rushed out into the street. Lesser mortals quailed in the corners of the tavern. It was into this atmosphere that Boombach and Monty returned.

Boombach assessed the situation in two seconds, cleared his throat and hit a high C. His shrill note penetrated every ear within a square kilometre of the tavern. Those inside its walls reeled backwards, ramming their paws against their ears. Those outside looked to the factories of the town, or to the port, thinking it was either the knocking-off whistle, or a ship in deep trouble out in the ocean. Boombach was able to hold the note for at least two minutes, during which lemmings and weasels had staggered out of the tavern and fallen in the street.

Monty, who had managed to cover his ears very early, was deeply impressed. 'I've heard you sing, but I never thought you could do that,' he said. 'If the military could get hold of you, there would be no more wars.'

Maudlin and Scruff were climbing to their feet as Bryony came running along the dock side. 'Quick!' she cried. 'Get under cover! I heard a warning siren. The town must be under attack.'

Florette managed to hop, skip and catch up with her. 'No, no, I try to tell you. That is Boombach. He made the high C note. He does this to make people stop what they are doing.'

'And what were you doing?' asked Bryony accusingly of Monty.

'There was a tavern fight—' he began.

'Oh, *Monty*.'

'Not me, silly. Those two.'

'Not me,' said Scruff. 'Him.'

'Me,' Maudlin cried proudly. 'I started it.'

'You should be ashamed of yourself,' said Bryony.

'Well I'm not, so there. I've never been in a tavern fight before now – well, only that one where we bashed Falshed when the mechanical barman knocked him off the bar – at least, I've never managed to start one before. It was easy. I just tipped over a table. You should have seen it, Bryony. Just like in books.'

'I'm glad I didn't,' she snorted. 'Jacks!'

'Well, there's one tavern where we won't be staying tonight,' Monty said. 'Did you manage to book us some rooms, Bryony?'

'At the Weremouse Inn.'

'The Weremouse Inn? Why not the Vampire Arms?' said Monty.

'Could've been. They've all got those sort of names. Frankinstyn's Monster House, Drakula's Castle. It's part of the tourist trade, I suppose. Anyway, did you get the coach and twelve?'

'Yes,' replied Boombach. 'He make a special

price for me, since I am local lemming. I pay him, now you pay me.' He held out a fat paw for the money.

Monty shook his head sadly. 'Boombach, I happen to know you didn't pay a pfennig. I understand enough of your language to know the lemming coach-master said we pay when we collect the coach.'

Florette flicked Boombach's ear. 'If you are going to try such tricks, Boombach, please do them properly.'

Boombach looked disconsolate. 'I *did* try, my little Florette, but he is such hard weasel to cheat. I think he asked for double dollops of brains, like some mammals ask for two puddings. It is most irritating for jokers like myself. I think I stick to Maudlin in future. He is much more the idiot.'

'Hey!' cried Maudlin.

Scruff put a forelimb around his friend. 'Well, Boombach did catch you out on the boat, didn't he? Speaking of puddings, I'm hungry. Can we go and eat now? I saw a place where you can buy pancakes with what looked like jammy centres. Can we go there?'

'Yes, except we do not call them pancakes here,' said Boombach, 'we call them panbreads.'

'Really?' said Maudlin.

'Ha! Caught you again,' clicked Boombach. 'He is so *easy*, that weasel. Soon it will not be any fun. Anyways, is not *jam* middles. Lemmings do not make jams. Only have honey.'

'Yeah,' cried Maudlin. 'Pull the other one.'

They all stared at Maudlin. He shifted uncomfortably.

'What?' he said.

Florette murmured, 'Is true. Our last king choked on a strawberry, from strawberry jam, and he died. Since then there has been no jam allowed in this country.'

Maudlin's eyes narrowed, and again he clicked his teeth. 'Tell it to the marines,' he said.

Still the blank faces. Some – like Bryony's – looked shocked.

'Aw,' said Maudlin, squirming. 'I really thought you were having me on again. I'm sorry. I don't mean to make these mistakes with your culture. I really thought . . .'

They all twisted their mouths and let out sounds of merriment.

Boombach choked on his mirth. 'He is *so* easy,' he cried.

They all began walking towards the inn, with Maudlin grumbling, 'That's not fair. Why always me? Why not pull somebody else's leg for once. I wish you wouldn't do that. You're supposed to be my friend, Scruff. You're the worst of the lot . . .'

Chapter Ten

Spindrick stood on the deck of the sailing barque and stared at Keng's Island, which had been shrouded in mist the day before. In fact the pine-marten captain had thought it was just a fog bank. But they had put out the sea anchor for the night to do some repairs to the ship, and during that time had heard the beat of the island's drums. There were mammals inside that cloud resting on the waves.

Spindrick was a curious weasel, highly intelligent, but just a bit loopy. Like most middle-class Varicosian mustelids he was interested in all things 'scientific', which covered just about every aspect of life. Monty always felt that Spindrick had been kicked in the head by a mouse when he was very young and that accounted for the loopiness.

'We're not staying here,' said the captain of the barque firmly, 'and that's that. I'm the captain.'

'I hired this ship,' replied Spindrick, even more firmly, 'and that makes me its temporary owner. I want to see what's on that island. If you don't do what I want, you won't get paid at the end of the voyage – it's as simple as that. No stay, no pay.'

'But what if something happens to my vessel? Some of these tropical island mongooses can be very savage. I've been a castaway, so I know. They cooked one of my crew and ate him.'

'That was a different set of islands, and anyway I heard it was *you* who ate him, when you ran out of grub. They composed a song, a sea shanty about the incident if I remember right. Doesn't it go: *Poor Billy, he was ate by Captain Spreng, belt, buttons and boots and all*? Your name is Spreng, isn't it?'

'Yes, but there are many Sprengs sailing the seven seas.'

'*Poor Billy, he was the cabin jack, and lordy did he bawl . . .*'

'All right, all right!'

'*Some say he cried for mercy, most say he cried in vain, for Captain Spreng had Billy chops, for starters and for main . . .*'

'Yes, yes,' growled Spreng, 'we know how the song goes.'

'*Young Billy, he boiled down to lard, of that there is*

no doubt, while Spreng cracked open all his bones, to suck the marrow out . . .'

'No need to go on,' muttered the captain, absently licking his lips. 'These songs can start very cruel rumours. I'm sorry, Jal Spindrick, we're moving on. I heard a rumour about a giant marmoset in these parts. They say there's a great wall built to cut an island in half. On one side, the local mammals; on the other a flesh-eating monster. They say he peels mammals like bananas, dips them in fat, and bites their heads off.'

'Flesh-eating,' said one of the crew. 'Yuk!'

'Yummy,' murmured a dreamy-looking Spreng, a little too loudly. 'Oh – oh, I mean, yuk.'

'Bogey-mammal gods and witchvets – I've heard it all,' grumbled Spindrick. 'Those are just stories. I'd like to see the *real* islanders. I understand they build huge canoes which carry a hundred mongooses and sail thousands of miles across unknown waters with nothing but a few coconuts and half a dozen prayers. I've heard they navigate by nature alone: just the sun, the stars and sightings of birds. But I suppose we don't have the time. Maybe on the way back.'

They continued their voyage to Tarawak without further incident, but Spindrick, writing in his notebook, was already making plans to return to Keng's Island.

Tarawak was a vast continental island with wall-to-wall jungle, most of it unexplored. On arrival, Spindrick set about organizing his expedition to search the interior for Margery Spred and Speckle Jyde. He found some local mongooses who were prepared to act as guides and porters. It wasn't easy, for they were in high demand. There were other expeditions being formed at the same time. One was led by a stoat named Alan Barrelbung, who was off looking for another lost professor, the father of a jill stoat who had gone searching for some lost diamond mines. Then there were two weasels who wanted to find the source of the Klangalang river, which they believed to be in the Mountains of the Moon. Finally there was a group of badgers who were determined to find the mythical graveyard of bearded hogs, whose tusks fetched a high price in Muggidrear. The whole place was humming.

Spindrick managed to get his porters, but failed to find a good guide, and decided to book into the local hotel before resuming his search. He was not impressed by the expatriate stoats, who sat on the veranda all evening, drinking mango dew and moaning about how hard life was on Tarawak. However, he did hear some story about a weasel who had been raised by wild fruit bats and could hang upside down from the tops of palm trees by his claws. Spindrick wrote this down in his notebook, thinking that if ever he became a writer, stories like this would come in very useful.

While Spindrick sat on the veranda listening to these wild tales of the dark continent, he was visited by a tall, elegant mongoose who seemed more regal than those he had employed as his porters.

'My name is Rakki-Takki,' said the creature. 'I

wish to return to my homeland in the south. I know the country well – its rivers and mountains, its lakes and whatnot. I would be willing to act as your guide for nothing, if you will have me.'

'Oh, I wouldn't take him,' said the expat stoats. 'He's a prince of some tribe or other, who chucked him out. He'll get you into all sorts of trouble, he will.'

But Spindrick liked the look of this wiry creature with his noble bearing. 'You're hired,' he said. 'Three square snakes a day and a loan of one of my sleeping bags.'

'Done,' replied Rakki-Takki. He pointed to Spindrick's pith helmet. 'Do I get one of those?'

'No,' said Spindrick, who was rather possessive of his helmet. 'Only the leader of the expedition gets one of these, but you can wear a turban, or fez, or anything else you like.'

Rakki-Takki was rather disappointed, but he tried not to show it. He draped himself over a chair in a lithe, willowy fashion, much to the disgust of the expat stoats, who didn't approve of mongooses hobnobbing with weasels or stoats. There was no such prejudice in Spindrick, however. Anarchist as he was, he saw all mammals as equal, and would blow them all up given the chance to create chaos.

'So, will you have a glass of mango dew with me?' he asked Rakki-Takki. 'Or don't you drink?'

'I'd rather not.'

'Suit yourself – blast, don't these mosquitoes bother you?' Spindrick swatted at a particularly persistent buzzer.

'Rotten blood,' explained Rakki-Takki. 'They don't like it.'

'How do you get it rotten?'

'You have to drink the water of the Klangalang river for half your life. It's got some terrible diseases in it, but it does thicken your blood and gives it a foul smell. Keeps away flies as well as mozzies. Well, I'd better turn in, if we're going early tomorrow.'

'Crack of noon.'

'See you then.' Rakki-Takki unfolded his long lean self from the raffia chair and stood up, knocking his head on an oil lamp. He sloped out into the night, leaving the tongues of the expats wagging.

'You lot make me sick,' cried Spindrick, as he rose to go to bed under his mosquito net. 'I've a good mind to blow you all up before I leave in the morning.'

When he had gone the wagging tongues began again, only it was Spindrick's name on the end of them.

'Demned impertinent weasel!'

'Too uppity by far.'

'Doesn't know Tarawak at all. Newcomer here.'

'Doesn't know our ways.'

'Send 'im back to Welkin, I say.'

And so on. And so forth. Idle bodies, busy tongues.

CHAPTER ELEVEN

The coach and twelve, with its six passengers,
set off for Krunchen on a cold and frosty
morning. All the visitors were wrapped up in
coats, scarves and mittens. The two natives –
Boombach and Florette – wore simple country
smocks. They were used to the weather in
Slattland. In fact Boombach professed himself to
be quite warm. 'I am not so good with the
heat,' he told them. 'My weight, you know. Such
a trial to me.'

'Why don't you go on a diet?' said Bryony
primly. The 'healthy vet adviser' in her had been
dying to say something to Boombach, but she had
held back out of politeness. Now here was an
opening. She could speak freely.

'Diet?' asked Boombach, looking puzzled. 'What is that? I am not familiar.'

'Eat less,' said Maudlin, who hadn't forgiven Boombach for telling him untrue stories.

Bryony tempered this. 'Eat the *right* kind of food.'

'Eat less, I do not like,' said Boombach, looking worried. 'Eat different, I think I can stomach. What must I eat?'

'Vegetables,' replied Bryony eagerly. 'Plenty of fruit and vegetables, and nuts. Very little meat. No starchy things though, like potatoes. No sweet things, like cream.'

Boombach looked horrified, then he shuddered violently. 'I must have my meat. I must have my fried potatoes. I must have my double cream on steamed pudding. You ask me not? It is impossible. I would die. I would surely die.'

'Of course you wouldn't die,' snapped Bryony, losing patience as she always did when someone failed to take her good advice. 'You might *yearn* a little, but you won't die.'

Boombach shook his head determinedly. 'I eat what Florette eats – we eat together.'

'You surely don't eat the same things? The same amounts?' asked Bryony.

'Yes, we surely do,' said Florette. 'Yet, as you see, I am the thin one, the dancer, and he is the fat one, the singer.'

'So much for science,' Maudlin said.

Bryony didn't understand it. She didn't understand it at all.

The coach rumbled over tracks with iron-hard

furrows. They went through woodland most of the way. Dark, dense pine forests spread from one end of the country to the other. Maudlin stared into these forests and wondered what they harboured. Surely they were chock full of gothic monsters? He mentioned it to Scruff.

'I make you right there, Maudlin. Crawlin' with 'em, I suspect. Lots of tragedy in them woods. Littered with red hoods thrown off by young jills. Woodsmammals' axes lyin' rustin' on the ground. Lost kittens, lookin' for houses made out of marzipan. You wouldn't want to go in them woods, Maudlin.'

And the towns they passed through were equally sombre and dark. Tall cathedrals threw shadows down narrow alleyways. Even the inns looked like homes for wayward bats.

Of course, it was between such towns that Maudlin found he just *had* to go to the toilet. 'Stop the coach,' he said, after ten minutes of crossing his legs until it hurt. 'I must find a bush.'

Monty yelled at the coachmammal. The guard thought something was chasing them and fired his blunderbuss into the trees. The explosion frightened Maudlin so much it nearly meant that a stop was unnecessary. Finally it was all sorted out. Maudlin stepped out of the coach into the crisp air. He was a very shy weasel, so he went quite a way into the trees before he felt safe relieving himself. Having finished, however, he looked around him in quiet panic. It swiftly became noisy panic. 'Help! Monty! Scruff! Bryony! I'm lost.'

There was no answer – simply an eerie silence. All the trees looked alike. He listened hard for any answering sounds, but there were none. Staring at the forest floor, he could see no tracks of any kind: it was covered in a soft carpet of brown pine needles. Maudlin began walking the way he believed he had come.

When he had been walking for twenty minutes, he realized he was not heading in the right direction, and began backtracking faster. Again he found he was passing ground nests and fox holes he had never seen before. 'Awwweee,' he whined. 'I'm lost.'

The forest, he knew, was almost endless. It covered thousands of square miles. When he came across the skeleton of a badger, he almost broke down and wept. Instead, he wept, then broke down. 'Scruff,' he whined. 'This is all Scruff's fault.'

Just when he had given up hope, Maudlin came to a clearing in the trees. In the middle of the clearing was a tree stump. Sitting on the tree stump eating a sandwich was a creature Maudlin had never seen before. Maudlin decided it was a furry goblin. Leaning against the tree stump was a sharp axe. Maudlin didn't like the look of that axe. It might be a tool, but then again, it might be a weapon. He wasn't sure.

The creature looked up. Its strangeness seemed to be all about its ears. They were huge. They hung from its head down to its back feet. In all other aspects it seemed to be a rat of some kind. There was a pointed nose, the visible teeth, the long bare pink tail. Maudlin was not fond of rats, be they foreign or home grown. He approached warily.

'Hello, do you speak Welkin?'

'I might,' replied the rat, pushing the last few crumbs of bread through his whiskers, 'or I might not.'

'You obviously do.'

'So? I was in the merchant navy, once upon a time. I speak several languages. What are you selling, anyway? Cuckoo clocks? I've got a hundred. Leather breeches? I'm wearing some. Glockenspiels? I can't play.'

'I'm not selling anything. I'm lost. I wonder if you would show me the way out of the forest,' asked Maudlin weakly.

'Not selling anything?' The rat's whiskers twitched. 'No point in talking to you then, is there?'

'No, no – please. I'm lost. Do you have a cabin near here? I'm tired, thirsty and hungry. I have money to pay.' Maudlin showed the rat his purse.

The rat picked up his axe and Maudlin took two steps backwards.

The rat scowled. 'I'm not going to hurt you. I'm not one of those woodsmammals who chop off the first head they see. As for showing you the way out of the forest. Which way? You can go in any direction and get out, but where you'll be when you do is another matter. Which direction were you travelling? North, south, east or west?'

'South,' murmured Maudlin miserably.

'Can't help you,' said the rat, shouldering his tool. 'I only know the other three.'

'Then you must know the fourth!' cried Maudlin.

'I must not,' replied the rat firmly. 'Come along then, if you want food and drink. It'll cost you coin though.' He walked off.

Maudlin followed him, realizing that he would have to get friendly with this creature in order to obtain assistance for himself. 'My name's Maudlin,' he told the rat, catching up and keeping pace with him. 'What's yours?'

'Karl Kribbelig.'

'Um, what do you do?'

The rat indicated his axe. 'I'm a woods-mammal. I chop wood.'

'Do you get bothered by vampire voles here?'

Kribbelig stopped and stared at Maudlin with hard eyes. 'With what?'

'Vampire voles.'

'South?' cried the woodsmammal. 'That way.' He pointed with a paw. 'Get thee gone, o vampire hunter.'

'Oh, so now you know the direction,' cried Maudlin sarcastically. 'Well, thank you.' Then he added pitifully, 'I'm going to die, aren't I?'

'No,' said the rat. 'You're going to live for ever – as one of the undead – if you don't turn round and go back to Welkin.'

'You're just trying to scare me.'

'And doing a good job, by the look.'

The rat then melted into the trees. Maudlin shuddered and went off in the direction indicated. Finally he came to the coach party again.

Scruff cried, 'Where've you bin? We looked everywhere. We was just going on to the next turnpike, to organize a search party.'

'I want to go home,' whined Maudlin. 'I met a rat who said I was never going to die.'

'Lucky you,' replied Bryony.

'You don't understand! We're all going to live!' cried Maudlin, in melodramatic tones. 'We're all going to live for ever!'

'What is it with this weasel?' laughed Scruff. 'He looks death in the face and laughs.'

Full of merriment, they bundled Maudlin into the coach and sped on their way along the dark forest road.

CHAPTER TWELVE

The coach rattled along the highway. They finally came to a wayside inn where they were to stop the night. As usual, Maudlin and Scruff shared a room between them. When they had unpacked their cases and were sitting around a roaring log fire down in the parlour, Monty asked Maudlin, 'What exactly *did* happen in the forest?'

'I – er – I met a rat called Karl.'

'And what did Karl tell you?'

'He said I would become one of the undead.'

Monty nodded, satisfied. 'We're definitely on the right track here, if locals in the middle of the forest know of the vampires. Well done, Maudlin, I would hate to think we were on a wild wren chase.'

A full tankard of pear dew sat before Maudlin and he reached down to take a sip of it. At that moment the innkeeper yelled something in Slattlandish and mammals began diving for the cellar door. They scrambled down the steps in a great panic.

'What's going on?' cried Monty.

Florette said, 'Quick, down the steps. The were-foxes are coming! The werefoxes are coming!'

Monty, Boombach, Bryony, Scruff, Florette and, lastly, Maudlin scampered down the cellar steps. The innkeeper locked and bolted the thick door behind them. Everyone – all the animals who had been in the parlour – sat around on barrels and casks, listening. The eyes of the local mammals were on the ceiling of the cellar, above which presumably the werefoxes were roaming. There was a tense atmosphere – one or two lemmings were restless, pacing up and down, glancing up at the ceiling every few seconds.

'What exactly does that mean?' asked Maudlin. '*Were*foxes?'

'Well,' replied Monty, 'the word *were* actually means "man". A werewolf, is a man-wolf. A wolf that changes into a man, usually at full moon. These supernatural men-beings go out into the night seeking the blood of victims. Here we have foxes who change into blood-drinking humans, ranging at night, seeking to quench their terrible, driving thirst. It doesn't do to get in their way. They have the strength of ten foxes. If you get bitten by one – they usually rip you apart anyway

– they're not like subtle vampires just sucking gently on your throat: they tear open your chest and gorge on the heart's blood – anyway, if you get bitten, you turn into one of them.'

'A werefox?'

'In your case, a wereweasel.'

'Um,' said Maudlin, in a disbelieving tone.

After quite a while the innkeeper, his ear to the great oak door, nodded and signalled the all-clear. Lemmings began chattering in that harsh tongue of theirs, climbing the steps to the parlour.

When they reached their table, however, Maudlin let out a loud, 'Hey! Someone's drunk all our pear dew.'

True enough the tankards were all empty.

'Never mind,' said Boombach, collecting them up, 'I will fetch us some more drink.'

The corpulent lemming had the tankards filled again, but just as they were about to drink them, the landlord yelled in Slattlandish, 'The wererats are coming! The wererats are coming!' Everyone rushed for the cellar again, went through the same agonizing wait below stairs, and finally came up to find all the tankards empty.

Maudlin's eyes narrowed. 'Something's going on here,' he said, looking down into his empty pot.

This time Bryony refilled the tankards. Just as they were raising them to their lips, the now familiar cry went up: 'The werestoats are coming! The werestoats are coming!' The anxious scramble for safety began again. Only the name of the mammal had changed. The supernatural nature of the invaders remained the same.

Maudlin went down with the others, but very reluctantly. He was now convinced that one of the landlord's serving jills was emptying their tankards back into the barrels while everyone was in the cellar. Sure enough, when they all came up again, Maudlin's pot was empty.

Right, that does it, he said to himself. I'm not going down into the cellar again.

A few minutes later the cry went up: 'The wereweasels are coming! The wereweasels are coming!'

Maudlin hung back and ducked away, just before the cellar door closed. He sneaked behind the bar, where he had seen the guard on his coach put the blunderbuss. With this weapon in his paws he resolved to fire into the air should he see anyone emptying the tankards, to scare the living daylights out of them. That was the plan, anyway.

After a short while he heard the front door open. There was the padding of bare feet on the flagstone floor. Maudlin peaked over the top of the counter and stared at the shadowy figures moving around in the lamplight. Man-weasels. Foul-looking creatures with no hair on their bodies. Bare as a rat's tail. They looked pink and evil, with their red eyes burning feverishly in their faces. Seven of them in all: given their small stature, clearly once weasels in shape, now horribly human in form. Their large, slavering mouths were full of oversized teeth. Their claws were long, dagger-like and vicious-looking. Distorted weasels, with human features, but weasel tails and weasel litheness about their movements.

Here were seven wereweasels indeed. They had left the front door open, through which Maudlin could clearly see the full moon. It was a strange-looking moon, scarlet with splashes of shadow about its face. No wonder all the werecreatures were about tonight. They roamed the parlour, sniffing at this and that, drinking down pots of pear dew when they found a full one. Finally they gathered in the middle of the room, their red eyes glaring, and took one last look around. Finding no mammals to rip open, they began to leave.

Six of the wereweasels left the inn, dashing out into the moonlight with eerie yells of 'Ercha!' and 'Watchit!' One remained behind, sniffing the air. Maudlin crouched down lower behind the bar, but as he did so the blunderbuss barrel chinked against a glass bottle. Instantly the wereweasel ran forward, snarling, its mouth wide, its claws raking air. Maudlin felt terror coursing through his veins. He was about to be torn apart by a small pink human with weasely swiftness. 'Help! Help!' he cried. 'I'm being attacked!'

He raised the blunderbuss and squeezed the trigger. The old blunderbuss kicked and boomed, sending out a deadly spray of nuts and bolts, old foreign coins, paperclips, collar studs, pen nibs and other various unwanted pieces of metal. The wereweasel was struck full in the head and body with this hail of shot. It stopped it in its tracks.

Maudlin felt both relieved and triumphant. He had destroyed a wereweasel!

But when the smoke had cleared, the wereweasel was still on its feet. Its body was full of holes, through which bright moonlight was streaming – but it wasn't dead. It snarled its anger at Maudlin, who felt the fear start bubbling up in his stomach, then enter his veins as cold as ice. This was surely the end. If a full barrel of grapeshot in the chest did not stop this creature, nothing would. Maudlin was doomed.

The wereweasel sprang forwards, latching onto Maudlin's throat with its nasty teeth, digging its claws into his fur. Maudlin felt all his confidence drain from his body. He was a dead weasel. Perhaps one fated to become like this bare-skinned, hairless creature of the night, roaming the earth for ever in search of blood.

Suddenly a shot rang out.

CHAPTER THIRTEEN

The wereweasel gave a strangled cry. Then its teeth loosened their grip and it slipped away from Maudlin, its eyes still glaring its ferocity. Finally it fell in a heap of disgusting pink skin on the floor. Its mouth gaped open and the tongue lolled out onto the inn floor. Clearly it was dead – or what passed for dead with wereweasels. Gradually, before Maudlin's eyes, the corpse began to change. It grew hair, a nice pointed nose, some decent fluffy ears. It had changed from human form into an innocent-looking weasel which looked tranquil and sweet in death.

Maudlin turned to look at who had fired the single shot. There was a smell of cordite in the air. When the smoke cleared, Monty stood there, a pistol in his paw. He lowered his forelimb, letting the weapon rest at his side.

Maudlin was astonished. 'How did you do that? I shot him full of holes and it just irritated him a bit.'

'Silver bullet,' murmured Monty, reloading the pistol carefully. 'Silver bullet in the heart. The only thing that will kill a weremammal of any kind.'

Maudlin nodded. 'Thank goodness you came up! I could've been torn to bits. That thing could have been chomping on my heart this very moment. As it is, I've just been bitten in the throat. Not serious. Bryony will soon put it right with some ointment and a dressing.'

'Mmmm,' murmured Monty, closing the chamber of his pistol with a loud click.

'Why – why are you looking at me like that?' asked Maudlin. 'What've you loaded the gun for? There're no more wereweasels to shoot. Is that a silver bullet in there? Answer me.'

'Yes it is,' said Monty, raising the weapon. 'You did say you'd been bitten.'

Maudlin choked. Of course! Monty had said earlier that anyone bitten by a werecreature became one of those creatures themselves. Monty was now going to kill him because he had become one of the supernatural creatures of the night.

Just as the other weasels and the lemmings were coming up out of the cellar, Maudlin screamed, 'Please don't shoot me, Monty!'

Monty frowned and shook his head. Scruff came across the room and sidled up to Maudlin.

'Hush,' he said severely. 'As if our friend and benefactor would kill you.'

'He thinks I'm a wereweasel,' sobbed Maudlin.

Boombach stepped forward. 'Does he indeed? Please to tell me what has happened?'

Monty said, 'He was bitten, but very slightly. I have no intention of shooting him of course. I loaded my pistol in case we were attacked by any more weremammals.'

Boombach nodded. 'So – bitten? By the were-creature?' He suddenly lurched at Maudlin and sank his teeth into the small wound on the weasel's neck.

Maudlin screamed. 'He's a werelemming!' Then when Boombach let him go, he swung away and into a corner, clutching his throat.

Bryony went to him, opening her vet's bag at the same time. She dabbed and dressed the wound, which in truth was not at all deep. Then she went to remonstrate with Boombach. 'You made matters worse, Boombach. I'm surprised at you.'

'But that was not intention. You see, I have a silver tooth – so.' He opened his mouth to reveal a fang of pure silver. 'I think it is like the silver bullet. It makes the weremammal ordinary again. It drives the *were* from the body like bad spirit. It silvers out the demon. I think I cure him of his were-problem.'

Maudlin's eyes suddenly filled with tears on hearing these words. He came over to Boombach and hugged him. 'My hero,' he said.

Boombach shrugged him off. 'Oh, it is nothing.'

Monty said, 'Nevertheless we'll have to keep a close watch on our Maudlin, in case he starts developing any strange symptoms.'

The evening's entertainment started: Boombach sang and Florette danced, much to the delight of the local lemmings. Later, as Scruff and Maudlin went up to their bedroom, their shadows wavering on the walls in the candlelight, Scruff let out an audible gasp.

'What is it?' asked Maudlin, whirling round.

'Your fur – it's all comin' out! You're – you're turning furless.'

'Oh, Gawd!' cried Maudlin. 'I'm changing.' Then he looked up to see a smirk on Scruff's face.

Scruff said, 'Gotcha there, Maud, eh?'

'You rotter,' growled Maudlin. 'I'll be ready for your jokes, next time.'

Scruff went into the room first and checked to see if there was a chamber pot under the bed. Finding one in place, he was satisfied. But he also came across something else, which he didn't mention to Maudlin.

It was bitterly cold outside. Through the window, they could see large flakes of snow drifting by in the moonlight. Surely by the morning the snow would be waist deep? They wondered what the journey to Krunchen would be like. Some coaches allowed small coal stoves inside, but most passengers had to make do with blankets to cover the legs. There were coach-drivers who still had a wild mammal's fear of fire and didn't want their vehicle going up in smoke. The weasels' coach-driver was one of those.

The two weasels changed into night-shirts and lay down in bed side by side, staring up at the ceiling in the gloom. Maudlin, still nervous after his experiences with the wereweasel, started to hum, but someone in the next room hammered on the wall with a shoe and he shut up.

'Did you know,' said Scruff quietly, 'that there was a lemming count once, who had a blue room and a red room in his manor. He always asked his guests which one they wanted to sleep in. If they slept in the red room, they died during the night. Those in the blue one disappeared, never to be found again. None of 'em knew this, of course. They was just asked which one they wanted.'

'How – how did the ones who vanished – I mean – where did they go?'

'They found out years later, after the count was dead, o' course, that the bed opened up and swallered the sleepers. They would be trapped in a box under the bed and suffocate and die. Then they would just rot away. There was quite a few skeletons in the box, when they opened it all up.'

'D-didn't they suspect anything? The guests?'

'Not a thing. Oh, yes, one or two of them wrote in their diaries before they went to sleep in the blue room, sayin' they thought they smelled somefink like rottin' flesh comin' from under the bed.'

'It – it was the corpses, wasn't it?'

'I s'pose it must 'ave been, yes.'

Maudlin sniffed. He thought he could detect a faint aroma of something rotting. In fact he was sure of it. Meat? Perhaps not like meat. More like silage. More vegetable in nature. That was a relief. He tried to take his mind off this latest unpleasant suspicion by asking more questions. 'Where did the count live?' he asked.

'Oh.' Scruff waved a paw vaguely. 'Around here somewhere, I think. Yes, definitely somewhere near Krunchen. Hey!' He sat up abruptly. 'You don't think . . . nah. Well, I s'pose it's possible, but it would be a bit of a coincidence, wouldn't it?'

'What?' asked Maudlin nervously.

'Well, this could be the count's manor, couldn't it? Maybe he fell on hard times and had to sell his house, which is now an inn? It makes sense but . . .'

'But what?'

'Well, it's all a bit far-fetched, ain't it? You think *this* inn might have once been the count's manor?' Scruff shook his head violently. 'Nah, nah. Too much of a coincidence really.'

'You haven't told me about the red room. How – how did the guests in the red room die?'

'Oh, that was easy. The pillow and sheets had poison in 'em, which only came out as a deadly gas when the sheets and pillow was warm. So, you're cold when you get into bed, see? But you warm up, and you warm the pillows and sheets when you do. That's when the gas came out and killed whoever was in the bed.'

'And did this gas – well, what did it smell of?'

'Hmm? Oh, it had a sort of old-vegetably smell. Like rottin' potatoes, or cabbages – or fruit. Yes, that was it.'

113

'Fruit?'

'Yep, somethin' like that.'

Maudlin sniffed. Yes that was it. Definitely. Rotting apples. He leapt out of bed and yelled at Scruff: 'Get up! Get up out of bed!'

'What's the matter?' cried Scruff. 'What's up?'

'This is the count's red room bed! I can smell the deadly gas. Rotting apples. I can smell them!'

There was silence for a while, then Scruff clicked his teeth in the equivalent of a weasel's snigger. Maudlin, shivering in his night-shirt, lit a candle with a match. He held the candle up and asked in a frustrated voice, 'What are you so amused at?'

'Under the bed,' clicked Scruff. 'Look under the bed.'

Maudlin did so, finding a box of bruised apples there, next to the chamber pot. Someone had left them behind, perhaps a guest, or maybe even the innkeeper himself. There they were, rotting away slowly, giving off that particular odour. He snuffed out the candle and jumped back into bed. 'You're rotten, you are.'

'What,' clacked Scruff, unable to contain himself, 'like the apples under the bed?'

At that moment the door flew open and Boombach stood there. 'One more sound,' he said in that booming voice of his, 'and I must come and jump on the two of you. I am very fat. It will hurt very much. Please, I am trying very hard to sleep in my bed. You two are making the most unholy racket. Is it the same with all weasels? I think not. The rooms of Jal Sylver and Jis Bludd

114

are silent. Only from this room comes the noise. Be quiet.'

'Sorry, Boombach, it's Maudlin,' said Scruff, trying to blame his friend. 'He keeps tellin' me ghost stories – scarin' me to death, he is.'

'Maudlin, this is not kind to a friend in an unfamiliar old house like this one, once owned by an ancient count by the name of Stretchikoff. Not kind at all, when many mammals have died here by the paw of Count Stretchikoff, who used to murder his guests. There are many ghosts. Many. Try to contain your mirth, and your noise, if you please.' Boombach left, closing the door quietly behind him.

There was a terrible silence in the room for about half a minute. Then Maudlin let out a thin whimper. Scruff swallowed hard.

The door opened quietly again and Boombach peered in. 'Got you!' he said. 'This wall between our rooms is quite thin. I hear the whole story from Scruff's lips. Now go to sleep, or I really must come and jump on both you Welkin weasels. It is understood? Good.'

CHAPTER FOURTEEN

Mayor Poynt was in his element. He was presiding over a private function attended by all the mayors of smaller northern towns. He held a similar one for southern town mayors but it was best to keep the two apart if Muggidrear was to stay intact. The two groups tended to start off friendly and end up running riot through the streets, chasing each other with custard pies and chair legs. Mayor Poynt's private functions were jackish do's, where stoat behaviour was at its worst.

Stout male stoats stuck their thumbs in their waistcoat pockets and said things like, 'Hey oop, jack, 'ow's thee, mate? Does she know you've robbed kitten's mousie bank of all them farthin's?' To receive a reply in the vein of 'Like as 'eck. What she don't know won't 'urt 'er, will it?'

Jeremy Poynt held most of these jack mayors in contempt (a jill did once stand for mayoress in Mackleswipe, but was driven off the platform by jeering stoat louts who said jills were good for nought but making jellied rabbits' blood) but he held this annual dinner to curry favour. He needed their support for various provincial projects and it did no harm to lord it over them for a day. So here he sat, with an object covered by a large piece of cloth by his side. Most of the mayors present thought that a silver cup or trophy lay under the cloth, ready to be presented to the mayor displaying the most jackish behaviour of the day.

'Gentlemammals,' he cried, hammering the table with a mouse leg cooked in rosemary, 'let the games begin.'

Forelimbs shot out and grabbed jugs of honey dew, plates of mouse- and vole-meat, chips, crisp toasted bats' wings, sparrows' liver pâté, and whatever else lay on the table in front of them. Weasel waitresses tried to replenish the dishes on the table as fast as they were gobbled down, but the provincial mayors were giving them a hard time, leering at them and making ill-mannered remarks.

Falshed, attending the dinner for the first time, was disgusted by the behaviour of the stoat mayors. 'Is it like this every year?' he asked Mayor Poynt. 'Where do these mammals come from?'

'It gets worse than this, Chief. But don't be so nicey-nicey. Let your pelt hang down. You could have some fun if you weren't so uptight and prissy.'

A Fearsomeshire pudding flew through the air – the first of many to come – and Falshed grimaced. If this was fun, give him a quiet day at home any time.

'Now, before I have too much to drink and forget why I invited a twit like you to my dinner, Falshed, let me tell you. It's a sort of farewell meal, the last rites, if you like.'

'What?' cried Falshed, alarmed, thinking he was being sacked.

'Don't look so shocked. I'm not throwing you out on the street. You're going on your holidays.'

Falshed brightened. 'Oh, where to?'

'Slattland.'

Now, the chief of police knew very well that Montegu Sylver and his troop had gone to Slattland to seek the source of the vampire voles. 'Oh, Slattland,' he said, depressed; then, with an attempt at humour, added, 'I'd rather go to Tarawak, where it's warmer at this time of year.'

'You may be going there too,' muttered the mayor, ducking a flying slab of pâté. 'Spindrick Sylver is up to no good in that particular region of the world. But first I want you to follow the other Sylver to Transylvladia and make sure he's not up to anything either. I don't trust those weasels. You'll take a ship tomorrow morning with the turn of the tide.'

Slattland! What a terrible blow. Falshed was in

the process of making progress with the mayor's sister, Sybil, who was recovering from her terrible ordeal of first being bitten by a vampire vole and secondly being sprayed with holy water. Falshed had been most understanding, sitting by the bed of the pale and wan princess, reading to her, discussing light and airy subjects with her (which was good, since Falshed was not at all happy with heavy ones), and generally making himself useful. Now he would have to forgo his ministering to the sick in order to take a horrible voyage, at the worst time of the year, across giant seas to a country that was clad in ice and snow, and was full of foreigners who spoke funny. 'What if I refuse?' he said to the mayor. 'You have no right to send me away on such errands.'

Mayor Poynt fluffed his white fur and narrowed his eyes. 'You don't want to try me, Falshed. You know I play dirty.'

This was true. Jeremy Poynt's dirty tricks were legendary. The deputy mayor, who had once disagreed with Jeremy on something or other, was now cleaning toilets on Whistleminster Bridge.

'Just kidding, Mayor,' said Falshed, forcing a look of good humour onto his pointed face. 'Hey – we're out with the jacks! Can't you take a joke?'

'I can take anything. Anything at all,' replied the mayor, with quiet menace. 'Just remember that.'

The air was now thick with pies and tarts. The weasel jills had retreated to the kitchens. Furniture was being broken up. A full pot of stew had just gone through the window, breaking several panes, to land with a terrible crash on the pavement below. It was at this point that the mayor unveiled the object by his side. It was not a cup or trophy. It was a steam-powered catapult, invented by Wm. Jott. Already chugging away and loaded with mouse pies, at the flip of a small lever it began to send its missiles hurtling down the length of the table. These swift meat messages struck the mayor at the far end of the table with full force.

This same mayor suddenly reached down by his side and picked up a suitcase. He opened it quickly to reveal a similar machine, this one powered by clockwork and invented by Thos. Tempus Fugit. Custard tarts hurtled towards Jeremy Poynt, striking him in several places on his ermine-covered body at once.

'Touché,' yelled the mayor at the other end. 'Got you back for that, Poynt.'

Falshed sighed. He got up and left the room, leaving the brainless stoats to their brainless games. He made his way to Princess Sybil's chambers and, after being announced by the weasel chamberjill, he entered her room.

Sybil was sitting up in bed, two pillows bolstering her weak frame. She was knitting. Falshed blinked, astonished. In the normal run of things the princess was no knitter. She hadn't the patience or the inclination to sit still, clicking two needles together.

'Princess? What are you doing?'

'I'm making my own shroud,' she said

brightly, holding up a horrible shapeless garment for him to approve. 'I've changed, Zacharias, since my ordeal. I'm more contemplative. I've taken up ki lok and that enables me to look upon my life as worthless. I want to go out in something warm, though, so I thought I'd knit this . . .' She put it down despondently. 'It's awful, isn't it? You don't need to say anything. As a knitter I'd make a good dustmammal, wouldn't I?'

'Well – it's just not your thing, Princess.'

'Oh well, I'll give it to the poor.'

'And how are you feeling now? What's all this ki lok business?'

She brightened again. 'Oh, my laundry-mammal, a weasel named Foo Fum, suggested I try it. It's exercises in breathing and stretching the claws, which can be done in bed. But it's more than that, really. It's a way of life and a way of death. You sort of do this.' And she put on a fierce expression, crossed her eyes, touched her nose with her wet pink tongue, and went, 'Hooommmmmmmmmmmm.'

'And that makes you feel better?'

'Much better. You should try it.'

'Maybe I will,' he lied. 'In the meantime, bad news, I'm afraid. I've been sent to Slattland by your brother.'

Sybil looked at him innocently. 'And why is that bad news?'

'Well, er, I shan't – shan't be able to come and read to you in the evenings if I'm over there, will I?'

'Oh, that's all right,' she said airily, picking up

121

her looking glass and inspecting her whiskers. 'One of the servants will be just as good.'

Falshed's heart plummeted. 'I did so enjoy your company.'

'Yes, I know you did, but I'm not coming to Slattland, so you'll have to get on without it, won't you?'

'I suppose. Look, you couldn't speak to – to Jeremy?'

She looked up from the mirror. 'Whatever about?'

'Well, about me. Couldn't you change his mind?'

'Whatever for?'

Falshed ground his teeth. The princess could be incredibly dense at times. He wondered whether it was deliberate. Did she have no feelings for him whatsoever? It was too bad. Too bad. 'Well, I thought you'd miss me if I went away, but obviously I was wrong.'

She looked at him with round eyes and placed a paw on his shoulder. 'Oh, Zacharias, you *know* I will.' Then she went back to primping her whiskers. 'But you know Jeremy. Once he's set his heart on something, nothing on earth will move him.'

'You could.'

'No – no I couldn't. I've never had any influence over Jeremy. He's a law unto himself.'

But Falshed knew this was not so. When Sybil wanted her own way, she could get it. But obviously her feelings for him did not run deep. Rather than a river, they were the trickle that goes along the gutter after a shower of rain. It was too bad. 'Goodbye,' he said. 'I shall miss you, anyway.'

'Pardon?' she said, as he reached the doorway. 'Did you say something?'

CHAPTER FIFTEEN

Monty and his companions arrived in Krunchen
when the snow was as thick as bedding over
the whole town. It was as if pillows, bolsters,
linen sheets and great white mattresses had been
dropped from the sky. The air was cold, but
there was no really sharp wind blowing, so the
weasels – unused to such quantities of snow –
could appreciate the charm of the scene. For
under that white covering were towers, domes,
turrets and green cupolas. Krunchen was a city
of high and dark gothic beauty. She was the
jewel of southern Slattland and her inhabitants
were justly proud of her.

'We have many fine buildings,' said Florette. 'I
hope you will find the time to visit them.'

'We'll certainly try,' Bryony replied, staring through the coach window at the architecture drifting by. 'Oh – look – a canal. Several canals. There're lemmings skating on them. How wonderful.'

The weasels in the coach could just see the heads of the skaters, level with the roadway, as they whizzed back and forth.

Boombach said, 'You must go in the evening. Yes, this is the best time for the skating. You see there are stalls now closed along the edge of the ice? In the evening this will be open, with many pretty lights. You will buy roast nuts and hot drinks. This is what you must do in Krunchen. This is what we are famous for in this time of year.'

'Oh, yes,' cried Maudlin. 'I want to skate. I'm an expert skater.'

'Have you ever skated, Maudlin?' asked Monty.

'No – but I just feel it in my bones.'

'You will do,' said Scruff, 'when you fall over tonight. I'd like to learn to skate proper, though. Then I'll give you a race, Maud. I expect you'll beat me, being an expert an' all, before you even start.'

'Yes, I expect I will.'

While they were in Krunchen, Monty was treating them all to a grand hotel. It was a magnificent building, built in the city's gothic style, with many tall, thin windows and rounded towers and a wonderful roof which at the moment resembled a ski slope. There were

125

statues everywhere. And fountains too, some frozen into ice umbrellas. Both Maudlin and Scruff were very excited about staying somewhere so posh. They each told the other that he must be on his best behaviour and not do anything that would shame his companion.

A lemming took their luggage up to their room. Maudlin and Scruff followed him up. When he had left they both bounced on the bed several times, finding it incredibly soft and springy. The big white duvet was filled with sparrow down.

'Bet you didn't think you'd be in a place like this,' said Scruff, 'when you was a kitten.'

'Oh, yes, I always saw myself using a bathroom with gold taps and a loo shaped like a swan.'

'Nah, did you?'

'Naturally. I think my mother picked up the wrong kitten after my birth. I think I actually belonged to another jill weasel – royalty, probably – and was robbed of my birthright. I'm convinced of it. Look at the way my fur gets all matted when I wear anything but silk. I mean, if you wanted proof of nobility, there it is. As soon as I put on something satiny or silky, why, I feel right at home.'

'There is that, grant you,' replied his faithful friend. 'But the way you hollered in the streets as a nightwatchmammal, shoutin' "Eight o'clock and all's well!" – why, you'd have said you were born to that too. I remember your mum. She used to speak to her nex' door neighbour, Lill, without

126

leaving her kitchen. You remember! She used to shriek, "Lill!" at the top of her voice. "Lill – you goin' to the fish market today for some stickle-backs?" She had a voice like a foghorn, your mum, except it was sharper and more penetratin'. I liked your mum.'

'She was not my mother, she was someone else's mother.'

Scruff looked shocked. 'How can you say that about your own mum?'

'I told you, I was born to the silk. She made me wear cotton all my life. My *real* mother, who was probably a duchess at the very least, would have had me wrapped in the finest fabrics—'

Scruff hit him with a pillow. 'You just keep quiet now, Maud, 'cause I'm not happy with you. First time in my life. You just keep your peace for a while and perhaps in a bit you'll be better.'

Maudlin did as he was told. Scruff could be a really fierce fighter when it came to it. It would be a brave weasel who could go up against the lamp-lighter in a contest of claw and paw. Maudlin was not brave, not when it came to physical violence.

When evening came the weasels set out for the nearest canal. Here there was a shed where they could hire skates. True to form, Scruff took to skating as if he were born to it. Bryony wasn't bad either. Monty soon learned to skate after a fashion, but he was rather stiff and upright in his movements on the ice. Maudlin spent more time on his backside than he did on his feet. He told the others he chose to do it that way. He would flail, forelimbs and hind limbs thrashing like mad, for about ten metres, then fall onto his back and slide twenty more.

There were strings of coloured lanterns lining the canal. Under these lights were the stalls and kiosks. Soon the four were stopping for mugfuls of hot cider and roasted chestnuts. Well wrapped up in high-collared coats, scarves and mittens, they were warm and enjoying themselves. When they weren't skating or falling over, they stopped at the sides of the frozen canals to watch the other skaters. The lemmings were fantastic. They glided by in their droves, chattering to one another, occasionally doing some twirls and loops, making it all look so very easy.

'I'm just going over there to practise,' Monty said, in truth a little upset that Scruff and Bryony were doing better than he was. 'I need to find my equilibrium. My centre of gravity. My balance. Something like that, anyway.'

He made his way to some railings underneath a bridge, where he could slip and slide in the shadows as much as he wanted without being observed by too many experts. It was while he was resting from his labours that he saw someone he recognized instantly. She was standing on the far side of the canal, about thirty metres away, also keeping to the shadows. Monty realized that she was studying the rest of his group – Bryony, Scruff and Maudlin – as they floundered around under the lights of the kiosks and stalls, near the steps which led up to the road.

It was definitely her.

Sveltlana.

Sveltlana in short, fur-collared coat and fur hat. Fur on fur. It was just like her to sneer at convention. Usually furry mammals avoided furry clothes. It was somehow abhorrent to clothe fur in fur.

Monty tried to melt even further into the shadow thrown down by the bridge. Unfortunately, the movement attracted Sveltlana's attention. She turned quickly and saw him. Her eyes immediately narrowed with hatred. Then, swiftly, she swung round and began skating away, gliding rapidly down the canal.

Monty could not help admiring her grace on the ice. She was like some celestial dancer with magical feet: an angel on skates. Impulsively he decided to follow her. If he could confront her now and get any unpleasantness out of the way, perhaps she would leave the group in peace. Of course, she could be the evil genius behind the vampire vole invasion of Welkin, but Monty very much doubted that. Sveltlana, much as she detested Welkin, liked to be at the forefront of any attack. Monty could not see her doing damage to his country remotely. She would want to see the effects at first paw.

He set off after her, but of course he was very inept. Lemmings in his direct path had to scatter to avoid being run down. However, the more he skated, the better he became. After about a mile, with his muscles aching like mad, he began to improve. He could stay on his feet for at least a hundred metres, and his movements were getting smoother and more accomplished by the second.

There was Sveltlana in the distance! The evil lemming was weaving casually through the other skaters on the canal.

Monty glanced up at a clocktower to see that it was close to midnight. Midnight skaters! There was something a little eerie about that. The moon was out. It shone on the thin ballroom floor on which Monty was now gliding. Then he felt his feet going from under him. He skidded along on his back, crashing into a stall, sending cups of hot cider flying onto the ice. When he looked up from his crumpled position, there was Sveltlana, staring down at him. He gazed into those wonderful brown eyes and, evil though they might be, he was lost in them.

'Help me up,' he said, putting out a paw. 'I want to speak to you.'

Sveltlana ignored him and skated away.

Monty somehow managed to get to his feet and follow her, a little shakily, racing under bridge after bridge. Just before he entered a midnight shadow he looked down and was shocked to see faces peering up at him through the clear ice. There were figures under there – demonic, they seemed, dressed in ragged frock coats and tail-coats, battered top hats and worn dancing shoes – and they were following him along, shoe to skate, foot to paw. When he did a turn, so did they. When he curved out of the bridge's shade, they curved with him. When he – at last – managed a circle, they traced the same figure. It was uncanny, weird and scary.

There were devilish imps down there too: tiny creatures with black bodies and white faces and tiny hooked claws, jumping around like fleas.

Then Monty saw something – someone – who made him catch his breath. 'Oh, no!' he cried.

Sveltlana was down there, peering up at him, swathed in white diaphanous veils. She seemed to be beckoning him. He was still beguiled by that dark beauty which had first attracted him in his flat in Breadoven Street.

The demons clustered around her. Those electric eyes drew him onward, into dark, unknown byways, until he realized he was thoroughly lost. There were no lemmings around him. Only he, Monty, remained on the ice in this deserted area of the city, overlooked by great warehouses and grain mills. Cranes and derricks towered over the icy canal, like carnivorous steel birds waiting for their prey.

That paw again, beckoning, beckoning.

'Arrggh!' Monty shouted. He had gone over the jagged edge of a hole in the ice.

'Haaarrrrghhh!' A hard splash. The coldness of the black water took all the breath out of his body. His shout for help was drowned as his mouth and lungs filled with water. He went under, numb in every part of his body. The hole in the ice closed over him, so that when he rose again, he smashed his head. There was no way out now. He was entombed in ice. Desperately he scrabbled with his claws, trying to scratch his way out of his freezing prison. To no avail.

Sveltlana swept up from the depths, clutched his ankles – and drew him down.

CHAPTER SIXTEEN

Monty opened his eyes. He could see nothing but an endless white expanse before him. A celestial white. It was somehow comforting. He had heard that when one died it was like going through a dark tunnel with a blinding light at the end. Perhaps what he was witnessing now, this beautiful desert of wan nothingness, was the equivalent of that? There was light, but not at the end of any tunnel. Light seemed to be coming in from somewhere to the sides.

Was this weasel heaven? Was he in Noguns at last? If so, where were his ancestors? Where indeed was the original renegade, Lord Sylver of medieval Welkin? Where was Capel St Sylver, the gentlemammal thief, who had escaped from more prisons than any creature on earth, then or since? Where was Bonnie Sylver, the greatest female of the family, who had led the Jillobite Rebellion against the Poynts, a century ago?

'How are you feeling?'

The Creator's voice was distant, but warm and comforting. A jill's voice. Funny, Monty had not considered that the Creator might be female. It made sense really, for jills were the main creators of life down on earth, so why not in heaven, here in Noguns?

'It's so white,' he said. 'I never imagined it would be so white.'

'What?'

'There!' He pointed with a wavering claw.

'The ceiling?' The light, a paw-held lamp, swung in front of his eyes and Bryony's face appeared with it. 'What are you talking about? It's just been painted, I suppose. I'm not sure there's anything so wonderful about a decorated ceiling, though, whatever the colour of the paint.'

Monty was suddenly aware that he was in bed and making a fool of himself. He sat up with a jerk, almost knocking the lamp from Bryony's paw. 'Where am I?'

'In the Krunchen mammal hospital. The vets say you'll be fine, though *I* could have told them that.'

'What happened? Did you catch her?'

'Catch who? You fell through a hole in the ice. You almost drowned. Luckily a number of lemmings were near by and they managed to pull you out. I gather they're rather good at that sort of thing. It happens all the time. Who's this *her*?'

'I thought . . . never mind.' He felt it best not to mention Sveltlana. Bryony went funny on him whenever he did. 'Did you bring my chibouque?'

'Here it is. I knew you'd want your comforter. It was the first thing I packed.'

'It's not a comforter.'

'If you say so.'

Monty chewed on the stem thoughtfully. 'There were lemmings around, you say, when I went through the ice?'

'Yes.'

'Hmmm. I thought I was on a deserted part of the canal.'

'You were on the main part. You slipped, slid about twenty metres and crashed through a barrier which had been placed around a hole. Did some jill push you? Was that it? What would she do that for?'

Monty realized what had happened now. Sveltlana had hypnotized him. She was an expert at that. Some of what he believed had happened was true and the rest was false. But the real and the unreal were so enmeshed it was impossible to separate them. He decided he would just have to accept that he had seen her, and that it had not been an accident, his falling through the ice. Somehow she had engineered it. 'The cunning jill,' he murmured out loud, without meaning to.

Bryony stood over him, folding her forelimbs. 'Come on, there's more to this than you've let on. Tell me who this female is. You know her, don't you?'

'Sveltlana,' he said. 'I think she tricked me.'

As predicted, an icy change came over Bryony. 'You saw Sveltlana? And I suppose you looked into her eyes? Oh, Monty, how can you be so foolish?'

'I don't think I'm that bad. One can't avoid looking into a pair of eyes when they're looking into yours. I'm doing the same with you, now. Anyway, I want to go back to the hotel now.' He threw off the sheets and stood up, feeling a little wobbly. 'You'll have to help me until I find my feet. It was quite a shock, that cold water. I'm surprised my heart didn't stop.'

'It did. Someone started it again.'

Something in the way Bryony said this made Monty stare harder into *her* eyes. 'You,' he said. 'You saved me.'

Bryony turned away and snorted. 'I'm a vet. It's my job to save lives.'

Monty felt very warmly towards his best friend at that moment. He reached out with his paw and touched her shoulder. She shrugged his paw off, though not with any irritation. It was more out of embarrassment than anything else. Monty could feel the awkwardness between them. He was intensely grateful to Bryony – that was to be expected – but there was something deeper there too: something that hadn't been there, or had grown much larger, much more powerful. 'You saved my life and I'll never forget that.'

'Well, I hope you won't mention it at breakfast every day, instead of hiding behind *The Chimes*, pretending to catch up on the news.' She still had her back to him.

'I *should* do, to remind me how wonderful you are – how expert, how brilliant—'

'Oh, shut up,' she said, whirling round on him. 'Come on, it's time we got back to the hotel. The other two are waiting outside. They'll be worried. I think I'll ask the hospital vet to put you in my charge. Otherwise they might insist you stay in for observation. I would insist on that, too, except that I know you wouldn't do it. Now, are you ready to take a few baby steps?'

'I am.'

She took his forelimb and led him to the door.

Scruff and Maudlin were sitting outside, staring gloomily at posters depicting the horrors of foot-and-mouth disease, mange, mustelid flu, and all the other terrors of the mammal world. Scruff was thinking how healthy they made him feel, these posters. He was knotting and untying a piece of dirty string. His coat had been plastered down with water to make him look half-respectable in a place of clean-bibbed surgeons and nurses. The water was drying now, however, and his fur was beginning to stick out in all directions.

Maudlin, on the other paw, was imagining that he had every single one of those horrible illnesses. One of the symptoms of mange was a headache. *He* had the most awful head pain. Another spoke of mouth blisters. Surely those were blisters he could feel with his tongue? He wondered if he should tell one of those vet lemmings who swept by in white coats. Perhaps they'd tell him he was fine. On the other paw, they might tell him he had only days to live. It was a terrible dilemma for a hypochondriac.

Both loyal creatures leapt up when they saw Monty on the forelimb of Bryony.

'Hey, guv'nor? You all right?' cried Scruff, looking pleased.

'I – I think so. Just a bit waterlogged.'

'Did you see me?' cried Maudlin in a high, squeaky voice. 'Did you see me skate forty metres without falling over?'

'You mean before or after he fell in the hole?' snarled Bryony. 'Really, Maudlin, have you no sense of timing?'

But Monty could see that Maudlin had spluttered out the words without thinking about what he was saying. He had obviously been so overwrought he had said the first thing that came into his mind. Monty did not want this weasel to suffer such agonies. 'I did see your amazing flight,' he told Maudlin. 'I'm all admiration. You must show me again, soon.'

Maudlin looked miserable.

'No, really,' confirmed Monty. 'I never thought you had it in you, Maudlin. I'm most impressed.'

This brought a look of joy to the other weasel's eyes and he glided up to the far side of Monty and took his other forelimb. 'Let's get you into a coach and back to the hotel,' he said. 'I'll fetch you a nice bowl of soup.'

'I'll be the ministering angel, if you don't

mind,' interrupted Bryony, but more gently this time. 'That's my job.'

The four got back to the hotel, where Boombach and Florette were waiting anxiously. They too had heard the news from the hotel staff and were very relieved to see Monty alive.

'So many mammals fall through those holes,' said Florette. 'We should have better warnings.'

'Yes,' nodded the fat Boombach, 'too many holes. Where do they come from? Some vandals, I think. They break the ice with metal poles to make good citizens to fall in.'

When they were seated around a table in the dining area, drinking campion tea, Monty enquired of the two lemmings, 'How are things treating you here in your capital city? Are you in work? Where are your performances?'

'We do one at the big opera house tonight,' replied Florette, 'but tomorrow is the masked ball. We will entertain there too. I must dance and he must sing.'

'A masked ball?' cried Scruff and Maudlin together.

Monty saw what was coming. 'We must be getting on to the heart of Translyvladia. We have work to do. No time for frivolous pursuits.'

Rescue for Scruff and Maudlin came from an unusual direction.

'My dear Monty, you're forgetting you're not well enough to travel just yet. It's one thing to sit here in a warm hotel, drinking tea; quite another to be out on the open road in a draughty coach. I think you'll need time to recover.'

Monty demurred, but Bryony was insistent. 'You won't be pleased if you come down with pneumonia or bronchitis, now, will you? Better to travel in health. We'll start the day after tomorrow, if I think you're well enough by then. As for the ball, I see no reason why these two should not attend. I take it we can get tickets?' Bryony's question was directed at the two lemmings.

'Oh, yes – I get you tickets,' said Florette. 'Four tickets.'

'I'm not sure Monty's up to going to a ball,' said Bryony. 'But the rest of us—'

'If you're all going, I'm going,' snapped Monty, determined not to be left out of this continental experience. He fended off objections. 'Don't worry, I'll be sure to wrap up warm, but I'm sure the ballroom will be heated in any case. And you'll be there, Bryony, if I suddenly collapse with chronic respiratory failure.'

'I'm not sure I want to save you twice in one week.'

CHAPTER SEVENTEEN

'You have to go to the wax mammal,' said Boombach. 'To have your mask made.'

The four travellers were sitting with the two lemmings in the foyer of their hotel. A five-piece orchestra was playing from a high gallery. There were waiters sliding about noiselessly and every table was covered with a crisp linen cloth. One of the hotel staff had made kangaroos out of the table napkins, which raised a few weasel eyebrows. None of them could understand what kangaroos had to do with Translyvladia.

'On Welkin we have our masks made too,' said Monty, 'but they're usually masks of ferocious animals, or human faces, or simple black patches with eyeholes, such as burglars wear.'

'No, no,' interrupted Florette, 'here it is different. Everyone gets a mask made of their own face. This goes into a box along with all the other guests' face masks. As you go into the ball you reach into the box and take a mask out. You're not supposed to look at it, so you don't know who you are. So, you see,' she cried brightly, 'everyone goes as everyone else. It's great fun and a little spooky, too.'

'Yes,' replied Monty thoughtfully, 'I can see it *would* be a little eerie to have someone walking about with your face on.'

'Exactly!' boomed Boombach. 'You can all be each other for a night. This encourages international understanding. If I am you and you are me, there is no need for fighting, ja?'

So, after tea, the four weasels made their way to the shopping district of Krunchen. There they found several mask-makers. Settling on one, they entered.

An elderly lemming looked up, peering over his small, square spectacles. 'Death or dance?' he said.

The weasels were a little taken aback by this direct confrontation and asked the lemming what he meant.

'Death mask, or dance mask?' he said. 'Death is more expensive, but I make both.'

'Oh, dance, please,' said Bryony. 'But if we ever get a death in the family, we'll come to you.'

They each had to sit in a dentist's chair to be smothered in wax. At the end of the session they walked out of the shop with their masks. These

142

they had to take to the ball organizers straight away, so that they could be put in the box and jumbled up.

'I can't wait till this evening,' said an excited Maudlin. 'Fancy! A masked ball. Wait till we tell your auntie Nellie, Scruff. Won't she be astonished! Two lower-class weasels like us, going to a masquerade.'

That evening Bryony wore a 'green weasel' outfit, saying that she preferred wearing nature. Scruff went as a lion with a great mane around his head. Maudlin went as a harlequin, in a costume of black-and-white diamonds. Monty went as fire, in a flaming-red cloak which covered the whole of his body.

As they went in through the grand doorway, lemming officials told them to turn round. When they did so a mask was taken out of the box and placed on their faces. They were told it was totally against the rules to tell *anyone* at the ball whose face they were wearing. Only when the ball was over could the masks be removed and the secrets revealed. It would have been difficult, anyway, to say who was who once they had their new faces on.

The great hall was packed. It seemed that every citizen in Krunchen was there. Boombach, of course, was easy to recognize by his shape, and Florette, who never left his side (or vice versa!), was also easy to identify. Just whose faces they were wearing was a mystery to all the weasels, who had no idea who anyone was. There was loud clicking in various parts of the room, as mammals came across their own faces on somebody else's body. The weasels went in search of themselves.

Monty found his face quite quickly, on a female lemming. It was quite eerie to be suddenly confronted by his own features and a chill went up his spine. He wondered why the others thought it was amusing to run into themselves. He found it very disturbing, especially since the features were frozen into a – yes, yes, it was – a *death* mask. For in truth there was no difference between a dance mask and a death mask, except that for one, the mammal was alive, and for the other, dead.

'Hello,' he said to himself. 'Might I know your name?'

'You're not supposed to ask such questions,' replied the jill lemming in a husky voice. Was there an attempt to disguise the tone? He wouldn't know her anyway, he was sure, unless she worked at the hotel where he was staying.

'Sorry, I forgot. Would I like to dance – I mean, would *you* like to dance? This is very confusing, to be confronted by one's own image. It knocks identities all into a cocked hat, doesn't it?'

'If you're sure of yourself, it doesn't matter.'

That was not a very comforting thing to hear, either. However, Monty followed himself onto the floor and began to dance.

Now, weasels have a most distinctive way of dancing, which involves a rippling movement from toe to head, creating a weaving effect.

144

Lemmings, on the other paw, tend to jump up and down, in very springy movements, mostly at an angle. So one mammal was doing serpentine, sinuous movements, while the other was boinging around as if made of rubber. It was an uneven contest and Monty, for one, was quite glad when it was over. 'Thank you,' he said, taking his partner to the edge of the floor. 'A most – er, interesting, exercise.'

'It was supposed to be enjoyable.'

'Well, it was, in a way.'

Monty slipped away from his partner. He then stood in the shadow of a pillar and surveyed the room. Good Noguns! he thought, as he stared across the floor. There was Prince Miska! Though, of course, the prince was no longer a prince, having given up his royal station in order to become the first democratic president of Slattland. Monty almost crossed the floor to speak to him, when he suddenly remembered that there would be a different creature beneath the mask. President Miska was in the room, obviously, but not behind that particular face.

'How interesting,' muttered Monty. 'Of course, it is quite probable that Sveltlana is here too! I must look for her mask. If I find it, I should beware, since it means she will be in the room somewhere, but hidden behind someone else's face. She's a game player, that one. I'm sure she already knows I'm here . . .'

While he was searching the room for Sveltlana's face, he heard Maudlin's excited voice asking Boombach, 'Who am I?'

'I'm not supposed to say.'

'Oh, go on. I know you're Boombach, by your girth. I'm Maudlin underneath. Whose face have I got on . . .?' His voice sounded so eager, so full of enthusiasm. Poor Maudlin! By some irony of fate he had picked out his *own* face. He was wearing himself. How sad. It could only happen to Maudlin.

Being a creature of science, Monty mentally divided up the great hall into sections, and searched each section for the mask of Sveltlana. There was not a great deal of movement: mammals generally stood in their own little groups, fearful of losing contact with their friends. It was very unsettling not to be able to recognize one's friends, and if you lost them you had to remember who they had become for the night. This made Monty's job a little easier.

He ran into Scruff's mask, his own again, and Bryony's, but there was no Sveltlana there. He began to relax. There was no point in becoming paranoid about the whole thing. If he had not seen her by now, it meant she was not there. It allowed him to enjoy himself.

Monty went in search of Bryony's body, which he knew almost as well as his own. When he asked her to dance, she became a little frosty, and he supposed it was because she did not recognize him. That was peculiar, since there were only a few weasels at the ball. However, she accepted his invitation and they were able to synchronize their willowy, shimmering forms, as dancing weasels were supposed to. It was an impressive

146

display which more than one lemming paused to watch in admiration. Both were left breathless. Bryony, who was wearing the face of some seed merchant or local cobbler by the look of the leathery, creased visage, again became distant once they had to talk.

'Are you having a good time?' asked Monty. 'Isn't that Scruff over there, looking very like the matronly jill who sold us watermelons in the market yesterday?'

Bryony replied curtly that she was having a 'super time' and then melted into the crowd with a shrug of her shoulders. Monty was a little put out. He couldn't think what he'd done or said to make her so offish with him.

Towards the end of the evening Monty felt the need to visit the toilets. Until now they had been off limits – the guests had been warned – because there were mirrors in the loos. One could see one's face in a mirror and discover the identity of one's mask. However, festivities were drawing to a close and the rules had been relaxed. Monty climbed the great staircase leading to the upper rooms and went looking for the toilets. There were no lemmings up on the landings, since most mammals were now drifting towards the doors, and out into the street.

The toilets were empty. After he had relieved himself, he went to the wash basins to clean his paws. Standing in front of the mirrors, he stared at the mask he was wearing. A cold shock went through him. Of course. He should have guessed!

At that moment the door behind him flew

147

open. He himself came flying in with a dagger raised. Had Monty remained where he was, the weapon's blade would have been firmly planted between his shoulder blades. As it was he managed to skip aside. The lemming wearing his features shouted in fury as she missed her mark. Monty then lurched forward, trying to grab her forelimb. She evaded him by jumping backwards, with great alacrity and athleticism. Then she was gone through the double doors, vanishing onto the landing.

Monty tore off his mask and gave chase, but the landing was empty. He tried several rooms, looking behind the great velvet curtains, and even behind the pictures on the wall in case they hid secret passages, but he found nothing. She had simply vanished.

'How frustrating,' he muttered. 'No wonder Bryony was so cold towards me.'

He glanced down at the mask he held in his paw. It was the replica of Sveltlana's features. All the time he had been wearing *her* face. Why hadn't Bryony said something? And behind the mask of his own face had been Sveltlana herself.

'She engineered this,' Monty told himself. 'She planned the whole thing and executed it somehow. She obviously knows the organizers of the ball. How clever she is.' There was more than a tinge of admiration in his softly spoken words.

Nevertheless, they had been overheard by someone who had followed him up the great staircase. 'Who's clever?' asked Bryony, her own mask now in her paw.

'Why – why, *you*, of course,' cried Monty. 'For not telling me I was wearing this grotesque face. You let me think I was a handsome young creature!'

'So you are,' she said in a contrite voice. 'You couldn't help it – wearing that face. I loathe her so much. Come on, let's go back to the hotel. I'm exhausted.'

'So am I,' replied Monty, linking forelimbs with her.

They went down the great staircase to see Scruff and a dejected-looking Maudlin waiting for them.

'I was just myself,' said Maudlin. 'How boring. I wanted to be someone exotic and all I was, was *me*.'

'I think you're a very exotic mammal,' said Scruff. 'I would've been proud to be you, if it was me.'

This piece of flattery did nothing to lift the spirits of the despondent watchmammal, as they made their way back to their gothic hotel through the snow-covered streets of Krunchen.

CHAPTER EIGHTEEN

Two canoes set off up the Klangalang river containing, among other things, one Spindrick Sylver, who sat quietly under the shade of his wide pith helmet. His forelimb was dangling out of the boat, running his claws through the cold water.

'I wouldn't do that if I were you,' said Rakki-Takki from behind him. 'Nasty things in this river.'

Spindrick wisely drew his paw back inside the craft. 'Where are we staying the first night?' he asked Rakki-Takki.

'There's a tribe in a longhouse about a day's journey from here. They're land mongooses, like me. Those mongooses you met at the port were sea mongooses, who live on the coast. We don't like each other very much. We've had some terrible wars.'

'Interesting. So, it *is* mongooses, and not mon*geese*. I'm glad we've cleared that up.'

'Yeeesss,' replied Rakki-Takki doubtfully, 'but you've got me thinking now.'

The journey down the Klangalang was fascinating for a Varicosian weasel like Spindrick. He saw all sorts of bird life, from beautiful kingfishers to much larger fish eagles. In the dense forest which bordered the river on either side were monkeys and snakes and other creatures of hot and sticky climes. The monkeys shouted abuse at them, making gestures with their forefingers. The snakes merely hissed and spat at the mongooses, who were their mortal enemies. Spindrick even saw a reticulated python, one of the largest snakes on earth, and he wasn't keen to make its acquaintance.

In the water itself were turtles, some rather nasty-looking fish and crocodiles. They all seemed to be lurking. Most life in Tarawak lurked. It was a disturbing business, floating in a little container amongst so many lurkers, up to no good.

The river was not always as tranquil as it had been at its mouth. Very soon it became rather bad-tempered and started foaming and thrashing amongst rocks. The ride became rather bumpy and Spindrick's bottom took the brunt of the turbulence as it banged up and down on the wooden canoe. Rakki-Takki employed one of his mongooses to stand in the prow of the boat and look out for logs, which belted along on the current and threatened to smash into the canoe. Every so often they came to a waterfall, or some unnavigable rapids, and had to resort to portage – carrying the canoe around the obstacle – before going on. It was a slow business.

At midday they stopped for a meal on the bank. It was here that Spindrick first experienced leeches. 'What's this?' he cried, finding a worm buried in his fur.

'Leech. Don't pull it out – you'll leave the head in your skin and it'll fester,' explained Rakki-Takki. 'Here, let me burn it out with a glowing twig from the fire.'

'Like cracky, I will. You'll set light to my pelt!'

'In which case, you'll be sucked dry of blood and fall over like an empty sack,' replied Rakki-Takki.

'Really?'

'Really.'

'All right then, burn away – but be careful, I've got delicate – *ow*!'

'There, it's all over. Till the next time, anyway.'

This afforded much amusement to the other mongooses, who clicked their teeth and shook their heads. Spindrick wrote all their names in his little black book.

Going down the Klangalang was not as much fun as he had first imagined. There were the ants, too, who tended to get into one's fur and bite like billy-o. Then there were the mosquitoes. And finally, the sea mongooses who formed the expedition were very superstitious creatures, who constantly delayed departures by finding bad omens amongst the natural surroundings.

'They won't move for at least another hour now,' explained Rakki-Takki, as Spindrick displayed impatience. 'One of the bearers has seen a bumble bee flying backwards.'

'So?'

'Very bad omen. The spirit of the bumble bee is warning them not to proceed until they see a good omen.'

Spindrick stared around at the lounging mongooses, who were draped over every available root or hump of grass. They seemed quite unperturbed by this 'bad omen'. He wondered if this were just an excuse to extend their lunch hour. 'Oh, come on, this is the nineteenth century. Omens?'

'Not for us mongooses. We started to count much earlier. To us it's the twenty-third century. We've been around longer.'

'Says who?'

Rakki-Takki was not about to get into this argument. 'I'm just telling you, they won't move.'

One hour later to the second by Spindrick's pocket watch, one of the mongooses spotted a red caterpillar.

'Good omen,' cried Rakki-Takki. 'Now we can proceed.'

The expedition continued up the Klangalang. It was a long, tiring day and at nightfall they arrived at a longhouse. Local mongooses ran down to the jetty to meet them. They waved their spears and flashed their shields. Some of them carried blow pipes; others wore swords at their sides. They all looked pretty formidable to Spindrick, who was a little disturbed by the dark, brooding atmosphere.

The wooden longhouse, built on stilts, had a front veranda which extended along the whole length of the dwelling; behind this were individual rooms, all in one long line. Everyone gathered on the veranda when they wanted company, to sit and mend nets, sharpen weapons, weave cloth and carve carvings. If they wanted a bit of peace and quiet they went back into their own rooms. The yard in front was running with domestic sparrows, kept for the pot and for their eggs. They were too fat to fly, having been fed on limitless oleander seeds their whole lives. They pecked and chattered the whole while, filling the air with their irritating noise.

Spindrick was treated to a tribal dance, in which one of the mongooses weaved and leapt around, waving a sword and shouting terrible threats at an imaginary enemy. This warrior had shaved tattoos onto his pelt, the white bits in the shape of tropical toads and other creatures of the forest.

'Very impressive,' said Spindrick to Rakki-Takki. 'Now I suppose I have to offer him some gifts.'

Spindrick had brought a whole sackful of mirrors and beads with him, which he now proceeded to paw out to the mongooses with great ceremony. They looked at these in disgust, having expected bottles of mango dew or the latest novel. Still, this was a friendly tribe and they soon forgot the insult.

Spindrick was sharing a room with Rakki-Takki. In the middle of the night there was a terrible commotion which woke them both. Spindrick asked what on earth was going on.

'Sounds like someone's in pain,' said Rakki-Takki, rising. 'Come on.'

Spindrick reluctantly went out onto the veranda to find the tribe and his porters clustered around a wailing jack mongoose. The poor creature was clutching his abdomen. His face was screwed up into a grimace of pain.

'Possessed by a demon,' explained Rakki-Takki to Spindrick. 'The witchvet's going to drive it out.'

'Looks like belly-ache to me,' snorted Spindrick.

'You mustn't interfere with tradition and culture,' replied Rakki-Takki. 'If they think it's demons, demons it is.'

Spindrick watched, fascinated, as the witchvet went through various rituals, scattering ash on the individual, marking his face with a charcoal twig, and beating on a bronze dinner plate with a wooden spoon. Finally, he took a sparrow and held it up while dancing around the ailing mongoose and letting out weird chants. Then he rubbed the body of the sparrow onto the sick mammal's chest, and everyone cheered. Spindrick swore he winked at him once the whole thing was over.

'What's happening?' he whispered.

'Well,' replied Rakki-Takki, 'the demon has been forced out of the mongoose and into the sparrow. Tomorrow they'll take the sparrow up-river and let it loose somewhere where it won't be able to return. Thus they will rid the longhouse of the bad demon for good.'

'Why not kill the sparrow?'

'Because when it dies the demon will jump into some other creature.'

'Gotcha. Not very fair on the sparrow, though.'

'Ah, that's the clever bit,' said Rakki-Takki. 'This is a female sparrow. When it next lays an egg, the demon will escape from its body into the shell. There it will remain until someone breaks the egg, which might not be for another hundred years.'

'Be a bit high by that time.'

'Demons stink anyway.'

'What do they look like, these demons – in the raw, I mean?'

'Pretty disgusting things. They're green, as you would expect, and fearsome looking. They have long, sharp teeth for clinging on inside a body, and claws to match. They make a dickens of a racket, shrieking and screaming their heads off. Your normal sort of demon, really.'

'Common or garden variety?'

'Precisely.'

The following morning preparations were made to continue the expedition up the Klangalang. However, the tribal chief asked Rakki-Takki if Spindrick would mind taking the possessed sparrow with them, to save the tribe a trip. Spindrick readily agreed. He intended to keep the creature and take its egg, when it next laid one. It would be wonderful to have a demon bomb in his possession. If there *was* a demon in there, he was going to let it loose at a special occasion, like the mayor's annual garden party, and cause all kinds of havoc amongst the ruling classes.

Thus the expedition continued up-river, now going into mountainous terrain, now through a plain. Spindrick gradually got used to the mosquitoes and ants, to the whacking great spiders and scorpions. Soon he was the veteran traveller and, not long after entering the heart of darkness, he got his demon egg.

The sparrow he set free. The egg he put into a box padded with cotton wool. He regarded it with great joy. Here was something that could cause a stampede without any effort. A jewel from the Orient. How lucky he was to have found this curio.

CHAPTER NINETEEN

Monty found he could not sleep after returning
from the ball. He rose from his bed and got
dressed. When he was in this kind of mood, he
found that walking was the best cure. It was a
strange city, it was true, but he had familiarized
himself thoroughly with the street plan. He did
not think he would get lost, even though it was a
misty night. Krunchen seemed to have the same
problem as Muggidrear, when it came to river
fog.

'If my friends wake up and find me gone,' he
told the night clerk at the desk, 'please tell them
not to come looking for me.'

The lemming at the desk nodded sleepily. She
had just been enjoying a little doze when Monty

had tapped on the counter with his silver-knobbed cane.

Monty stepped out into the street, buttoning his overcoat to the throat. In his pocket he had his single-shot pistol. It would be silly to venture out at night into a city like Krunchen without some sort of protection. The continent was going through a period of turmoil, with neighbouring countries suspicious and nervous of each other. Enemy agents walked the streets at all hours, seeking good information, planting false, and generally causing havoc amongst an otherwise peaceful population. Monty passed many a high-collared, low-hatted character hurrying along the cobbled streets, eyes peering between folds of cloth.

'Ah, intrigue and suspense,' muttered Monty. 'I remember my young days as a secret agent, how exciting they were.'

Actually Monty was still quite a young weasel, but so much had happened in his short life it felt to him like a long one.

He rounded a corner into the Old Square, where the great toy clock stood. At noon and midnight a clockwork coach and mice came out of the doors of the clock and raced around the dial, before disappearing back into the depths. The time was now showing two o'clock. In and around the square were elaborate wrought-iron gas lamps, spilling their light onto the slick cobbles. In the corner, by the gothic cathedral known as 'The Grong', stood a group of lemmings. One of them looked at Monty sharply, then disappeared down a side alley. With a shock, Monty recognized the lemming and he hurried to catch up with him, pursuing him through the narrow streets, until finally the heavy-cloaked form turned to confront him.

'Prince Miska,' said Monty – for it was he – 'why are you running away from me?'

'Please, do not call me that, Monty,' hissed Miska, recognizing his weasel friend immediately. 'I am now president – and, what's more, I'm not supposed to be here.'

'Not supposed to be *where*?'

'Out, wandering the streets. I like to sneak here at night and listen to the conspirators on street corners, pretend I'm one of them, to find out what rumours are going around and who is planning a coup against whom. This is important to me, to stay one step ahead of such cunning creatures as Sveltlana.'

'Ah, dear Sveltlana. She tried to stab me just a few hours ago.'

Miska's head went back in surprise. 'She tried to kill *you*?'

'At the masquerade. I won't bore you with the details, but suffice it to say I'm lucky to be here talking to you now. It was a close thing.' Monty didn't add that it was partly Miska's fault he was a hunted weasel. Sveltlana had been Miska's rival for the presidency and Monty had prevented Miska from being late, or dead, for the election. Sveltlana had never forgiven the Welkin weasel for that.

'Ahhh, she is so devious, that one. Her father was a viper and her mother was feline.'

'A rather strange and difficult union, I imagine, but I know what you mean.'

'Come,' said Miska, looking round suspiciously, 'there is an all-night coffee house where we can sit and talk. It's one of my safe cafés. I own it and my uncle runs it for me. I can go there and not have to watch my back for the knife. Come, let's go and talk.'

Once they were seated in the dimly lit coffee house, Miska plied Monty with questions. 'So, what are you doing in my capital city? Why do you not come and see your old friend, Miska? It seems you were here and not planning to visit me, yes?'

'I'm here on an errand. We've been plagued with vampire voles in Welkin. I and my friends have come here to seek the source of those creatures of the night, the undead. Now that you're here, perhaps you might give me some guidance on where I might start looking? I intend setting out for vampire country tomorrow.'

'In the dark hills and forests of Transylvladia? I know nothing about the country there. I am from the north, originally. But I do know one or two of the old nobles who live out there. There is one stoat, Count Flistagga, who lives in his castle in the Forest of Gnarl. He knows a great deal about vampires, having studied the subject at great length. I once saw his library and it was full of books on the occult.'

'Count Flistagga? Interesting.'

'How so?' asked the president, pouring himself another cup of coffee and putting seventeen spoonfuls of sugar in it.

Monty stared at the brown sludge which Miska was stirring and shook his head in wonderment. 'How so? Because there was an old stoat by the name of Flaggatis, who lived in Welkin in medieval times. He was responsible for an uprising amongst the marsh rats which has never been resolved. Each century sees some progress, but the war with the rats continues to this day.'

'Flaggatis?'

'It's an anagram of Flistagga.'

The president's brow furrowed for a moment and his lips moved silently, until finally he remarked, 'So it is!'

Monty had forgotten how dense politicians could be. They might be nice and they might be rotten, but they were all lacking a little in common intelligence. It seemed necessary for the job. If you were bright, you didn't get in. Possibly that was why Sveltlana was still roaming the streets, instead of being elected to a nice political post. She might be evil, but she was very intelligent. It was one of the qualities which attracted Monty to her. That and her eyes.

'So,' the president was saying, 'what is the significance of this discovery, if not coincidence?'

'It might be just that, a coincidence. I simply think it is an interesting one, that's all.'

'You think our Count Flistagga might be your

Flaggista, back from the dead?' Miska was a little brighter than he first seemed, after all.

'I think that would be unlikely.'

'So do I. Count Flistagga has been a respected member of our aristocracy for I don't know how long.'

'Exactly.'

'What – exactly what?'

'You don't know.'

Monty left the ex-prince in the coffee house and walked back to the hotel. It was now daybreak. The sun was prising the fog apart to let the daylight in. Green and bronze buildings blazed in the early brightness of the morning. Monty remained deep in thought, though one eye remained on the emerging alleys, in case a female lemming leapt out of one of them and tried to pin him to the pavement with a knife.

At breakfast he told the others they were taking another coach trip into the interior. He had taken the liberty of ordering them walking boots, flannel suits and stout sticks with little badges stuck to them. Bryony told him he was foolish for trying to do too much too soon after his encounter with Sveltlana, but Monty insisted he was feeling fine. Four mouse-stalker hats completed their outfits. Bryony was delighted with hers, as was Scruff, but Maudlin thought the jackets looked rough and itchy.

'If you'll remember,' he said, 'I like silk next to my fur.'

'I took the liberty of ordering silk underwear for all of us,' replied Monty, '*not* because of your pretensions to royalty, Maudlin, but because it's warm.' He then told them what they were going to do. 'We're going to pay a Count Flistagga a visit.'

Bryony started, then said, 'Flistagga? But that's an anagram of . . .'

'Exactly,' said Monty, remembering why he admired Bryony so much, too.

They climbed into a coach and twelve just before noon. The driver, a thin lemming, seemed reluctant to take them into Count Flistagga's country, but he said he would carry them as far as the bridge. 'After that, you must go on the feet. I cannot risk my coach.'

'On the feet it is then,' agreed Monty, pleased that he had had the foresight to purchase knapsacks full of food, drink and a blanket. 'How far is it from the bridge to the castle?'

'Half a league to the woods – then half a league to the ruined tower – then another half-league to the castle grounds. If you go onward from there, you'll be at the door.'

'Half a league, half a league, half a league onward,' muttered Scruff.

'That's daft,' said Maudlin. 'Why not just say one and a half leagues onward?'

'Sounds more poetic, the uvver way.'

'No it doesn't.'

When they reached the appointed bridge, the coachmammal stopped and ordered them from his vehicle. Next he threw down the four knapsacks tied to the roof. As he did so the poor lemming was shivering and the mice were skittish, scraping the ground with their claws and flicking their tails. Clearly both coachmammal and mice were fearful of this countryside. Even before the group had walked through the dark tunnel of the covered bridge to the other side of the chasm, the coach and twelve were disappearing fast around the curve of the road, the driver's whip lashing out at the rumps of the yellow-necked mice, who needed no encouragement to flee the region.

'Well, here we are then,' said Monty, as they emerged on the far side. 'Knapsacks all right and tight, everyone? Good. Step it out then.'

'*I love to go a wanderin', along the hill-vole track,*' sang Scruff, '*an' as I go, I love to sing, a knapsack on my back.*'

'Stop that noise,' growled Maudlin. 'It's giving me a headache.'

'Weren't you ever a kitten scout?' asked Scruff. 'My auntie used to send me along to our local pack every Wednesday. I used to love it – songs around the camp fire . . . camp-fire shouts: *One thousand volts, two thousand volts, three thousand volts – SHOCKING. Three thousand volts, two thousand volts, one thousand volts – REVOLTING.* Knottin' ropes. Bangin' staves into the ground. Camping. Great fun. Burnt bits of bread dough on the end of sticks which used to taste wonderful.'

'My mum thought that kitten scouts were full of thugs.'

'Nah, great bunch of young weasels, they was. You missed out there, Maud. Hikin', canoein', buildin' bridges out of bits of rope and poles.

Nothin' like it. Made a jack weasel out of you. Ain't that right, Bryony?'

'Well, it certainly didn't make a jack weasel out of me,' she replied cheerfully, 'but it gave me good strong legs.'

This was quite apparent from the way she was striding ahead through the gloomy forest – which was growing more gloomy by the second – and leaving the other three to trail on behind her.

CHAPTER TWENTY

Falshed was very ill on the voyage to Slattland. It was something to do with greasy larks' eggs and vole-bacon – that combined with mountainous seas and a businessmammal who shared his cabin and sang in the bath like a frog suffering with appendicitis. By the time he had made the crossing, he decided he was too sick to carry on. The first thing he did was ring Mayor Poynt.

'. . . so you see, Mayor,' he finished his long rehearsed speech, 'I have to take the next ship home.'

'Next ship home? I've sent you out there to do a job,' said the mayor. 'Look, I can't talk now, Falshed. I'm at the annual stockholders' meeting of the poor houses. We hardly made any profit from the paupers last year and I'm feeling a bit upset about it.'

'But, Jeremy,' cried Falshed, who felt that after all he had been through he was entitled to call the mayor by his first name, 'I've had a very bad time. I need rest. I need a vacation. It's *freezing* over here. There's ice on the inside of my hotel-room window-pane. They don't let you have hot-water bottles. They keep calling me a cissy, when I complain that the bed is cold.'

'So you are a cissy,' snarled the Mayor. 'And what's all this "Jeremy" business. It's Mayor Poynt, to you, Chief. I'm your boss, not one of your pals.'

'We might be brothers-in-law one of these days,' replied Falshed, feeling reckless with so many miles of ocean between them, 'and it'll sound silly if I call you Mayor.'

'Over my dead body!'

'If you like.'

There was silence at both ends as they seethed.

Finally the mayor said, 'Look, Falshed, I'm not an unreasonable stoat. You do this job for me – follow those arrogant weasels – and I'll see if I can put in a good word for you – with my sister, I mean. I don't think she knows you exist, but I'm willing to try. How's that?'

Falshed wanted, above all things, to be the mate of Sybil. It would be the culmination of a lifetime's secret desires. 'Oh, all right.'

'Good stoat. Right, see you then . . .'

There was a clunk at the other end and Falshed realized the mayor had not put the receiver back

168

on its hook properly. He tried whistling into the phone, but to no avail. Then, as he listened, he could hear the mayor talking to his cronies in the background.

'. . . wants to marry my sister, Sybil. Can you warrant the nerve? A nobody like Falshed in my family? I'll put Sybil into the ground first. Blasted cheek. That's what you get for being nice to stoats like Falshed. Airs and graces . . .'

Falshed felt like weeping tears of frustration. Instead, he went to another phone and called Sybil. 'How are you?' he asked her. 'Any better?'

'Who's this?'

'Zacharias Falshed – Chief of Police,' replied Falshed automatically.

'Who?'

He repeated the words with gnashing teeth.

'Oh – you. What? Am I under arrest? Why are you telephoning me, Chief Falshed? Is this how you badger your witnesses? Of what am I accused? Am I under suspicion on some trumped-up charge? I'll have you know my brother . . .'

'No, no,' groaned Falshed. 'I'm ringing in a private capacity, just as a concerned friend, to find out if you're well and happy.'

'Oh.'

'Yes, well, I can see it was a mistake.'

There was quiet on the other end for a while, then Sybil's voice came back. 'You – you're just enquiring after my health?'

'That was the idea.'

'Oh, I'm dreadfully sorry – Zacharias, isn't it?

Yes, I'm so sorry. I naturally thought, you being the chief of police – well, you know. Were you calling to invite me to dinner? If you're ringing to find out if I'm free this evening, I'm happy to say I am. I washed my fur last night. Shall I expect you around six?'

'I – can't,' he groaned.

'What?'

'I'm over here – in Slattland – over *there* to you, of course. Your brother sent me. Tomorrow I have to travel down to Krunchen. I just thought I'd see if you were all right. The last time I saw you, you were wrapped up in bed with two puncture marks on your throat. You looked so pale and ill, I was afraid for you.'

'Did I? But, oh, how disappointing – you're in Slattland? Well, perhaps when you return from your travels, you'll call on me?'

Excitement welled up in Falshed's throat. 'I'd – I'd be honoured.'

'Good. Until then?'

'Until then.'

Falshed hung up the telephone with a pleasant feeling washing through him. At last. Sybil knew who he was and that he was alive and kicking. She had asked him to call on her! (Falshed did a little skip and a hop, clicking both back heels together.) How wonderful. How very very marvellous. What a coup! Jeremy Poynt, you pompous podgy stoat in an ermine pelt, prepare to die of shame. You're going to have a common-or-garden-variety Falshed for a brother-in-law!

The next day in the coach down to Krunchen

Falshed found he was facing the stoat business-mammal who sang in the bath. He was too sunny in his heart to feel any sorrow at this turn of events. He clicked at the stoat, showing he was prepared to be friendly.

'You kept pulling out my plug, you did,' snarled the stoat. 'I don't forget bad treatment, I don't.'

Falshed's goodwill evaporated immediately. 'You deserved it. You sing like a hedgehog with asthma.'

'How dare you! I'll have you know Jeremy Poynt, the mayor of Muggidrear, is a distant cousin of mine.'

'You deserve each other. Actually, the mayor's sister and I are engaged to be mated, so there. How's that for checkmate?'

The businessmammal's eyes bulged. 'You don't know the mayor's sister.'

'Don't I just? Her name's Sybil, she's recently been bitten by a vampire vole, and she and I are like that.' The rash and foolish chief wound two claws around each other on his left paw.

Falshed was astounded at the effect this news had on the businessmammal. All the puff went out of him. He looked deflated. Somehow the creature looked quite overwhelmed. Falshed wondered if he had gone too far. After all, this stoat was a distant cousin of *both* Poynts.

'Well – I'm astonished,' cried his companion, aware that the other three passengers, lemming nuns, were regarding this developing situation with great interest. 'Utterly astonished. My

171

cousin Sybil and I plighted our troth when we were just young things. It's been an understood thing: the whole family expects us to unite in matery one day. You say she's now your fiancée? I'm thoroughly gobsmacked. It just shows you can't trust a jill, doesn't it? She'll get a nasty letter from me the minute we reach Krunchen. I'm – well, I just don't know.'

The nuns nodded their heads in sympathy.

A horrible sickly feeling crept through Falshed's stomach. 'You – Sybil? Oh, well, she never – that is to say – you haven't cropped up in conversation. This – this engagement of ours is a secret, see, so I'd appreciate it if you didn't go blurting it out to anyone. Or speaking to Sybil about it, either, because it's a secret, you understand?' Falshed was sweating under his fur.

'A secret? What, from her too?'

The nuns all tutted in unison.

'No, no, not exactly from her, but she doesn't like it mentioned. She's – she's afraid her brother will find out. He doesn't approve of secret engagements, Jeremy. In the general run of things, he's against them.'

'I'm not sure I like them much myself,' snapped the stoat, much aggrieved. 'They're horrible things, especially when they're sprung on you in front of half the world's sisters of mercy. Not nice at all. Not your fault, of course, though I don't like you much. Sybil is entirely to blame. She promised herself to me. She should have broken that promise before promising herself to you. Now there're promises all over the place. It just

172

isn't good enough. I'm not sure I shouldn't take it up with the queen. She's the moral head of the country, isn't she? I'm not sure what I should do about this situation now.'

Falshed's heart was racing like mad now. If any of this ever got back to Sybil he would be dead in the water.

'Get thee to a nunnery?' he suggested, trying to make light of the situation.

The nuns all frowned in unison.

'Look,' he said, 'perhaps I'd better own up—'

At that moment a shout came from outside and the coach was stopped abruptly. Falshed stuck his head out of the window to see two masked lemmings swaggering in front of the coach. They had pistols in their paws. 'Highway robbers,' he told the nuns. 'Don't be alarmed.'

The nuns all screamed in unison.

'You there,' cried Falshed. 'I'll have you know I'm chief of police in Muggidrear city. You would be well advised to—'

A shot rang out and the wood splintered on the coach door.

'Welkin, is it?' cried one of the robber lemmings. 'Stoats, is it? Your money or your liver. Which is it to be? I warn you, I'm a dead shot. I'll part your whiskers with the next one.'

The occupants to the coach were made to step outside. The businessmammal was trembling and the three nuns were sobbing. Falshed was inwardly quaking, but he had too many other worries to concern him to be thoroughly afraid. He was so distracted by his spiritual agony that he failed to watch where he trod. As he stepped down from the coach he tripped over his own tail and went headlong into the two robbers, sending them sprawling onto a snowy bank. Immediately the guard on the coach leapt down and disarmed the pair. He and the businessmammal trussed the robbers, while Falshed calmed the terrified nuns. It was all over in minutes.

'Well done,' said the businessmammal, clutching his breast pocket as if his heart were going to fall out. 'You saved our bacon. I have some very valuable diamonds in my waistcoat pocket. Had they fallen into the paws of these two thieves I should have been ruined. Can I reward you in any way, sir? Will you accept a cheque for a thousand guineas?'

'No,' replied Falshed, 'but I wish you wouldn't mention me to Princess Sybil. Our – our engagement is not yet formalized. Perhaps, in the end she might still choose *you*. She hasn't said yes *emphatically*. You know how jills are – they can't make up their minds. The two of us, for example, we know what is within our grasp in life, but jills, they want everything and anything. They say yes here and yes there, hoping things will sort themselves out without having to make a choice.'

'How true, how true,' murmured the other stoat. 'I shall say nothing – nothing. We must both hope and may the best stoat win.'

Falshed almost melted with relief. 'Thank you,' he said.

The coach stopped at the next inn and, to Falshed's surprise, a jill stoat got in. When they

174

set off again, she looked significantly into Falshed's eyes and gave him a nod and a wink. Falshed was astonished. Who was she? A tourist? He had the feeling he had seen her before, but couldn't remember where. There was something in her clumpy movements, her clod-hopping bearing, that was familiar.

Then it came to him. 'Constable Debbie,' he said, 'what are you doing here?'

CHAPTER TWENTY-ONE

The four intrepid vampire-hunters came out of the forest to be confronted by an enormous Transylvladian castle. It was a monstrous, dark dwelling of tall towers, high battlements and lots of spikes on top of round rooms. It stood, in the growing gloom, silent and dismal on a turfed bank above the trees. Maudlin, for one, was daunted by it. Two of the other three felt certain misgivings, which they did not voice. Only Monty felt calm and strong and able to handle the situation.

'We'll give that bell-rope a pull,' he said cheerfully, 'and see what happens.'

The door opened, creaking and groaning as any door to such a castle should, and an elderly

176

stoat stood before them. He stared at them with narrowed eyes. 'Weasels? What do you want?' he said. 'I'm busy.'

'Count Flistagga?'

'Yes – yes, come along, out with it.'

Monty saw no reason to be secretive. 'My name is Montegu Sylver. I'm from Muggidrear on Welkin. These are my companions, Bryony Bludd, Scruff and Maudlin. We wondered if we might talk to you on the important matter of vampire voles?'

'Bryony *Blood*? Interesting name.' The stoat's eyes narrowed even further, until they were just pencil lines on his furry face. 'Vampire voles, you say. What would I have to do with vampires? Have you been listening to those silly yokels? Their heads are full of old religions, old legends. You mustn't take heed of them. They are a simple set of mammals. They have the brains of gadflies.'

'Really? But just the same, it's well known that this part of the country has spawned vampires in the past. I was given to understand that you are an expert on the matter. We've come to seek your advice.'

'Expert? Well, I suppose so. Yet,' he added quickly, 'you must understand that vampires are mythical creatures.'

'If you say so.'

'I do.' The count stared out at the deepening gloom. 'Look, where were you proposing to stay? At the local inn? You'll only hear more stories about me down at the Gutted Rabbit. You'd better spend the night here. The only trouble is, I have no servants. I'm alone in the castle. So you'll have to take us as you find us. You may use the kitchens. I've already eaten. After you've had a meal, join me in the great hall.'

The count then led them into the house, which was as dusty and bleak inside as it was forbidding outside.

Maudlin hung back, saying, 'I might just as well go down to the inn. I think I'd like a pint or two of pear dew. I won't listen to any stories, Count, don't you worry about that. I'm good at not listening. You ask Scruff. All right? You lot can fetch me later, when we're ready to go home.'

He started off back down the track, only to find that it was getting darker and darker all the time. The forest looked positively black inside. The wind had got up and there was rustling in the leaves of the bushes. In his mind's eye was the welcoming sign of the Gutted Rabbit, but he realized he had absolutely no idea how to find it.

'Make sure you keep to the path,' called the count. 'We lose tourists all the time in that forest.'

At that moment the howl of some wild beast rose above the trees.

'On second thoughts,' said Maudlin, returning, 'I just *might* get lost, mightn't I?'

They followed the count through the castle to the kitchens. Studying him from behind, they could see he was lean, grey-whiskered and slightly bent. Yet there was a strength, a vitality about him which belied great age. His tread was sure, his movements quick and fluid. True, his coat looked coarse, the hair on it stiff and starchy, but his eyes were full of fire.

'Here – here they are. I'm afraid you'll have to light the fire under the range, but you'll find kindling and logs in the corner over there, and matches in that drawer. As for food, there are turnips and potatoes stored in the back, but no meat, I'm afraid. I'll see you in a short while.' With that, the count left the room.

The weasels set about making turnip and potato soup.

'Notice,' said Monty, 'the cobwebs on the wood pile. And how cold the cooking range is. There are no ashes in the grate. It's as clean as a whistle. I would swear they've not been used in a very long while.'

'So what?' said Maudlin aggressively.

Bryony said, 'And turnips and potatoes are easily stored.'

Scruff added, 'An' the candles are all new, ain't they?'

'So what? So what? So what?' cried Maudlin.

'Oh you know,' replied Bryony, 'they don't eat or drink, do they? Has anyone seen a mirror yet? I haven't. One usually has a mirror in a hallway, to check on one's appearance before leaving the house. There was no mirror that I could see.'

'What are you trying to tell me?' Maudlin cried.

'Nothing really,' replied Monty, tasting the soup. 'Just circumstantial evidence. Not conclusive at all. Please don't alarm yourself.'

Maudlin tried not to alarm himself, but there was a loud voice inside him which told him to run, run, run.

Once they had eaten the weasels each took a lit candle in a holder and went searching for the count. They found him in the great hall, where there was a long dining table, several uncomfortable-looking chairs, and a roaring fire. The flames from the fire danced on shields and swords which decorated the walls. Large tapestries hung from brass poles, covering those walls not littered with weapons. An enormous chandelier full of lit candles hung from the very high ceiling.

'We don't have the luxury of gas in these remote parts,' explained the count, seeing them stare. 'Nor that new-fangled stuff they pump along solid wires – what is it?'

'Electricity,' replied Bryony.

'Yes, that's it. We have a lot of storms here in the mountains. I've spent my life avoiding lightning; now they produce it from magnets, I understand, and soon it will be entering houses of common mammals. Quite extraordinary – and quite unnecessary. What's wrong with good old tapers and candles? I say.'

The count was sitting in a huge armchair by the fire and they joined him, dragging up seats in front of the flames.

'So, you're vampire-hunters,' murmured the count. 'Got your hammers and stakes with you?'

'Nothing like that,' replied Monty. 'We simply want to find the source of a plague of vampire voles, who have suddenly descended on Muggidrear.'

'How do you know they're not home grown?'

'We found the ships which were bringing them in.'

'Ah – so. And you're sure they're vampires? I have always regarded the legends with some scepticism, you understand. One tries to live a peaceful life in these mountains, and hordes of vampire-hunters descend at a moment's notice to disrupt it. I'm not blaming you, but rumours start, usually in local inns, and then spread far and wide.'

'This is no rumour. We've experienced them at first paw,' said Monty.

'If you say so, then I must believe you. But I think you'll find that it's all some kind of prank. An elaborate joke. In the meantime, you are welcome as my guests. I've put aside four rooms for you. When you're ready, I'll show you to them. Perhaps in the morning we could have a much longer chat. I'm rather tired at the moment. I'm not as young as I used to be, you know.'

The count sprang from his chair like a two-year-old and led them up a grand staircase to some bedrooms on the second floor. Before he left them he said, 'Weasels and stoats used to drink blood at one time, you know.'

'Yes,' replied Monty, 'they did. The blood of rabbits, usually. Some still do. But it doesn't turn them into undead beings.'

The count clicked his teeth and shrugged.

Their rooms were all next to each other.

Maudlin went into his and came out again immediately. 'There's no key,' he said hoarsely. 'No bolt on the door. There's a horrible old four-poster bed with dirty rotten curtains that fall to bits in your paws. There's a washing bowl and jug, but no water. An' there's dust everywhere you look.'

Monty advised. 'Prop a chair against the door knob and try to sleep lightly.'

Maudlin shuffled next to Scruff. 'I'm coming in with you,' he said. 'I'm not sleeping in there alone.'

'Suit yerself, Maud,' said Scruff cheerfully. 'I won't say no to comp'ny.'

'Oh, by the way.' Monty undid his knapsack and took out four strings of garlic bulbs. 'Hang some of these on your window and around your doorway. They might just work.'

Later that night Monty was lying awake and heard a scratching at the window. He rose and went to look. Finding nothing, he went back to bed. A short while later he heard the door knob turn as someone tried to force their way in, but the chair held fast. Shortly after this he managed to fall asleep.

He woke in the morning with the sun streaming through the dirty window. Looking out, he saw a herd of water voles down by the lake at the bottom of the garden. Now, the bank vole and the field vole were domestic creatures, one farmed for meat, the other for milk, but water voles were no use to mustelid or lemmus and why anyone would want to keep a herd of them was a mystery.

Or perhaps not?

Monty woke the other three, who had survived the night – Maudlin by refusing to go to sleep. They scoured the castle in search of Count Flistagga, finding a note pinned to the fireside chair. '*Gone to town,*' it read, '*C.F.*' Nothing else.

'Well, well. Let's go and have a look at the cellars, shall we?' Monty suggested. 'Perhaps we'll find something to our advantage down there?'

'Pear dew?' said Maudlin hopefully.

'No, silly – *vampires,*' answered Scruff.

Maudlin shrivelled into his pelt. 'Vampires,' he repeated. 'How nice.'

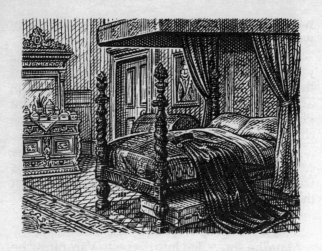

CHAPTER TWENTY-TWO

The cellars revealed nothing but the usual junk. No coffins, no grave earth, no horrible smell of vampires. Monty was absolutely sure they were on the right track. Everything added up to the count being the source of the vampire voles. All the circumstantial evidence pointed to that fact. Yet there was no *direct* evidence.

'Something doesn't add up here,' he said to the others, as they gathered again in the hall. 'Something's not quite right. I suggest we begin searching the rooms. We'll have to split up, because we've got an awful lot of them to get through before nightfall.'

Maudlin said, 'Look, the count might come back at any minute – then we'll look good, won't we? Guests rummaging through his castle. That's bad manners, that.'

'He won't be back,' said Bryony. 'He's hiding somewhere until the deadly daylight has gone.'

Maudlin refused to search on his own. He said he would accompany Scruff. So they split into three parties and divided the castle between them.

Monty began in the west wing and made his way to the centre of the castle. It was a quicker business than he expected. Most of the rooms were empty, containing little but dust. Seventeen of these dusty, tomb-like rooms he inspected, finding little to interest him. Finally, he struck gold: an occupied room, just above the grand staircase. It proved to be the count's bedroom. There was the count's evening cloak, draped over the bed, which looked as if it had been slept in. 'Curiouser and curiouser,' muttered Monty. He inspected the dressing-table, finding rather a lot of make-up there for a male weasel, unless that weasel was quite vain. 'Or hiding something,' he murmured. Finally, looking under the bed, he discovered a suitcase.

'Hello! Anyone home? Where is everybody?'

The shout went through the castle. The count? Monty looked at his pocket watch. It was just noon. Would such a creature be abroad in the middle of the day? 'Stranger and stranger,' Monty said, nodding to himself, 'yet it's *becoming* clearer.'

Going down to the great hall, Monty found the count with a shopping basket in his paw, wearing a red riding hood. Bryony had got there before Monty, and she was saying, 'You really *have* been shopping.'

'Yes, of course,' said the count. 'I said so in my note, didn't I? I thought you might like some meat, so I brought four steaks. I don't eat meat myself . . .'

'You don't each much of anythin', do you?' announced Scruff severely, entering the room with Maudlin at his heels. 'In fact you don't eat anyfink at all, eh?'

'What is the fellow talking about?' said the count, with what sounded like a false clack of the teeth.

Maudlin went straight up to the count and confronted him. 'Those water voles in your garden! What are they doing there?'

Again that clack. 'A question I ask myself quite frequently. They seem to wander up from the river. But, you see, I value *all* mammal life, that's why I'm a vegetarian. I couldn't chase them away. They're the Creator's creatures, just like you or me. There's food in my garden. I cannot deny it to them.'

Bryony folded her forelimbs. 'So you're just generous towards all mammal life, is that it?'

The count nodded gravely. 'I hope so. I try to be. We are all the . . .'

'Creator's creatures,' finished Monty. 'Yes, yes, we heard you the first time.' The weasel looked around him. 'Don't you find it rather dark in here, with the drapes closed all the time? We can hardly see anything in this gloom. Why don't I just go and draw them? Let's have a window or two open, let the winter sunshine in for a few moments.'

'No – no, that won't do,' cried the count, moving to intercept Monty, as the weasel went towards the windows. 'I like it dark. The light – the light hurts my eyes. I can't allow you to dictate to me in my own home.'

Bryony dashed over to the far side of the room and placed her paw on one of the drapes. 'The light hurts your eyes? Perhaps it hurts more than that? Let's see what you do with *this*.'

She whipped the curtain open to let the bright sunlight into the room. The rays struck the count squarely. He reeled backwards, his paws over his face. 'No – please,' he cried.

'Ha!' yelled Maudlin. 'Ashes to ashes, dust to dust.'

'No need for that, Maud,' said Scruff, a little severely. 'No need to be so smug, old matey.'

But, astonishingly, the count did not crumble. He staggered, it was true. He moaned and groaned, that was obvious. But he was not destroyed by the light, as he should have been.

The only one who was not surprised was Monty, who went up to the count and, when that stoat lowered his paws, stared into his face. 'You're not old at all,' he said, nodding his head. 'I knew it. That's make-up on your face – stage make-up. You're an actor, aren't you? Footlights and greasepaint?'

'Yes,' groaned the stout.

Bryony said, 'But why was he afraid of the

187

light . . . ?' Then it dawned on her. 'Oh, he didn't want us to see through his disguise.'

'Exactly,' said Monty. 'I think you owe us an explanation, count, or whoever you are.'

The stoat drew himself up and stared at the four weasels coldly. 'I don't think I need to explain anything,' he said. 'This is my home. You will kindly leave. Goodbye!'

Bryony said, 'But *is* it your home? Or does it belong to Count Flistagga? What have you done with the count? Murdered him? Have you taken over his life? Why are you pretending to be someone you are not?'

The stoat looked as if he were about to burst into tears. 'I haven't murdered *anyone*. I love all life. As Billy Daggerwobble once wrote in his marvellous play, *Two Weasels from Verona*, "Life is like the humming bee, stripy-bottomed, winged and free." I wish you would leave now. I have nothing further to say.'

'Where's the real count?' asked Monty.

'I don't think I have to answer that.'

'You should do, if you value life,' said Bryony. 'He may be a vampire.'

'Oh, that old story,' said the actor, clicking his teeth. 'How many times have I heard that from local villagers and the like?'

'It might not be just a story,' said Monty. 'It would be wrong to accuse the count of something without proof – but tell me, why would he hire an actor to live in his house and pretend he was the real count? He *did* hire you, didn't he?'

'Yes,' replied the actor defensively, 'but maybe he just wants to be left in peace? That's what he told me. He said he was fed up with being bothered by mammals accusing him of nefarious activities . . .'

'What?' asked Maudlin.

'Dirty doings,' replied Scruff.

'Oh,' said Maudlin.

'Look,' said Monty, 'we have no wish to invade the count's privacy, but this is a serious matter. It is a certain fact that vampire voles were sent to Welkin aboard ships. Voles are not intelligent creatures, as you know. They wouldn't be going there of their own accord. Someone is shipping them over there— What is it?'

The actor's eyes had gone a whiter shade of pale. 'Shipping?' he said faintly.

'That's what I said.'

The actor sat down in the nearest chair. 'Have a look in that desk over there,' he said. 'The top drawer on the left.'

Scruff went immediately to the drawer and opened it. He reached in with his paw and took out a sheaf of papers. Looking at the top one, he nodded. 'Shipping invoices. Here's one for the *Mosquito*. You remember, guv'nor. That was the ship what brought them vampire voles in – the one with the coffins and grave earth?'

'I remember very well indeed.' Monty turned to the stoat. 'What's your name?'

'Lillie Longtree,' he said.

'Lillie?' questioned Scruff.

'I usually play females in Billy Daggerwobble's plays, so I chose a jill's stage name to go with my roles.'

'Is that why you wear a red riding hood?' asked Maudlin, with a touch of envy in his voice.

'No – that's just to confuse the beasties in the forest.'

'Look,' said Monty, 'you must realize we are in deadly earnest. We have to find the count before he does any more damage. Will you take us to him, please? I'll absolve you of all blame. I'll say I forced you at gun point.' Here Monty produced his pistol.

Lillie's eyes opened wide. He stood up. 'You're not going to shoot me, are you?'

'I'm merely playing a role,' said Monty. 'The role of the villain. Now, if you please?'

The actor led the way out of the house and into the garden. They followed a path through an orchard, at the bottom of which lay a cottage in rather bad repair.

'In there?' asked Monty.

Lillie nodded miserably.

Monty went up to the cottage door and rapped. He listened hard. No sound came from within. He knocked again, harder this time, and the door swung open on rusty hinges. Peering inside, Monty could see nothing. He entered cautiously, his pistol at the ready. The cottage smelt damp and – yes – of grave earth. It was very gloomy inside the single downstairs room. Monty went to the window and opened the shutters. Light flooded into the cottage. There in the middle of the floor was a coffin with the lid removed. In the coffin was grave earth.

'I think we've found what we want to know,' called Monty to his companions.

They came, they saw, they nodded their heads.

'Well,' said Bryony, 'it seems we were just too late. Where do you think he's hiding now?'

'I think I can tell you that,' replied Lillie Longtree, taking a letter from his pocket. 'This was at the post office this morning, waiting to be collected. I recognize the envelope. It's from the shipping company.'

'Would you mind opening it, please?' asked Monty.

'It's against the law.'

'But,' said Scruff, 'you've bin given power of attorney, so to speak, since you're standin' in for the count, eh?'

'Yes, yes, I suppose I have. Oh, what the heck.' Lillie ripped open the letter and read the contents. 'One coffin, due to be shipped in two days' time on the SS *Natterjack*. Bound for Welkin.' He showed it to Monty.

'The count's goin' to Welkin hisself,' cried Scruff. 'We got to stop him.'

'We have indeed,' replied Monty. 'We must leave at once.'

The four weasels swept through the doorway, leaving the actor standing holding the shipping invoice. '"I have a sealed letter from the king,"' he intoned in his actor's voice. '"Rosencrass and Guildenswine are yet undead."'

CHAPTER TWENTY-THREE

'The mayor sent me along to keep an eye on you, Chief.' Constable Debbie, a young policemammal with huge ambitions and a cunning character to go with them, grinned at Falshed smugly.

Falshed had a hard time keeping his temper in the packed carriage. He ground his teeth noisily before saying, 'Oh, he did, did he?'

'Yes, he did. He said you were not to be trusted. He said you always bungled things. I told the mayor I would make a far better chief of police than you, and he agreed with me. I shouldn't wonder if I'll be taking over soon.'

Falshed sneered. 'Better get your sergeant's stripes first, before going for the top job in the officer department. Who do you think you are, you jumped-up constable? I could sack you tomorrow for insolence.'

The rest of the carriage booed him softly.

'Well, I could,' he said.

'No you couldn't,' replied Debbie. 'I'd just go straight to the mayor and tell him how unfair you'd been and he would reinstate me. Jeremy likes me. I think *I* could get *you* sacked if I wanted to. But I wouldn't because . . .'

'Because what?'

'Because I would like you to suffer under my tyrannical paw. I can be a harsh jill, I can. You wouldn't know what had hit you.'

Falshed spluttered. What was happening here? He was chief of police, after all – and she was a mere constable, the lowest of the low. Did he have no power at all? Even the mayor did not have full command of him. Only the populace and the queen. It was too much. 'Listen, you evil little wych. You might *want* to be, and maybe one day you just might succeed, but at this present moment *I* am the chief of police. Any more of this nonsense and I'll order you home. If you think I can't do it, just try me.'

Debbie stared into his eyes and saw that this was the truth. This bumbling stoat was indeed the chief. She should not have forgotten that fact. 'Oh, you,' she said, slapping him lightly with her mouse-hide gloves. 'I'm just kidding, you know.' She turned the full force of her eyes upon him. 'I promise I'll be good in future.'

'You'd better be.'

She bit her lip to stop herself retorting something very hot and nasty.

When the train arrived at Krunchen, the two stoats made for the best hotel in town. After all, this was on expenses. They wouldn't have to pay for a thing. When it's not your money, why not choose the best? Falshed told her, and Debbie agreed. On the way they bought expensive continental chocolates and some new snow boots each. What was the point of having an expense account if you couldn't enjoy it?

'We could take a tour of the city,' said Debbie, 'after we've found out where those weasels have gone.'

'Good idea,' replied Falshed, feeling wicked.

They booked in at the hotel, made enquiries at the desk and found that the weasels had been in the company of two lemmings, a fat one who sang and a thin one who danced. They discovered where these two entertainers were performing and went along to the lemming equivalent of a music hall, which the Slattlanders called 'clopper theatre', and both weasels found it very boring indeed. The dancing was rather clumpy and the singing rather booming and in another tongue. Afterwards they went backstage to speak to the two lemmings.

'You, the fat one,' said Falshed, 'I'd like to know where your weasel friends have gone.'

'What if I don't tell you?' said Boombach, wiping the greasepaint from his fur. 'What if I say to you, "Go to blazes, stoat!"'

'Then I'll have to speak to your chief of police about you.'

'Fine,' said Florette. 'He is my big brother.'

'Who?'

'The Krunchen chief of police. He is my big brother. And we have different laws in this country. You can't just skip in here and order mammals about. You have no authority.'

'No authority?' snapped Debbie. 'What happens if I just bite your nose, you tramp.'

'What happens,' said the rather larger Boombach, 'if I push you over and jump up and down on you?'

A brace of seething stoats squared up to a twosome of stubborn lemmings.

'Look,' said Debbie after a while, 'be reasonable. We're not going to arrest your friends. We just want to know what they're up to, so we can report to our boss.'

Florette shrugged. 'They have gone into the hinterland, into the dark forests and purple mountains. There was no secret about it. They've gone looking for vampires.'

'Will they return here?' asked Debbie.

'I believe so,' replied Florette.

'Good, then we have no need to go chasing after them, Chief. We can relax and pick them up on their way through.'

'Excellent. I didn't want to go chasing about gothic countryside in search of vampire-hunting weasels in any case.'

The two stoats left Boombach and Florette and went to see the river. The lights were pretty on the water. Debbie wanted to go for a boat ride, but Falshed thought it was a bit late for that, so they simply strolled along the left bank. They seemed, after all, to have quite a lot in common. They both disliked Jeremy Poynt, for one thing, but of course pretended not to. They both liked to get the best out of the system. They both wanted to go home to Welkin but, failing that, they were going to enjoy themselves.

There were several craft still crossing or navigating the length of the river. One of these carried a tall, thin stoat in a broad-brimmed hat. He stood up in the boat, a long black cloak hanging from his narrow shoulders. They watched him curiously, since there were few stoats in Krunchen.

'Death warmed up,' said Debbie. 'Look at him! See how pale his eyes are. How his lip curls back over his fangs. Look at the way he leans over that boatmammal – good gracious, he's bitten him! He's bitten him in the neck!'

The phantom-like stoat had indeed bitten the boatmammal, a rather plump lemming, on the throat. The deed was done as if in response to the request for payment. The lemming had stretched forth his paw and the stoat had instantly fixed his teeth onto the lemming's throat. The stoat seemed stuck there for a while. Then, when the jaws opened and the boatmammal was released, the lemming collapsed like an empty sack, pitching into the bilge water at the bottom of the boat.

Debbie and Falshed were on the promenade above the river, when the dark stoat ascended the stone steps from the landing stage. Falshed stepped into his path. The stoat's face had been hidden by the broad-brimmed hat, but now he looked up and Falshed recoiled. The features were stamped with an ancient evil: there was utter depravity in the eyes, a viciousness in the lips and teeth. Falshed gasped in horror as the creature before him hissed, 'Get out of my way!'

To give him credit, Falshed held his ground. 'Who are you?' he cried.

'Stoats!' complained the other, as if recognizing his own kind for the first time. 'I hate stoats.'

'I repeat, who are you?'

'The name would mean nothing to you, stoat. I am Count Flistagga, of the old and aristocratic Nosfuratoo family, who came over here to escape the oppression of idiots like you. But see how you tread in my footprints. Beware of my shadow, stoat! It may shrivel your soul and freeze your heart. Let not my shadow fall upon you.'

'But you haven't got a shadow,' protested Debbie, stepping forward. 'Look, Chief, he's shadowless!'

'So he is!' cried the astonished Falshed.

'Oh what fools these mammals be,' muttered Flistagga. 'Send a worthy foe against me, you forces of Good, not these weak, feeble-minded, pathetic morons.'

With that, the figure swept away into the narrow streets beyond the promenade. Falshed was about to follow when he saw the shape grow monstrous wings to assist it to scale the side of a tall building. When it reached the gargoyles along the gutters, it seemed to vanish amongst the blackness of the steep rooftops.

'No footprints in the snow,' Debbie pointed out. 'What kind of stoat leaves no footprints?'

'The worst kind,' said Falshed. He stared down at the boat below, where the boatmammal still lay in the bilge water. Dead? Perhaps not. Later, when the clocks struck midnight, that poor creature would rise again, and itself go scouring the streets for nice throats to suckle. Falshed was beginning to feel he had got in over his head for once. What was the mayor thinking of, sending him to a country where monsters lurked behind every parapet?

'What shall we do now?' asked Constable Debbie. 'Shall we inform the local police.'

'Best not to get involved,' replied Falshed, hurrying away from the scene with Debbie on his heels. 'The police here don't know us. For all we know we'll be thrown into some medieval dungeon and forgotten. Do you think Mayor Poynt will bother to get us out? Not him. He'll appoint a new chief of police and strike one jill constable from his list. That'll be the extent of *his* involvement. Best to pretend this didn't happen. We'll go back to the hotel, have a nice cup of cocoa, and tell everyone what a wonderful city we think this is.'

'For once I agree with you,' Debbie said. 'I can't forget that creature's eyes! I shall have trouble getting to sleep tonight.'

When they emerged onto the street, something fell from above and hit the pavement with a solid thump. Feathers fluttered in the cold evening wind. Blood stained the white snow. It was a starling with its throat torn out. Falshed looked up, realizing that the vampire had found a nest in which to rest for a few hours. Up there it could restore its energy levels, before setting out again amongst the living.

Debbie shuddered and stepped round the fresh corpse. 'We don't know anything,' she said. 'We were never here.'

The pair made it back to their hotel without further incident. Falshed went thankfully to his room, picked up pen and paper and wrote his last will and testament. He put it in one of the envelopes provided by the hotel and addressed it to Sybil. He had left everything to her, his princess, and his testament was that he had loved her all his life, and would continue to do so unto death. What a surprise she would get when she received this letter!

Wait a minute! She would think he was close to death, that he had gone abroad to save her the suffering of his last few days. He could not put her through such torture. What a thoughtless individual he was, not to realize how such a misunderstanding could arise.

He opened the envelope again and wrote: 'PS, I'm not dead.' There, that would forestall any confusion.

Then he thought how silly that sounded – 'not dead.' Of course he wasn't, otherwise he wouldn't be writing the letter, would he?

He opened the envelope once again, adding:

'PPS, I'm not even ill.' There, that should do it.

Wait a bit. 'I'm not dead' and 'I'm not even ill' sounded as if he actually wanted to be both. He didn't want to give the impression that he was considering suicide. She might think he had gone abroad in order to end a futile life. His life wasn't futile. It was jolly good at times.

He re-opened the letter for the third time and wrote: 'PPPS, and don't even want to be.'

Now he was pleased with it. He sealed it for good and found a stamp in his wallet, the Penny Dreadful he always carried for emergencies. He stuck it on the envelope and left it where the chamberjill would see it and post it for him. Then he went to bed, to dream of a grateful Sybil.

Falshed was awakened by a sharp knocking on his door. He looked at the clock by his bed. Half an hour to midnight. 'Who is it?' he cried.

'Police – open up.'

Chapter Twenty-four

The rapping turned into a hammering before Falshed managed to get out of bed, put on his dressing-gown (the one his mother had bought him with seventy-nine different kinds of sea fish on it) and open the door. The hotel manager was standing there. So was Constable Debbie. There were also several lemmings dripping with gold braid, medals and weapons. One of these characters, a tall lemming in a black uniform with a sharply peaked cap and encrusted with the aforementioned braid and medals, spoke to him.

'I am Constable Zugspotz. I speak perfect Welkin. Good evening. We would be pleased to come in.'

The whole troop forced their way into the room, making Falshed back up until he was almost out of the window.

'By the way,' said Zugspotz, whirling on Falshed, 'that is a horrible dressing-gown. All those ugly fish. You could be arrested for wearing that alone.' He clicked his teeth and said something in Slattlandish, and his fellow police-mammals also clicked their teeth.

'You're a *constable*?' gasped Falshed. 'I wonder what the chief of police looks like.'

'That's what I said,' agreed Debbie.

'Please,' said Constable Zugspotz, 'not to talk until spoken to. You are under arrest.'

'What for?'

The hotel manager interrupted here. 'This is a scandal. A terrible scandal. You must pack your luggage and leave. Never have we had murderers staying in our hotel. The other guests would be horrified. I have barons here, earls, lords and ladies, baronesses, earlesses—'

'Murderers?' cried Falshed, interrupting the interrupter. 'What do you mean, murderers?'

Zugspotz immediately slapped Falshed round the face with a pair of leather gloves. 'Please, not to speak until spoken to.'

Falshed glowered. 'You do that once more and I'll stuff those gloves down your throat and make you swallow them.'

Debbie said, 'Oh dear,' as Zugspotz's eyes widened. He stepped aside and two of his non-Welkin-speaking comrades jumped forward and snapped some monstrous, medieval-looking pawcuffs on Falshed. They then proceeded to blow up his nostrils, which proved to be a torture Falshed could not endure for long. He cried for mercy.

'Now,' said Constable Zugspotz, sitting in one of the comfortable forelimbchairs, 'I must ask the questions. Firstly, why did you murder the boat-mammal down by the river this very evening. You must not deny it. You were seen from the bridge by the bridge-sweeper.'

Falshed gasped. 'He said he saw us killing the boatmammal? We didn't go near the boat-mammal.'

'He said a "thin stoat with an evil eye".' Zugspotz leaned forward and peered intently into Falshed's face. 'I think you have the evil eye.' He then said something to the other two constables, who peered likewise and nodded intently.

'This is not evidence,' spluttered Falshed. 'Did he actually recognize the perpetrator as *me*.'

Zugspotz shrugged. 'How many stoats in this city? You admit you were at this scene of crime. You say to me you did not go near the boatmammal. In which case, you were present, yes?'

'We were there, but the murder – if it was such – was done by another thin stoat. Count Flistagga, he called himself.'

Zugspotz showed his teeth. 'Listen, you must not try to implicate innocent citizens of Slattland.

We know this Count Flistagga. He is a very respected noblemammal, who has lived in this country for many, many years. Here we have one boatmammal, lying dead. You are responsible. You must show concern, show remorse, then we will hang you on the public gibbet as a warning to other murdering tourists.'

A chill went through Falshed. How did he always manage to get in messes like this?

Debbie was not helping. 'I told you we should have called the police,' she said. 'Now they're going to throw us in one of their foul, flea-infested cells and leave us there until the mayor finds a way of getting us out.'

Falshed turned to Zugspotz again. 'Look, I'm Muggidrear's chief of police. We're comrades in arms, you and I. What would happen if you ever came to Welkin? I would look after you, that's what. Why? Because we're both policemammals. We watch out for each other. I didn't kill the boat-mammal. He's not even dead yet. In quarter of an hour he'll jump up and start biting everyone in sight. You'll see.'

Zugspotz's eyes narrowed. 'You try to bribe me?'

'What? No. How?'

'You tell me to come to Welkin and you will see me "all right", as they say over there. I have been to Welkin. It is a horrible place. I do not like it. They have no good food there, the water is bad and the toilets are made only to sit on, not to stand over. It is very unhygienic to sit on a toilet. And everyone on the continent says how

204

arrogant they are in Welkin, how stupid is their language. There is foot-and-mouth disease in every corner of the rooms. Keep your bribe. I will tell the judge and you will get many more years on your sentence.'

'I thought you were going to hang me?'

'We will keep you many years in prison, then we will hang you. Then we will shear the fur from your dead body and make mats of it to wipe our paws on when we come indoors.'

'That's real justice, that is,' snorted Falshed.

Suddenly a voice came from the doorway. 'I'm looking for the hotel manager. What's going on here?'

Falshed recognized the voice instantly. 'The Right Honourable Montegu Sylver,' he said, relief in his voice. 'You'll tell these policemammals who I am, won't you? They think I'm a scoundrel and murderer.'

Monty stepped into the room. 'Well, your ancestors certainly were, but so far you personally haven't broken the law.'

Constable Zugspotz swung himself easily to his feet, his medals jangling on his chest. 'Who are you?' he demanded. 'Weasels do not put their noses in where they are not wanted.'

Monty cast a glaring eye on the constable. 'I am a personal friend of President Miska,' he said. 'And you are?'

The constable blinked. His comrades instantly let go of Falshed's forelimbs and gradually sidled away from him. Their body language said that they just happened to be on duty with Zugspotz, but did not necessarily agree with his methods of arresting foreigners. They were there more in the role of observers. Zugspotz was on his own, really, when it came down to it.

'I – I am Constable Zugspotz.'

'Good lord, I would have thought you were at least a general.'

'That's what I thought,' cried Falshed eagerly.

'This is a murder investigation,' said Zugspotz, trying to gain command of the situation. 'This is nothing to do with weasels, even if they do know the president, which I seriously doubt.'

'Oh, you do, do you?' responded Monty. 'Well, we'll just go downstairs and get the president on the telephone. I'm sure he'll be very pleased to be bothered so late in the evening. I expect we'll get him up out of his bed. But don't let's worry about that.'

'How – how do you know the president?' asked the constable, faltering.

'You may recall that when he was a prince he visited our country in order to find out how to shed his royal status. He was kidnapped and held captive. I was the one who set him free. I think he was very grateful for this service. He tells me quite frequently that he owes me his life.'

'Ah,' murmured the unhappy Zugspotz, 'which is the case, I am sure now. But I have to say, a murder has been committed. We have the body downstairs, in the police coach—'

At that moment the clocks struck midnight all over town, in the hotel, and within pockets where pocket watches were kept. Just a second later there was a roar from the street below. Everyone rushed to the windows to look out. The black police coach was crashing back and forth on its springs, startling the two yellow-necked mice who were harnessed to it. Two more lemming constables were trying to pacify the mice, at the same time as peering into the coach.

Under the eyes of all, the coach doors flew open and an enraged lemming boatmammal burst forth. This creature was clearly demented, for it sank its fangs into the nearest neck, which happened to be that of one of the two yellow-necked mice. The mouse squealed, a high-pitched sound that jarred on everyone's nerves. Then it sank slowly to its knees as it was drained of blood. The boatmammal, now bloated and rather dreamy, walked off towards the river. Its driving lust for blood had been satisfied.

The two constables below opened fire with pistols, hitting the creature several times in the back, but he hardly faltered. He swatted at his wounds as if bitten by mosquitoes and continued his stroll into the rolling mists which dampened the cobbles.

'There!' cried Falshed dramatically. 'There's your corpse. What did I tell you? Count Flistagga was responsible for that.'

'Count Flistagga?' muttered Monty. 'How interesting. Perhaps, Constable Zugspotz, you will remove the pawcuffs from Muggidrear's chief of police, now that you know the truth? I'm sure a crime was committed, but not, unfortunately, by this stoat. Your criminal is out there roaming the streets of Krunchen. I suggest you go out and arrest him.'

'Arrest a vampire?' cried Zugspotz, removing the offending fetters from Falshed's claws. 'Are you crazy?'

The police left the room. The hotel manager backed out, bowing, craving forgiveness, uttering a thousand apologies. Falshed and Debbie were left with an old enemy of the stoats.

'My friends have gone to bed,' said Monty. 'I just happened to be in the next room to yours and heard the commotion. Now, what's this about Count Flistagga? What are you doing here, anyway, the pair of you? Following me?'

'Certainly not,' snorted Constable Debbie. 'I don't think we have to explain ourselves to a weasel, in any case. The chief and I – well, we're here on a private holiday. Nothing to do with work. We're – we're walking out together.'

Monty saw Falshed's eyes widen and knew this was not the truth, but he decided to let it go. 'All right, have it your own way,' he said, 'but I would still like to hear about your encounter. You're very lucky to have escaped from Flistagga. From what I hear he would think nothing of killing anyone who got in his way.'

'It was an ugly experience,' admitted Falshed. 'He very nearly did for the both of us.' He then went on to describe his meeting with the notorious count and the subsequent events.

At the end of this tale, Monty thanked the stoat. As he was leaving the room, he added, 'By the

way, Chief, that dressing-gown is an affront to
every decent law-abiding citizen in the land. I
suggest that if you and this jill stoat here are
serious about each other, you get rid of it quickly,
before she changes her mind about you.'

CHAPTER TWENTY-FIVE

The next morning Falshed took Monty down to the river to show him where Count Flistagga, the master vampire, had struck. Monty had a good look round, but could find no clues to where the count might be hiding while he was in the city.

'So, master detective,' growled Falshed, 'where to next?'

'We must go to the port of departure,' replied Monty, ignoring the sarcastic tone in Falshed's voice. 'The coffin leaves on the *Natterjack* and I don't have to be a brilliant detective to guess that Count Flistagga will be inhabiting it.'

Once more a coach and six was hired from the livery stables. Falshed and Debbie decided they might just as well accompany the weasels and keep the cost down, since their sole reason for being in Slattland was to see what the devious creatures were up to.

Of course, the mayor might have been happy if the weasels never returned to Welkin, but Falshed was not made of the same metal as his master. He was not the sort of stoat that could do away with his fellow countrymammals, or even simply falsify evidence against them, so he continued to observe them. Poynt, on the other paw, would have done anything to get rid of his weasely nemesis Montegu Sylver. But then Jeremy Poynt was essentially lazy and would never have followed them here in the first place.

Boombach and Florette came to see them off. 'So sad you are leaving, weasels,' said Boombach. 'My Florette and I will miss you.'

'Yes, yes, we will,' confirmed the other lemming.

They were all having drinks in a famous coffee house called Ryk's Place when in walked Sveltlana, bold as brass. She was wearing a black boa and dress and hat, all made from ravens' feathers. In the corner of the coffee house a piano-player was tinkling the ivories. Sveltlana went straight across to him and whispered in his ear. A moment later he changed the tune he was playing, bringing a look of grim amusement to Monty's features.

'What cheek,' said Bryony, 'coming in here like that.'

'It's a free country,' replied Monty, 'and I don't think she's broken any laws.'

'What's that tune, then?' asked Scruff. 'Can't make it out, an' I know most of the popular ones.'

Florette replied, 'It's an old rafter rat battle tune – the sort army buglers use on the battlefield. I expect Monty knows what it means.'

'Yes, I do,' Monty said. 'It's the bugle call for "Take No Prisoners". She's trying to frighten us. It won't work.'

'It *might* work,' said Maudlin.

Monty got up and walked straight over to the jill lemming, who still stood by the piano. 'Of all the coffee houses in all the world, you had to walk into this one,' he said.

'You know I came for a purpose.'

'Yes, I suppose I do. Where do you think it will get you?'

'Oh –' she flashed her dark eyes at him – 'you never know.'

Monty leaned over the piano. 'Play, "Cheer, Weasels, Cheer".'

'No,' replied the lemming piano-player.

Monty glared. 'Play it.'

'No.'

'You played for her, now play for me.'

Sveltlana sighed and said, 'It's no good badgering him – I own this place. He works for me.'

Monty said, 'You don't look like a Ryk.'

'Ryk was an otter who once owned it. I won it from him in a game of hollyhockers. He's now walking the left bank of the river with holes in his shoes. He's a fool. I hate fools. That's why I admire you, even though one day I will have to . . .' She glanced down at the piano-player.

'Kill me?' finished Monty.

'You said it, not me.'

'Well, I'm flattered that you consider me worthy of such a fate – that you should spend your valuable time considering how best to put an end to my miserable life.'

'Actually, there is a foolish side to you which will be your undoing, in the end.'

'What's that?' He thought she was going to say that she knew she was attractive to him.

Instead, she said, 'That you would never consider killing *me*.'

'Yes, that is a disadvantage which we keepers of the peace labour under. We can't commit murder, you see, even when it would seem sensible to do so, because once we step over that line – the line between good and evil – we become evil ourselves, and we might as well not have fought the fight in the first place. I hope you understand what I mean.'

'I'm not an idiot.'

'No – you're not. You're a greedy, selfish, wicked, power-hungry lemming who feeds on revenge.'

Her eyes flashed with anger. 'How dare you insult me in my own coffee house. Get out.'

'Oh, I'm going. I wouldn't want to add to your profits. If I had known this place belonged to you I wouldn't have come here in the first instance. And don't try my patience too far,

Sveltlana. You have tried to kill me while I have been in Slattland – not very hospitable, is it? – and while I would not stoop to murder, I might find other ways of dealing with you. No – no, I'm not going to say what ways, for that would put you back at an advantage. Suffice it to say that I can't be expected to sit around waiting for the assassin's dagger to plunge into my back. Beware, lemming. I am a formidable opponent.'

'So am I,' growled a voice by Monty's shoulder, 'and with me murder isn't out of the question, you strumpet.' It was Bryony.

Sveltlana sneered. 'Ah, the jealous little weasel.' She flicked a paw at the pair of them. 'You are less than the dirt under my claws, weasels. I shall deal with both of you at once, one of these days. Play it, lemming, play it.'

The piano-player immediately attacked the ivories again, rattling out a speeded-up waltz, which made everyone in the coffee house look up in astonishment.

On their way back to the table Monty said, 'You wouldn't ever carry out that threat, would you, Bryony?'

'I might.' She sighed. 'Then again, I might not. Oh, why do we have to be so law-abiding all the time when there are creatures like that in the world?'

'Because we have to have rules, or we would spiral downwards into anarchy and disorder. What my dear cousin Spindrick never under-stands is that once he has his world where everyone is free to do anything, mayhem and

214

murder will be commonplace. Some mammals are always at the extremes. Moderation, boring though it seems, is the only path.'

On the way to the port Maudlin said, 'We came over here for nothing, didn't we? We might as well have stayed at home.'

Scruff demurred. ''Course it weren't for nothin', Maud. The guv'nor will tell you that if we 'adn't come over here, Count Flistagga wouldn't be on the run. We've frightened 'im, 'aven't we, guv'nor? We've got 'im chasin' 'is tail. What's more, we got 'im on our own territory – Welkin. Ain't that right, guv'nor?'

'As ever,' said Monty, chewing on the stem of his chibouque, 'you have followed events accurately. If we had not come to Slattland, and thence to the region of Translyvladia, Flistagga would still be sending shiploads of vampire voles to our country. This creature harbours a deep hatred for Welkin and all who live there. His resentment goes even deeper and is certainly older than that of creatures like Sveltlana. He is a stoat scorned. It is my belief that he is the resurrected Flaggatis, who encouraged the ship rats of the unnamed marshes to rise up and try to conquer Welkin in medieval times – which they are still trying to do.

'Yes, I do believe he is of an evil and ancient family, who were once disinherited by the Poynts. Such families, dispossessed by rulers, build up immense hatred, which sustains them from century to century, until they feel the time is right to strike.'

'But,' argued Bryony, 'wasn't that Flaggatis – the medieval one – wasn't he drowned off the coast of Dorma Island when the weasels brought the humans back to Welkin?'

'Who saw his body?' asked Monty. 'All they saw at the time was his ship going down with his body lashed to it. Perhaps Flaggatis actually escaped drowning? Perhaps he was cast away on some uninhabited island? Who knows what magical powers were available to such a creature?'

'How did he become a vampire, then?' asked Maudlin.

'A *master* vampire? There are strange celestial creatures called Vis who live in the air of tropical regions such as that in which Dorma Island lies. The Vis are vampires. Perhaps he was bitten there? Or perhaps, having found his way to Slattland by whatever means, he joined the clan of vampires in Transylvladia, willingly or unwillingly? It was certainly to his advantage to become one of the undead, since he could travel through the centuries until he obtained the revenge he seeks.' Monty paused, then continued, 'You or I, Maudlin, would not even contemplate such a step. To us, becoming a vampire is a fate worse than death – feeding off the blood of others, turning them into creatures of the night, is unthinkably horrid. We would rather live a natural lifespan and then either go quietly, or even raging, into that goodnight. We would have our souls. But to some, the price of their soul is not too much to pay to satisfy their lust for revenge.'

'But you live for ever,' said Maudlin in a wistful voice.

'Is that life?' Monty replied. 'I think not.'

Maudlin said no more, but it was obvious to everyone in the coach that his ideas did not completely dovetail with those of Monty.

Eventually, after another night's stop, they reached the port. Monty found that the *Natterjack* was due to sail in one hour. However, it was not going straight to Muggidrear but to another port on Welkin. Hearing this, Falshed and Debbie left the weasels, preferring to take a direct ship to the capital of Welkin.

Monty booked passage for the four weasels on the *Natterjack*. 'Now we have him,' he said in deep satisfaction. 'He'll be trapped on board a vessel – contained, so to speak.'

Maudlin said, 'But won't we be trapped too?'

'In a sense I suppose you're right. But we have the upper paw. He will only be able to move around at night, while we have both the night *and* the day at our disposal.'

It was late afternoon when the vessel sailed. Monty went immediately to the marten captain and asked if the ship were carrying a coffin in the cargo. The captain confirmed that it was.

'We need to open it,' said Monty, 'before dark.'

'Oh, I can't do that, not without proper authority,' replied the captain. 'More than my job's worth. Cargo is sacrosanct, you see. Private

217

goods. Only customs can open it. I'm afraid we'll have to wait until we reach Welkin.'

'We might never reach Welkin. It's my belief there's a vampire in that coffin. I strongly urge you to heed my warning.'

'Customs only,' replied the captain. 'You'll just have to wait.'

CHAPTER TWENTY-SIX

'As you are aware,' said the weasel vet to Mayor Poynt, 'stoats are stoats in the summer and *ermines* in the winter, when they change their coats from tan to pure white.'

'Yes, yes, blast it, I don't want a lecture. It may have escaped your notice, but I *am* an ermine.'

The veterinary surgeon blinked. 'I know, I know – but you, Mayor, are an ermine *all* the year round. I think this is where half the problem lies. Your white pelt is getting worn out. Why not consider changing this summer, into a nice browny-tan one, to give your white one a rest?'

Jeremy Poynt ground his teeth. 'I-would-if-I-could,' he snarled impatiently, 'but you see, my father, my grandfather and their grandfathers before them were ermines all the year round. We Poynts have got out of the habit of changing. We can't do it any more. And now *this* has to happen.'

By *this* he meant the reddish-brown stain which blemished the otherwise pure-white fur of his bib. It had suddenly appeared over the last few weeks and the mayor was devastated. Of course, he had never had what one might call classical looks. He was too chubby for that. But he had a certain panache, a devil-may-care sort of look, which was enhanced by the white coat of which he had always been proud. Now his suave and rakish air had been spoiled by this horrible stain on his pelt.

'Well what *is* it? You must know what it is.'

The vet adjusted his spectacles and peered hard at the offending mark. 'It appears to be a rust stain.'

'A rust stain?' cried the mayor. 'What? How? Do I look like I'm made of iron?'

'No, it will have come off some other object. You don't wear armour, do you?'

'Of course I don't wear armour. What do you think this is, the Middle Ages? I'm the mayor of Muggidrear, not Sir Limpalot.'

'Perhaps your chain of office?'

'My chain of office is made of gold, not ruddy tin, you nincompoop . . .'

'Mayor, Mayor, please – I'm a professional. You can't use that sort of language these days, even to weasels, you know. I'm only trying to help. If you are going to lose your temper you must leave my office. It's not the sort of behaviour which will get you re-elected, you know.'

Jeremy Poynt stifled a desire to strangle the vet with his bare claws and said, 'I'm sorry.'

'That's all right. Now, have you come into contact with ferrous metals lately? Garden railings? The parapet of a bridge?'

Something dawned on the mayor. His new bed! He had recently purchased a great iron bedstead of which he was inordinately proud (though not as proud as he was of his white pelt). It was a steam-driven bed, manufactured by Wm. Jott. It chugged gently all night long, simulating the movement of a railway engine, which naturally induced sleep. Being steam-driven, it had a water tank attached. Where there are water and iron together, there will eventually be rust. That rust had been transferred to his wonderful white bib.

'I know where I got it now,' he told the vet, 'but what can be done about it? How does one remove rust?'

'I've no idea. You must ask your local carpet cleaners for that information. I'm a vet. I pop blisters and take out thorns.'

'Fat lot of good you are,' muttered the mayor as he left.

He went immediately to his one and only friend in the world, Lord Haukin. Lord Haukin's house was in a white-fronted, terraced crescent, in the middle of Gusted Manor. Hannover Haukin was an unashamed blue-blood, with a fierce desire to see the restoration of the aristocracy. He collected everything from owl pellets (disgorged remains of devoured mice) to dried beetles. Hannover's ancestors were also historically friends of the Sylvers and he was no exception, counting Monty as one of his closest companions. This, of course, upset the mayor enormously, but Jeremy Poynt could do nothing about it.

'Hannover,' he said, entering the library, 'you must help me.'

Lord Haukin was poring over a sheet of glass on which were arranged some fifty different snails and slugs, all of different species. He was at that moment studying a Moss Bladder Snail – *Aplexa hypnorum* – which was slowly making its way to the edge of the glass.

Jeremy Poynt, unthinking as usual, absently picked up one of the snails and popped it into his mouth to crunch like a sweet. 'Hannover,' he said again, 'are you listening to me?'

Lord Haukin's eyes opened wide and he stared at the mayor with something close to anger. 'You have just swallowed my White-lipped Banded Snail – *Capaea hortensis* – which took me a week to find. Have you any idea how rare they are these days?'

'What? Eh?' said the mayor, genuinely puzzled. Then he realized what Lord Haukin was talking about. 'Oh, sorry, Hannover. I thought you were offering them. Mid-morning snack and all that. Didn't realize you were doing – just what *are* you doing with them?'

'I'm observing them, studying them. I'm doing

a paper on Welkin slugs and snails for the Royal Mollusc Society. Now you've just eaten two pages worth. It'll take me ages to find another.'

'Sorry, Hannover, sorry,' said the miserable mayor. 'Not up to snuff at the moment. Got a lot to worry about. This stain on me bib, for instance. I wondered if you had any idea how to get it off.'

Lord Haukin peered at the mark and then shook his head. 'Not me – but my butler Culver's good at that sort of thing.' He rang a bell. Nothing happened. He rang again. Still nothing happened. Finally, on the third ring a weasel-butler entered the library carrying an open book in his paw. He seemed a little perturbed at being disturbed.

'You rang, my lord?'

'Three times. Are you reading that blasted poetry again?'

'*Blasted* poetry? Poetry has little to do with explosives, artillery or pyrotechnics, my lord. Poetry lifts the soul but without the aid of gunpowder or cordite. It enthrals the spirit but without flashing lights or burning sulphur. It is simply exquisite words beautifully arranged on the page for the delight of the discerning reader. Your father appreciated poetry, as did your grandfather before him. Forgive me if I say there is something sadly missing in this generation of the Haukins.'

The mayor thought this weasel had the cheek of the devil, but wisely kept this opinion to himself, since Lord Haukin himself did not offer any criticism of this insubordinate behaviour.

Culver finished his speech with, 'Can I be of any assistance, my lord?'

'You certainly can. Jem here has a tea-stain on his bib. Can you get it out?'

'Rust,' corrected Jeremy. 'It's rust.'

'May I suggest bleach, my lord?'

'You can suggest anything you like,' said Hannover, 'that's why we called you in. All right, Culver. Get the fellow some bleach. Let's dab a bit on, see how it goes.'

Culver left the room and returned with some kitchen bleach. With a wicked look in his eye he daubed some of the liquid onto the mayor's stain. After a few moments all could see that it had done the trick. It had removed the reddish-brown mark. But in its place it had left another sort of yellowy stain which looked even more firmly embedded in the fur than its brown predecessor.

'What have you done?' cried the mayor. 'It's horrible.'

Culver straightened his shoulders. 'I'm sorry, Mayor. I thought I was helping. Clearly you have no more need of my assistance.' He left the room carrying the bleach before him.

'Now look what you've done,' said Lord Haukin. 'You've upset him.'

'Hannover – he's made things worse.'

'He was only trying to help. I think your bib looks much better now, anyway. Yellow suits the colour of your eyes.'

'My eyes are not yellow!'

'The white bits are – or at least, those bits which

are white on everyone else. You'll just have to get used to the mark. Pin a medal over it or something. No-one will notice.'

'*I* will notice.' The mayor liked to think he was perfect in every way.

'Well, if there's nothing more . . .' said Lord Haukin, putting a monocle to his right eye.

His tone was a little icy and Jeremy Poynt decided it was time to leave. He said his good-byes and made his own way out of the front door. As he passed the parlour he could see Culver draped over a chair reading *Verses* by Billy Birdsworth. The mayor sneered. 'Only wimps read poetry,' he said, but very, very softly, aware as he was that Culver had been to the Orient and was fully conversant with about five different martial arts and could take the wooden ball off a banister post with one swipe of his tail.

Miserable and at the end of his tether Jeremy Poynt made his way through the mists of Muggidrear, along cobbled streets lit with jaundiced gas lamps, to his home. He dragged himself into his study. There he flopped in a chair and stared forlornly at the wall.

'Nice day, brother?' It was his sister, Princess Sybil.

'Oh – you know. I've got this horrible stain on my bib. It won't come out.'

'Let me see . . .' Sybil inspected the mark. 'You've put bleach on it, haven't you? It'll never come out now.'

'Not me,' replied Jeremy angrily. 'Hannover's butler, Culver.'

225

'Brother, you should never trust a weasel with an ermine's fur, you know that. Anyway, you can't walk around like that. It looks as though you've spilled stew on your front. There's only one thing for it. You'll have to have a fur graft.'

Jeremy brightened. He sat up. Why was it that females were always so good at perking one up? You had a problem, which seemed like the end of the world, and a sister or a mother, or a mate, would come along and, in a very practical way, sort it out. No fuss, no bother. Just do this, do that, and everything will be fine. 'What a wonderful sister you are,' he cried. 'Of course – a fur graft.' Then he added doubtfully, 'Where will I get one of those?'

'At the veterinary hospital. You can go tomorrow. I'll make an appointment for you. There's a surgeon there by the name of Scrawbelly. He's the best they have. We'll get him to operate tomorrow.'

'Operate?' Jeremy gulped. 'Tomorrow? Will it hurt?'

'Of course not, they have a thing called chloroform now – it puts you to sleep while they cut. You won't feel a thing.' She frowned, looking down at a piece of paper in her hand. 'I've just received this extraordinarily silly letter from Zacharias Falshed. I do think he's going a little weak in the head, brother.'

'Always was, always was. Only employ him out of tradition. So, it won't hurt, eh? Not one bit?'

'Not one bit.'

Nevertheless Jeremy Poynt hardly slept that

night. When he went to the Royal Veterinary Hospital the next day, he found that his sister had been there before him. The famous cosmetic vet, Scrawbelly, a stoat wielding a sharp knife, stood there waiting. He wore a leather apron and a leather skull cap. Both were covered in blood and pus stains. Scrawbelly wore these red and yellow smears as if they were badges of honour. On his feet he had some boots with gore still sticking to them. He bared his teeth at the mayor and asked him to jump up on the operating table.

Jeremy didn't exactly jump. He climbed, shaking, onto the green marble slab, which had just been swilled down. Two weasel assistant vets strapped him down with great leather belts which went all the way round the table. He was bound and helpless. He felt like screaming.

Scrawbelly tested the sharpness of his knife on his thumb, and then prepared to slice into Jeremy's chest. The ermine mayor let out a great terrified whine, which stopped the vet in his tracks.

'Keep still, Mayor,' said Scrawbelly testily. 'I nearly cut myself then.'

'But – but aren't you going to put me to sleep, with that new stuff I heard about?'

'Chloroform? I wasn't going to. An operation is a serious business. You surely don't want to be asleep for it? I suggest you bear the pain with fortitude and watch what goes on. It's your flesh and blood, after all. I wouldn't trust *my* body to a stranger with a knife – without remaining awake to see what he was doing with it.'

'I'd rather go to sleep.'

Scrawbelly let out a great sigh. 'Oh, all right,' he said in an exasperated tone. He reached for a bottle of chloroform and a rag. 'All my patients turn out to be cissies.'

'By the way,' said Jeremy, just as the soaked rag was going over his nose. 'You have got a good match, haven't you? The fur?'

'A perfect match. Not *ermine*, of course – too difficult to get hold of. You won't find many stoats giving up bits of their winter coats voluntarily. No, no, we've got a mountain hare's pelt, supplied by Jals Herk and Bare. Mountain hares change white in the winter too, you know. Very little difference. No-one *you* know will be able to tell where the ermine finishes and where the hare begins . . .'

But Jeremy heard none of this. He was unconscious long before the surgeon got to the bit about hares. He was actually dreaming that he was dancing through some daffodils, their yellow blooms dusting his head with their pollen. Then he was down by a stream with sticklebacks darting beneath the surface and dragonflies above. When he came to a lovely arched bridge he skipped over it to a daisy patch on the other side. 'Fah-diddle-de-dee,' he sang, 'I love the flowers and me.'

Scrawbelly was at that moment peeling the offending bloody patch of fur off the mayor's chest. He tossed the amputated flesh into a bin marked MOUSE-SWILL. The mayor continued his tuneless song. Scrawbelly glared at the simpleton lying on his operating slab, wiped his bloody knife-blade on his encrusted apron, and snorted with disgust. 'Pass me that bottle of chloroform,' he said to one of his assistants. 'He needs a bigger dose.'

CHAPTER TWENTY-SEVEN

Jeremy Poynt shivered with the cold. Gradually, he opened his eyes. He sensed the room was vast and saw that it was cast in gloom. There were lots of strange loud noises – screams, wails, ranting, shouting – going on around him. He wondered where he was. It sounded awful, like being thrust into a colony of parrots. Wild-eyed mammals passed by and looked down on him with various strange expressions.

Slowly, slowly, his senses returned. Still he did not feel like moving. His chest felt sore and his head was swimming a bit. He reached up and felt his chest. There was a bandage around it. Of course! The operation!

'Welcome to the Underworld,' said a stoat,

leaning over him. 'Abandon all hope, ye who enter here.' The stoat had hollow eyes, with dark rings around them. He stared in a most frightening manner. His pelt was in disarray, he smelled musty and he had tics on his ears. When he opened his mouth to click, Jeremy noticed his teeth were yellow and his gums were bleeding. In three words, he looked awful, terrible, dreadful.

'Where am I?' croaked Jeremy, raising himself up on his elbows. Looking around him, into the dimness, he saw that he was in a kind of jail. There was a thick door with a barred window. What little light there was filtered through a dirty casement window high above. Shapes littered the room, sitting on mucky straw, or wandering around as if lost. There was a vacant look to the creatures of this nether world. They seemed like abandoned souls in a kind of limbo world. 'What is this place?'

'Hell,' replied the stoat. 'It is hell!'

A horrible piercing scream came from one of the occupants, an elderly jill weasel. Jeremy noticed she was in chains and she rattled her fetters and followed up with a mournful cry. Others were making noises too, some of them very unpleasant. Apart from several in chains, one or two were strapped to wooden blocks, foaming at the mouth, uttering gibberish, dribbling down their bibs.

Bibs! The operation. Something had gone wrong.

'Did I die on the operating table then?' cried Jeremy. 'Am I dead? Is that what's happened?'

231

The hollow-eyed stoat nodded gravely. 'Every mammal speaks his own truth here. If you say you are dead, then you are dead. What you perceive is what may be. This is neither heaven nor earth, but somewhere else, my friend. You and I are victims of time and space. We hover in the lost regions between. Once here, here you stay. Give up any hope of leaving this black hole. No-one will be able to reach you. Your loved ones will have forgotten you already. They are in another world, a world full of light and joy. This is the Kingdom of Despair.'

Jeremy screamed at the top of his voice. 'Sis! Sybil. Take me away. Come and take me away.'

The stoat, who wore a pointed hat made from a copy of *The Chimes*, had his paw tucked beneath the lapel of his ragged coat. 'It's no use, my friend. I feel for you. I, the great general Nippylion, was the same when I first found myself in this den of dead souls. Now I have come to accept that here is where I'll stay, for all eternity.'

Eternity. He *was* dead then. Jeremy would have got up and dashed around in panic, if he didn't feel so woozy and sore. As it was, he simply lay there, a pathetic creature full of woe. It was horrible to be dead. It was especially horrible to be dead and not in mammal heaven. How had that happened? Hadn't he been good, and wise, and just? Yes, he had made mistakes, but then he was only mammal, he was entitled to a few errors in his life. On the whole he had tried to make Muggidrear a decent and happy society to live in. Hadn't he? Hadn't he?

232

'When do the demons come in?' he asked his companion mournfully.

'The demons are *in* all the time,' came the reply; 'in here.' The stoat tapped his head.

'Oh.'

Then, just as Jeremy was about to give way to total despair, the great door opened and two angels in white came and whisked him away. He was wafted through the doorway on his wheeled trolley and out into the light. He left behind the screeching and wailing of the lost and forsaken.

'I knew it! I knew it!' he cried to one of the angels. 'I was good, wasn't I? You made a mistake and now I'm off to heaven.'

'I don't know where you're goin', guv'nor,' said one of the angels, who looked remarkably like a badger who had come up before Jeremy when he was a magistrate. 'Me an' Herk, here, we was just told to come and fetch you out.'

'Herk?' Jeremy's head turned to the side and he stared at the other badger. 'Why, you're the notorious body-snatchers, Herk and Bare, sons of Herk and Bare, grandsons of Herk and Bare . . .'

'An' so on, back through time immoral,' agreed Herk, with an amused click of his teeth. 'That's us.'

'Are you dead too, then? Are you angels?'

'Us?' roared Bare. 'Angels? I should say so. Nah, we're just working shift work here at the hospital to earn a crust. Mind you –' he touched his nose with the tip of his claw – 'if we finds a dead 'un, why I thinks we're entitled to a few trinkets before we takes 'im along to the morgue.

233

Herk here, he snaps off their claws like rotten carrots to get at the rings, while meself, I'm more your locket- and pendant-snatcher.'

'You rob the bodies of the sick and dying?'

Bare looked hurt. 'Not the sick – not so much, anyway. The dyin' – well, they got no use for it, where they're goin'. Have a heart, guv'nor. We got to eat. We got to feed our famblies. Five kittens, Herk's got. Me, I got six. Where's the bread to fill the mouths of the little mites?'

Jeremy's eyes narrowed. 'Are you sure you work here?'

'Unofficial like,' said Herk. 'Whoops. 'Ere comes the chief vet, Bare. Time to be gone, sunshine, time to be gone.'

The two badgers disappeared like magic into the surrounding corridors. The next moment Scrawbelly in his bloody apron was standing over the mayor's trolley, looking down on him. He waved his surgical knife, still dripping with gore from a recent operation. 'Naughty, naughty. What are you doing out here, Mayor? I left you to rest.'

'Yes, but *where*?' growled Jeremy.

Scrawbelly was not to be intimidated. 'Why, in our madhouse, of course. In Bedlamb. We had nowhere else to put you. The ward beds were all full at the time. We would have left you in the corridor, but that was rather crowded too.'

'Bedlamb! You left me to wake up in Bedlamb amongst all the crazy mammals? Have you any idea what I've been through?' Remembering Herk and Bare, the mayor looked at his claw. 'And my gold ring has gone.' He felt around his neck. 'And the gold pendant that Sybil gave me for my last birthday.'

The surgeon shook his head. 'Well, that *is* strange. The patients don't usually steal things. They sometimes poke other patients around or try to eat them, but they very rarely rob them.'

'It wasn't them, it was Herk and Bare, the grave-robbers.'

'Those two? Oh, dear.' Scrawbelly became brisk and efficient. 'Now, let's have a look at your . . . Oh, yes,' he said, lifting the dressing and peeking underneath, 'it's healing nicely. Wonderful. You can go home today, Mayor. Shall I call your sister?'

'Go home?' cried Jeremy, almost sobbing with relief. 'Oh, yes please. It is healing then?' He took a quick look himself. The stitching around the wound did not look very pleasant, but the actual fur which had replaced the stained bit looked a lovely white, a beautiful match. 'Oh, that's grand,' he said. 'There won't be any scar, will there?' he asked anxiously.

'You won't see a thing,' assured Scrawbelly. 'That's a prime piece of winter hare's pelt you've got there.'

Jeremy jerked upright. 'Winter hare?' he said slowly.

'Of course. We couldn't get ermine fur. Very difficult to get hold of at this time of year. But we had some frozen hare.' He saw the anxious look on the mayor's face and said, 'Don't worry. We use it all the time – fur from other creatures. You won't notice the difference, I can assure you.

235

Now, if you'll excuse me, it's my lunch-time.'

Scrawbelly took a sandwich out of the pocket of his apron and proceeded to cut it in half with his bloody surgical knife. He began to munch on half of it before he remembered his manners. 'Oh, I'm sorry, would you like the other half?' He offered it to Jeremy. 'Pickled stickleback,' said the surgeon, 'my favourite.'

'I won't, if you don't mind,' muttered Jeremy. 'I'm not at all hungry at the moment.'

'Ah,' nodded Scrawbelly, munching away, 'loss of appetite, eh? Quite common after an operation, I assure you.'

Sybil came to fetch Jeremy immediately. She took him home in a carriage and told him how brave he had been. The mayor was then put straight to bed with a hot-water bottle and waited on paw and claw. He told his sister he wanted to do something about the poor mad mammals in Bedlamb.

'Those poor devils have an awful time of it, Sib. I think we ought to build a hospital just for them and put caring mammals in charge. At the moment they're just left to rot.'

'Why, brother,' cried Sybil, 'you have become public spirited overnight! How very good of you. I keep telling other mammals that my brother is not the blackguard everyone says he is, but a thoughtful and caring creature with the welfare of others close to his heart.'

Jeremy ground his teeth at the word 'blackguard'. 'Yes, well, I just want to see them settled.'

'I'll get on to it right away. And by the way, we're still getting those vampire voles all over the place. I've arranged for every ship coming from Slattland to be inspected now. And I've got vets all over the city pulling vampire's fangs, when we find them.' She paused, then said, 'Unfortunately some of the less experienced vets are pulling the teeth of ordinary citizens. We've had a number of complaints and there's a string of law suits waiting for you when you're better.'

Jeremy winced. 'Can't these vets tell the difference between water voles and weasels and stoats? They started all this, those weasels. You can't blame everyone else.'

'Well, naturally they find them sleeping in gloomy places, where the light's not good. The "mistakes" are usually vagabonds, sleeping rough, but you'd be surprised how quickly down-and-outs can find a lawyer to take up their case for them.'

'No I wouldn't.'

'And there's been one or two rather more respectable citizens – Judge Bludgenbox had a few too many honey dews at a society dinner the other evening and woke up on a bench in Hide Park with two front teeth missing.'

'Oh, my,' groaned Jeremy. 'All right. I'll sort it all out once I'm back on my feet.'

'Don't worry, brother, I'm doing quite well myself.'

She left him sitting up in bed sipping a drink of hot rabbits' blood. After a while he stared at his scar. It was healing nicely. Hare's fur, eh? he thought. No difference really. He felt it with his paw. Yes, much the same as his own fur. *Slightly* coarser, but not so's you'd notice. Hare. Yes. Mountain hare.

He picked up the paw mirror on the bedside table and stared at his face. No change there, really. Wha— wait a bit. Was his nose looking a little rabbitish? Why was it twitching like that? He'd have to lay off the rabbits' blood in future, though he loved it so.

No, no, surely he was imagining it? He stared at his ears in the looking-glass. Was it *really* his imagination, or were his ears just a tad longer? Was it that the glass was warped? They looked a bit more pointy than usual. No, no, don't get obsessive, he told himself. Stay sensible and sane.

He got up to go to the toilet. As he passed a full-length mirror on his way to the bathroom, he suddenly felt the urge to box his image. His little paws came up and he flashed a couple of punches at the Jeremy in the mirror, who at the same time threw one or two rather good ones his way.

Funny, that, he thought. Fancy boxing himself.

WAIT! Didn't hares box each other in the spring?

And why was he walking to the bathroom in a zig-zag fashion?

His eyes opened wide as he realized what was happening. 'Sybil!' he shrieked. 'I'm turning into a hare!'

CHAPTER TWENTY-EIGHT

Once the ship was under way, Monty, Bryony, Maudlin and Scruff set about searching it. They had to do it discreetly, of course, for the captain would not have allowed it had he known. It was Scruff who found the coffin, in the forecastle, and he went to fetch Monty.

'Got it,' he said. 'Stuffed under some canvas sails, like someone wanted to hide it or somefink.'

'Right,' said Monty. 'I don't think we can fuss around with pulling teeth here. We're dealing with one of the world's most savage monsters. This is a stake-in-the-heart job. Fortunately I had the foresight to pack a hammer and wooden stake in my suitcase. I'll get it now. You find the other two and meet me at the fo'c'sle.'

'Is that how you say it? Folksell. I thought it was *forecastle*.'

'No, that's how it's spelt, not how it's pronounced.'

Scruff trotted off and Monty went to fetch his tools. Hopefully, he thought, as he took them out of his suitcase, this action would rid the world of its last really dangerous vampire. The oldest ones were the most difficult to destroy. They had the wisdom and craft of ages. They were stronger, far more cunning than new vampires, and highly intelligent. That's what made the chase so exciting for Monty. Of course, he could have done without vampires, but since they were around they made marvellous adversaries. They tried every corner of his intellect. Monty would have admired them, as formidable opponents, if their table manners and eating habits did not disgust him so much.

The three weasels were waiting for him in the dim reaches of the forecastle. Here there were ropes and spare sails, rusting marlinspikes, wooden pins, blocks and tackles, and various other sailing equipment. The four of them surrounded the coffin. Monty gave his instructions.

'Scruff and Maudlin, you lift the lid quickly. Bryony, you put the stake in place, ready for me to hit with the hammer. You know the position of the heart in the chest. We won't get a second shot, so do it swiftly and accurately. Now, don't be alarmed when we take off the lid. What light there is in here will wake him instantly. His eyes will snap open. Whatever you do, don't look into them. Master vampires are skilful hypnotists. Now, are there any questions before we go to it?'

'Yes,' whimpered Maudlin, 'can't we get the crew to help? They're stronger. I don't think I can lift this heavy coffin lid.'

Scruff nudged his friend. 'You're a card, you are, Maud. Always comin' up with a joke, even at times like this.'

Maudlin said nothing more. He had made his protest. Now he made his peace with his god. Today he prayed to the sea, which was about to embrace him, so he believed. The sea was big and wide, and very well able to embrace a weasel. The only thing was, it was so very cold.

'Ready?' said Monty, raising the heavy hammer.

'Ready,' said Bryony.

'One, two, three – go,' said Scruff, and he and Maudlin raised the coffin lid.

Bryony put the point of the stake over where the heart would be, if a heart lay beneath. Monty brought down the hammer, automatically, on the head of the stake. The stake was driven downwards into the grave earth which the coffin contained. It went in too easily.

There was no vampire beneath it.

'Well, well,' said Monty. 'We've been tricked yet again.'

Maudlin, who was so scared he could not see straight, asked what was the matter.

'No vampire,' said Scruff. 'Def'nit'ly an absence of vampires.'

Bryony said, 'Do you think he's on another ship, Monty?'

'Quite possible. Perhaps he's left several false trails – I don't know. He's a clever creature, that's for sure. It all seems quite logical now. We found out the name of the ship too easily, didn't we? I'd be very surprised if he's not still in Slattland, or on another ship. Just the same, we ought to continue our search of this one, just to make sure there's only one coffin.'

They split up again and gave the ship another thorough search. At lunch-time they met up in the dining-room and each gave his or her report. The gist of it was that no other coffin was found. Bryony had searched the lifeboats, Scruff had befriended the engineer and gone over the engine-room, Maudlin had pretended to be a steward and gone through all the cabins of the other passengers, though there were not many of them. Monty had been in all those secret places which one finds in a ship – galleys and heads and bilges. All to no avail. Not a trace of any other coffin was discovered.

'I think,' said Monty, as they sipped their grass soup, 'we can safely relax. I'm fairly convinced he's not on board. I suggest you all try to enjoy the voyage as much as you can, though it's coming on to a big blow by the look of those dark clouds.' He pointed with his fork through the porthole. 'Dirty weather ahead, I'll be bound.'

Indeed, the squall hit just a few minutes later. Plates and cutlery went sliding all over the table: there was a high rim which kept it from

242

falling on deck. Lightning flashed, thunder crashed. Rain lashed at the ship and the sea around it. Waves grew in size and white water ran along the decks. Officers left their tables and took up various stations about the vessel. Sailors came and went in streaming oilskins, their tails poking through slits in the backs of their garments.

After the storm the weasels gathered in the saloon to play a game of hollyhockers. Other passengers were beginning to emerge. The captain passed by their game, looking grave.

'Anything the matter?' asked Monty.

The captain sighed. 'We lost a sailor or two during that blow.'

'Or *two*?' cried Bryony. 'How many all told?'

'Seven.'

'What? Was they washed overboard?' asked Scruff.

'No-one saw what happened,' replied the captain. 'We mustered after the storm and found they were missing, that's all.'

'I don't need to ask whether that's usual,' said Monty. 'It's not. How very strange. A freak wave, perhaps?'

'Something like that,' said the captain. 'Now, if you'll excuse me, I have work to do . . .'

'Seven,' murmured Monty. 'This ship is sailing round the horn of Welkin this trip, which takes longer than our voyage going out. I would say we have about a week before we reach port. Seven marten sailors, seven days. Does that raise alarm bells in anyone?'

Bryony nodded. 'The vampire would need one for each day.'

'We need to search the ship again,' said Monty, rising from the table. 'He's got to be on board somewhere.'

Once more the intrepid travellers set about the task of scouring the ship. They found six of the pine-marten sailors, gagged and bound in one of the holds, but they could tell the weasels nothing. 'Just felt a sort of slight pressure on the back of me neck,' each one said. 'Then I went out like a light.'

The seventh sailor was never found. No doubt his body lay at the bottom of the ocean in Davy Jack's locker, drained of blood.

'I don't understand,' said Bryony. 'Why didn't the vampire just take one sailor, then let the others walk around and pick them off one by one, when he got hungry?'

Monty said, 'I've been thinking of that too. The only answer I can come up with is that Count Flistagga wanted to taunt us. He wants to prove he's so much cleverer than me – us.' Monty paused before adding, 'He'll take one when he needs one now, all right. You'll see. The next thing to do is watch to see if any of the passengers only appear at night. Flistagga might be one of them, of course. I've been aware of that from the start, and have been observing the other passengers closely, but I didn't want us *all* doing it. It might have been too obvious.' Monty imagined Maudlin staring every passenger full in the face from about three centimetres' distance. 'I haven't seen anything which would cause my suspicions to be confirmed, but I'm not infallible. I think we should all now be on our guard. This includes the crew too, of course. But be discreet.'

'Gotcha, guv'nor,' said Scruff.

The voyage continued and, much to the alarm and distress of the captain, his sailors did indeed begin disappearing one by one. And the passengers too. Eventually they hove into a small harbour on the south-west spur of Welkin. There the marten discharged all his passengers and sent the crew into the mariners' hostel. With everyone out of the way, Monty and the other three weasels, plus the captain, went through the vessel centimetre by centimetre, until they had covered the whole ship. Nothing was found. It was a blessed mystery to all concerned.

Then, by chance, Maudlin's hat was blown off. It went upwards, into the rigging, where it stuck between two stays. Monty stared at it, then clicked his claws. 'Of course!' he said, nodding. 'The crow's nest!'

The captain looked up and he too nodded. 'Why, *why* didn't I think of that?'

'The trouble with us mustelids,' said Monty, 'has always been the same. We *rarely* look up to the sky, to the stars, to the sun and moon. We have always been close to the earth, our noses attracted by its smells. We've never got into the habit of looking upwards.'

'Di'n't the sailors go up there?' asked Scruff.

'Oh, they went up into the rigging, but not all the way up into the crow's nest. What for? That's

245

for sighting land, or other ships. This ship knew where it was going – it's done the trip a thousand times before. There was no need for anyone to go up to the crow's nest. Well, let's go and take a look . . .'

Sure enough, the crow's nest was full of musty-scented grave earth. It was so full that a creature could bury himself in there and not see the light of day. Flistagga had obviously been up there most of the time, though during the storm and other dark hours he must have roamed the ship looking for food. He would have thrown the drained bodies overboard, so that there would be no rivals for the limited veins and arteries available on such a trip. Those he had turned into vampires would wake up to their undead state at the bottom of the ocean, where they would waste away, or be eaten by predators.

'Well, he ain't here now,' said Scruff, poking around with a marlinspike. 'Gone's what he is.'

'Must have slipped away just as dawn was breaking,' said Monty, looking around. 'My guess is he's in one of those warehouses over there. But which one? It would take a week to search them all and by the time this evening comes around he'll slip away from us again. I'm afraid Count Flistagga has beaten us this time. But we'll catch up with him, just you see. He's not got the better of Montegu Sylver for good!'

'That's the stuff,' said Scruff.

'My sentiments exactly,' said Bryony.

'Too right,' growled Maudlin, ferocious in the daylight.

'I'm sorry,' the marten captain said. 'I should have listened to you before we left port on the other side. Now there's a monster loose within our shores. A Nosfuratoo. Horrible to think of.'

Monty said it was always difficult to accept the existence of vampires, and the captain shouldn't blame himself. But now they had to be on their way to Muggidrear. Monty asked the whereabouts of the nearest railway station and the four took off in its direction.

CHAPTER TWENTY-NINE

Spindrick had been through all kinds of hell since going up the Klangalang, but he was nearing his journey's end in Tarawak's heart of darkness. In the distance was a high, active volcano, topped with sparkling snow. Below this great wonder of nature was lush forest which spread around and about its base. From this vegetation curled a snake of smoke, rising vertically in the windless air to the blue regions of the sky.

'That's their camp?' asked Spindrick.

'That's the village,' said Rakki-Takki, who had recently and inexplicably taken to wearing a batik turban. 'That's my homeland and that's where you'll find your two professors.'

'Excellent.' Spindrick took off his now battered

pith helmet and wiped the sweaty fur on his brow. He was half the weasel that had started out. He had lost several grammes in weight, his pelt was in a terrible condition and there were insect and leech bites all over his nose and other tender exposed parts of skin. As well as being run-down and exhausted he had lost half his mongoose bearers: some had left to join an angling contest run by local fishermen, others had fallen sick and died.

Yet he had made it. It was a tremendous achievement. And he had a notebook full of articles for *The Chimes*, who would pay him handsomely. There were also many drawings of plants, animals, birds, fish and all kinds of insects to take back with him. Spindrick had been quite good at sketching at school. Now that talent had been put to good use. He knew that when he returned to Welkin the newspaper would ensure that he became a famous Varicosian explorer and naturalist, to be lionized and fêted by the wealthy. For any other weasel this would have been enough. Not for Spindrick. He was still intent on carrying out his original plan of destroying organized society and reducing it to metaphorical rubble.

'What are you going to do now, Rakki-Takki?' he asked.

'Fight my half-brother for supremacy of the tribe,' replied the long, lean mongoose. 'I am the rightful chief, not him. It was my dad who ran things before he died. I was away at a Welkin boarding school when it all happened.

249

That Icki-Ucki is going to get a shock when he sees me.'

'You were at boarding school?'

'Yep, St Smidgen's.'

'Good lord, I was at St Smidgen's too. Do you remember old Chalky Chunker – used to throw blackboard rubbers when one couldn't decline ancient Stoatian verbs?'

'Do I remember him? I still have a lump behind my ear where that very same missile struck.'

'I say,' said Spindrick excitedly, 'you aren't the R. Takky (Minor) who captained the cricket team in 'thirty-seven, when we beat St Giblets in the final?'

'Yep,' replied Rakki-Takki, smiling. 'Actually my elder brother, R. Takky (Major), was the captain of the soccer team the year before me. Unfortunately he died of the mange in 'thirty-eight, which is why I'm the next in line for chieftainship of the tribe.'

'Good lord,' said Spindrick. 'To think we've travelled down this river over half a continent and we went to the same school. Put it there!' He put out his forelimb. Sure enough Rakki-Takki knew the school's secret paw-shake and they both clicked their teeth in glee.

Spindrick's tone was wistful when he said, 'I don't suppose there're any gold and diamond mines on the mountainside? Didn't King Slobbermon live around here somewhere?'

'Yep, but he spent the lot on mango dew, jills and song before he died. Slobbermon's motto was: "When the snake hunter follows the tortoise, the soldier ants feed," so you can see why he didn't leave anything behind. That was long ago, anyway. The gold and diamond mines have long ceased to produce wealth. You'd be lucky to get change out of sixpence now.'

By now they were at the jetty. Spindrick jumped ashore and walked up to the village, with Rakki-Takki just behind him. Two gerbils were sitting on the porch of a hut, swaying back and forth in raffia hammock chairs and being fanned by a punkah-wallaby from the antipodes: a castaway who had found his way up-river from the coast. The two gerbils looked up in surprise on seeing a weasel advancing towards them.

Spindrick took off his helmet and stretched forth his paw. 'Professor Jyde, I presume?'

'Indeed. Speckle Jyde, and this is . . .'

'Professor Margery Spred,' added Spindrick. 'Jal Spindrick Sylver, at your service. Sent by the editor of *The Chimes* to find you and write an article on your work. So pleased to meet you both. May I introduce my friend and guide in this river-mazed country, Prince Rakki-Takki, rightful heir to the chieftainship of this tribe of mongooses.'

The punkah-wallaby made a rather rude noise with his rear end. 'Flamin' chillies,' he muttered. He let go of the punkah string and wandered off towards an outhouse which had the words BRUCE'S DUNNY chalked on the door in large antipodean letters.

By this time several hundred native mongooses had surrounded the group from the northern hemisphere and a gasp went through

251

them at the mention of Rakki-Takki's name. There was a shout from the back and the mongooses parted to let an angry fellow through. He was waving a spear with his right paw and a sword with his left. He confronted Rakki-Takki and said with a sneer, 'You claim to be my half-brother? Prove it.'

Rakki-Takki unwound the turban on his head. There on his brow was a shaven area revealing his white scalp beneath. It had been cut in the shape of a king ragworm. This was his mark of princeship.

Icki-Ucki stepped backwards, quickly, his eyes pale. 'So,' he said, recovering after a few moments, 'my half-brother returns. But you are too late. I am now chief of the tribe.'

'There is a way of settling these things,' snapped Rakki-Takki, 'and I suggest we go to it straight away.'

'After you,' replied Icki-Ucki. 'You know where the killing ground lies – or have you forgotten after so long away from your mammals?'

'I haven't forgotten.'

Rakki-Takki set off for a clearing in the jungle. Icki-Ucki and the rest of the tribe followed. In fact everyone except the punkah-wallaby, who was still in the outhouse, which Spindrick noticed the tribal mongooses gave a wide berth.

Margery Spred said, 'I'm not sure we should witness this contest. They can be very ugly.'

'Yet, as mammalpologists we ought to record such rites at first paw. I don't think we have a choice,' replied Jyde. 'What do you say, Jal Sylver?'

'I believe we should watch it. If I'm not mistaken, our lives depend upon the outcome. Rakki was telling me on the journey that if a claimant to the chieftainship returned, and failed in his bid to convince the tribe of his superiority over the usurper, then three outsiders would have to be sacrificed to appease the god of the volcano, Jon Frum.'

Jyde counted. 'Why, that's all of us,' he said. 'There're no other outsiders in the village except the wallaby, and he's leaving tonight, having finally worked his passage. Remarkable.' He wrote something in his notebook. 'In that case, it's essential that we go and support Rakki, isn't it? Otherwise, we'll be cast into the boiling lava of the volcano. Not a very pleasant thought, you'll grant.'

At that moment there was an eclipse of the sun. The world was plunged into darkness for a few minutes. All the sounds of the jungle stopped suddenly. An eerie silence ruled. Gradually the sun began to emerge from behind the moon. First the twilight returned, then eventually full daylight, for it was close to a vertical noon. The group, who had stopped to witness this phenomenon, continued along the forest track.

'Well,' said Professor Spred, 'that was a waste. It's a pity it didn't come at a crucial part of the contest. We could have claimed to be gods and ruled in Rakki-Takki's favour. What a shame.'

253

'Never mind, they wouldn't have believed you. Just because they live in the jungle doesn't make them daft,' said Professor Jyde. 'Too many explorers make that mistake.'

'Perhaps there'll be another eclipse?' suggested Professor Spred.

'No, they don't come in bunches.'

The three weasels set off down the path to the killing ground. There they discovered a level stretch of turf with three strange sticks poking up at the far end. At the near end only one stick stood. Beyond these were two great squares covered with white clay, and a small white dwelling with a porch.

Professor Jyde had a theory. 'I think the three sticks represent the mystical trinity of savage jungle gods, Vyne, Kreeper and Brambel. In opposition to these is the trickster god, Munkee, the joker represented by the single stick, whose shadow points in jest and derision towards the solemn trinity. The single combat will be fought on the ground between, thus ensuring the support of all four pagan gods . . .'

'I think it's a game of cricket,' said Professor Spred. 'Those white squares are screens and that wooden building the pavilion.'

'I think so too,' said Spindrick, 'and I have the feeling that our pelts are safe.'

They were right. The two combating mongooses had already tossed a coin and it was Icki-Ucki who had won the right to go in to bat first.

'I have to warn you, brother,' he called, as

254

Rakki-Takki took his long bowler's run, 'I've been practising in the nets every evening.'

'You'll need all the help you can get,' replied Rakki-Takki through gritted teeth. At the end of his run he delivered a fast, spinning ball. Icki-Ucki knew the pitch and got its measure, even though it caught an awkward bump and threatened to leap over his bat. He hit the ball square. It was enough for two runs, which he took at leisure, not wishing to puff himself out.

Four more balls, resulting in seven more runs, and the sixth took the bails off with a clean *snick*. Nine in all.

Now Rakki-Takki went in to bat. 'Middle and off,' he said. The umpire, an elderly mongoose with a grizzled countenance, gave him what he wanted with an expert claw. Then Icki-Ucki came thundering down to the wicket to deliver a ball at high speed. It flashed through the air, hit a ripple in the pitch, shot up at a forty-five-degree angle and missed Rakki-Takki's head by a centimetre, to disappear behind.

'Hey!' cried Rakki-Takki, 'no bodyline bowling!'

''S not against the rules,' replied Icki-Ucki.

'Gentlemammals don't resort to bodyline bowling.'

'Whoever told you I was a gentlemammal?'

The next ball hit Rakki-Takki full in the stomach.

''Owzat?' cried his opponent.

'Not out,' murmured the elderly umpire.

'Blind old fruit bat,' muttered Icki-Ucki.

The next ball was a full toss, travelling straight for Rakki-Takki's chest. The prince stepped up with anything but a straight bat and whacked the ball. It sailed over the boundary. Six runs. Only three away from victory.

Another ball broke to leg, zipped in with a vicious curve to it, and missed the wicket by a mouse-hair's breadth.

'Right, that does it,' muttered Icki-Ucki. 'That was your last chance . . .'

But it wasn't. Rakki-Takki had his eye in now. He went for the boundary, making a four, then took two off the last ball. Twelve runs, not out. It was indeed an imperial score. The spectators all rushed onto the pitch to congratulate him. He was chief. Icki-Ucki slunk away.

'Where did the tribe learn to play cricket?' asked Spindrick. 'They didn't *all* go to boarding school in Welkin.'

'Oh, no,' replied an amused Rakki-Takki, 'we learned from books. Back in ancient times, we used to fight to the death, battling with iron-wood clubs and vicious hooks made from the wicked long-thorn tree. There would be blood everywhere. Messy business, really. Now we settle all disputes with cricket: fair play – that's the ticket. Care for a glass of squash?'

After the match Spindrick asked the two professors about the special soil. They took him off into the jungle and produced some home-made gas masks from a backpack. Then they led him to a flowering hibiscus, around which lay a multitude of sleeping creatures, including a sun bear, a whole hive of hornets and two very long and bumpy-backed crocodiles.

'Here,' said Margery Spred, pointing to the peaty soil below the plant. 'This is it. Deadly stuff. We must be sure it never falls into the wrong paws.'

'Quite right,' said Spindrick. 'The wrong paws would be disastrous.'

CHAPTER THIRTY

Once back in the foggy city of Muggidrear,
Monty went to see the mayor. He found him in
conference with Thos. Tempus Fugit, the weasel
inventor of clockwork machines, and Wm. Jott,
the stoat inventor of the steam engine. The two
inventors were arguing, while the mayor looked
on with big round eyes, occasionally scratching
his right ear.

'I say my Vampire Detector and Apprehender
is better than your Vampire Tracker and
Grasper,' said Fugit. 'The descriptive name is
much more scientific for a start. My clockwork
robot looks for shadows and, when it finds none,
it throws a net over the offending creature and
drags it to the nearest police station.'

'Ha!' cried Jott, destroying this comprehensive argument with a single syllable. '*My* steam-driven VTG holds a full-length mirror in front of the suspect and, if there's no reflection, it sprays the vampire with a sleeping draught and drags it off to the nearest police station.'

'Your VTG is nowhere near as good as my VDA.'

'Your VDA is so much clockwork rubbish.'

'Hip-hop,' said the mayor dreamily.

Monty decided to intervene. 'I see you have both invented something that will be invaluable to the mammals of the next century.'

'What's that?' said both inventors, whirling on him.

'The TLA. Marvellous. Think how much time it will save. How wonderfully brief conversations will become with your new discovery.'

'What's a TLA?' asked Jott.

'Why,' replied Monty, 'the Three-Letter Abbreviation. I'm sure it'll catch on. "Get it done PDQ" – Pretty Damn Quick. "See you at the BSC" – Big Shopping Centre. Why, it'll save hours. Wonderful! Well done, both of you. I'm all admiration.'

They glared at him. 'Listen,' said Fugit, 'I hope you're not making fun of our vampire detectors?'

'Yes,' said Jott. 'You'd be well advised to keep your opinions on our vampire trackers to yourself.'

'Gentlemammals, gentlemammals, what if it's night-time?'

'What?'

'What?'

'If it's dark,' explained the weasel detective, 'there will be no shadows and a mirror will be useless.'

'Who asked you?' questioned Jott.

'Yes, why are you butting in?' enquired Fugit.

'Hop-hip,' murmured the mayor, with a little sniff.

At that moment Sybil came into the room. She very expertly ushered the two inventors out of the same door, then asked Monty what he wanted. During this interruption Mayor Poynt was looking at his sister expectantly, as if he were waiting for something. When she continued to converse with Monty, he suddenly demanded, 'Where's my carrot juice?'

Monty turned to look at the mayor, who was now jumping from one foot to the other. He kept stretching his body to its full height and swivelling his head from side to side, his eyes wide and his ears pricked. Every so often he twitched his nose, as if sniffing the wind.

'What's the matter with him?' asked Monty.

Sybil sighed. 'He thinks he's a hare. Watch, he's turning his head to look for foxes creeping up on him. See that? Now he's drumming his hind legs. I don't know what we're going to do. I'm at my wits' end. I would put him in Bedlamb – oh, it's a better place now, don't worry – but I wouldn't be able to care for him myself. He's gone completely mad, you see.'

'What brought it on?' asked Monty.

'He had a fur graft, on his chest. When he found

out that the fur came from a mountain hare, it sent him into this nether world he now inhabits. Creatures like those inventors I've just turned out keep taking advantage of him. When I took him to see the queen the other day, she asked to keep him – said he was much better fun as a mad March hare than he ever was as a stoat mayor.'

'Hmm. I can see this is distressing for you,' said the understanding Monty. 'Perhaps Jis Bludd could help? She's not usually called upon to minister to those with mental problems, but I'm sure she could point us in the direction of someone who can. Now, on another matter, we have a terrible monster loose in the city.'

'Monster?' repeated Sybil calmly. 'What – a dragon, or giant, or something?'

'No, it's a vampire, but it's not like those others we've been plagued with. This is a master vampire, a creature so cunning and clever it's going to take all our resources to capture him. Count Flistagga. Ever heard of him?'

'No, I don't believe I have.'

'Where's my carrot juice?' demanded the mayor. 'If I don't get my carrot juice, I'll go blind.'

Sybil turned to the mayor. 'That's not true, Jeremy, and you know it. Carrot juice *may* help one see better in the dark, though I have my doubts about that, but your eyesight is certainly not dependent upon it. Now behave, or this right honourable weasel will take all your nice lettuce leaves and give them to the poor.'

Will he? thought Monty.

The mayor glared at Monty. 'I could box your

ears for you,' he said. 'I could thump you with my big back legs.'

'I expect you could run faster, as well,' replied Monty, 'but I'm not inclined to race you, Mayor.'

Jeremy Poynt pouted and then hip-hopped over the window to stare out over the gardens.

'Well,' said Sybil, now that her brother was quiet, 'how do we get rid of this Count Flistagga?'

'We need to mobilize the whole police force. We need a thorough search of all the cellars, the attics, the newly occupied houses, the graveyards – in fact, a search of the whole city. He's here somewhere and we've got to find him.'

At that moment Chief Falshed and Constable Debbie arrived. 'Ah, Mayor,' cried Falshed, ignoring Monty. 'You see, I tailed him all the way home again. I have my reports here. Shall I leave them on your desk? You will see I have commended Constable Deborah, here—'

'Debbie,' interrupted the constable. 'It's just Debbie.'

'– who did an excellent job. It's my recommendation that she be promoted to sergeant forthwith. I'm sure you'll agree with that. Oh, hello, Princess Sybil, didn't see you there behind the door.'

'Zacharias?' she said. 'You've been to the continent.'

'Yep. Sent you a postcard. Didn't you get it?'

Sybil ignored this question, asking one of her own. 'You – you have been touring abroad with – with this constable?'

'Ah, yes,' he shifted his feet, clearly uncomfortable. 'Mayor's orders, you understand, Sybil. Not my choice at all.'

'Oh, really?' said Debbie coldly.

'Well, that is to say, it wasn't exactly a *chore*, but it was not my idea in the first place.'

Monty whispered to Falshed, 'Shut up, Chief. You can't win this one.'

Falshed recognized the wisdom of these words. He shut up. Monty then launched into his plan for searching the city, asking for the direct involvement of the chief of police. Falshed kept nodding, glad to be off the hook, yet wondering who Monty thought he was, ordering mammals about like this, with the mayor just across the room.

At the end of it all Falshed said loudly, 'What do you think, Mayor?'

'FOX!' yelled the mayor, pointing out of the window with his claw. 'SNEAKY FOX!' Still agitated, he ordered the chief to go out and shoot the offending creature.

They all went to the window and looked out. Sybil said, 'That's Jal Billingslab, the fox who owns the fish market. He's a respected citizen, Jeremy. You can't go shooting fish magnates.'

There were one or two foxes in Muggidrear – not many, for the houses and buildings were built for smaller creatures. Like badgers, foxes tended to live on farms out in the countryside, but there were, of course, exceptions, and Jal Billingslab was one of them. Highly educated, highly respected, rich as Crowsus, this fox was not one to upset.

'I say shoot the blighter,' cried the mayor. 'Look how sneaky he is. Cunning fox. Trying to creep up on me.'

'I would say he's on his way down to one of the river taxis,' said Monty. 'I don't think he's sneaking, Mayor.'

Falshed was now looking at the mayor with great concern. 'Mayor, are you all right?'

'Of course I'm all right. I'm fine. You want a race? I'll show you how all right I am. Listen . . .'

They all listened.

'I can hear that fox coming back,' murmured the mayor darkly. 'You won't be able to hear him, because you haven't got tall sensitive ears like me. Us hares can hear a beetle scratching its armpit from a hundred paces. That fox is coming back, I tell you. Sneaky blighter.'

'I think I'd better leave you all to it,' Falshed said, backing away from the mayor. 'Look, Jal Sylver, if you think the police force is needed to track down this master vampire, then I'll get it mobilized. Princess Sybil, may I call on you this evening?'

'You may,' she said, 'but I won't be here.'

'Oh?'

'No, I've been asked out by someone. I'd rather not say who. He's going to take me – oh, everywhere. On a world tour soon, I shouldn't wonder. I'll be very busy. You can call if you like, but I think you'll find me out with – with my special friend.'

'Who is it?' demanded Falshed, grinding his teeth.

'You wouldn't know him. He's . . .' Sybil glanced across at Monty. 'He's a weasel. Yes, that's what he is, a very important weasel. He treats me very well. He treats me like a princess.'

'But you are a princess,' said the ruffled chief of police.

'Yes – yes, I am, aren't I? And this special weasel friend of mine – oh, he knows how to treat a princess all right.'

'It's not *him*, is it?' cried Falshed, glaring at Monty.

'Him?' said Sybil. 'Oh – no, it's not him. It's a *much* more important weasel than him. Someone you don't know. He's very rich and good looking, and lots of things like that. I shouldn't try to find out who he is, if I were you. Now I suggest you and your Constable Deborah –'

'Debbie,' corrected Debbie.

'– go and look in spidery attics and dirty basements together. You're obviously suited to such things. You seem to get on so well together, trotting all over the continent and whatever. So, off you go.'

Falshed, slow on the uptake, now got the drift. 'Oh, so *that's* what this is all about. Me and Debbie. Well, there's no "me and Debbie". We're just work colleagues, that's all. We work together.'

'Except you did take me to the theatre in Krunchen,' Debbie said, devilishly. 'And on that canal trip.'

Falshed glared at her. 'That was work.'

'Oh, was it?' said Debbie innocently. 'Right.'

265

At that moment the mayor zig-zagged across the room, crashing into three chairs on the way, and out through the doorway. Once out in the street, with the whole roomful of mustelids chasing him, he yelled after that most respectable citizen, Jal Billingslab, in a high-pitched voice. The strolling fox stopped and looked back at the mayor.

Jeremy Poynt cried, 'Here I am! Come and get me. Think you can outrun me, eh? You sneaky fox in your suit and waistcoat, with your watch-chain dangling, and your shiny top hat, and that brolly on your arm! See if you can catch a mountain hare with legs that go like the wind!'

Jal Billingslab raised a foxy eyebrow and shook his head sadly.

CHAPTER THIRTY-ONE

Count Flistagga was running across the rooftops of Muggidrear at an incredible speed. He was as light and easy as a shadow, passing chimney pots, domes, spires. At this level the world was a silent jungle of brick and metal projections. Yes, there were birds up here, but they took to the air at his approach. To have a dark stoat tripping lightly over their normally deserted grounds was somewhat disconcerting.

It was late evening. There was a bunch of stars in the corner of the sky which let some light fall on the city, illuminating the waters of the river Bronn as they flowed beneath the bridges. The mammal in the moon was peering down. It seemed to have two rather long and sharp teeth in its mouth, but that might have been due to a cloud passing over its face.

During the day the count spent his time in the crypt of St Pompom's, though he knew this would soon become unsafe. He was skilled at outguessing his enemies and he knew that very soon Montegu Sylver would organize a search of the city. That was what Flistagga would do in the weasel's place.

The count reached the edge of the west side of the city. Between him and the animal side was the river. He would have to descend to street level and cross by a bridge or water taxi. Vampires generally disliked crossing running water, but the count had long ago overcome this weakness. He scuttled headfirst down a sheer wall, clinging to the brickwork like a spider. A bat flew by his head, curious to see this creature who defied gravity as much as it did. Flistagga hissed at it, 'Don't come too close!'

'Master,' said the bat, now recognizing his lord. 'You are here! I must inform the others. We need to welcome you properly to this city of weasels and stoats.'

'No, no, tell no-one. If I am to wreak havoc and instil fear into this country, I need to remain hidden.'

'Yes, master.'

By the time the count reached the street, the bat had gone. A human came clumping along the pavement, its big feet crashing down on the flag-stones. It was wearing boots with metal studs which sent up sparks as it walked. The count melted into the shadow of a lamp post, lean enough to be swallowed by the dark stem. Once the human had gone, he emerged again, and made his way to the river.

Looking over the parapet, he saw a rowing boat below, with an otter at the oars. 'Ho!' he called.

'Ho yourself,' came the reply. 'Who do you think you're ho-ing?'

'Are you for hire, otter?'

'Depends for what. I'll take you across the river, if that's what you're askin'. Otherwise, no, I'm a free mammal.'

'Yes, I wish to traverse the river. I can pay you in gold.'

'Gold, is it? Shillin's and pence will do. Use them stone steps over there to get down to the jetty. I'll pick you up.'

Soon the count was in the boat, and the boat was on the move. He looked down to see a name carved in the gunwales of the boat. 'You are Jaffer Silke? Are you the water taxi?'

'No, normally my job's fishin' dead bodies out of the river. But if someone's offerin' me money, I'll be a water taxi if you like.'

'You find many bodies in the river?'

'Lots of 'em. More than is necessary, if you ask me. Some get drowned by accident. Some drown themselves. Some is drowned by others. Some's dead before they even hit the water. This is an evil world, stoat, with little bits of good in it, here and there.'

'Ah, I see you don't subscribe to the view that

the world is good, with bits of evil here and there?'

'Not me – not in my job. If I was in another job, maybe I'd 'ave a different view. But as it is, I sees the worst. However, what I do say is that one bit of good is worth ten bits of evil. It's more precious, the good, you see. It's like comparing a diamond with a chunk of coal. The coal's bigger, there's much more of it, but it's not so valuable.'

'Because good is rare, like diamonds?'

'No, because good is simply worth more. Evil is like trash. It piles up, but it's not worth nuffink. Good is priceless stuff. That's why it only comes in small doses.'

'I think I see what you mean, though I don't necessarily agree. You think good is intrinsically precious. That it has that within it which is priceless in a universal sense?'

'Couldn't put it better meself.'

Flistagga was quite enjoying this social discourse. He was not often in a position to enjoy a chat with another mammal. This Jaffer Silke he found curiously interesting. However, he despised this view that evil was, in itself, inherently valueless. He, Count Flistagga the vampire, was the embodiment of evil, the manifestation of iniquity, and he thought a great deal of himself. 'I think you're wrong, Jaffer Silke. I think evil is just as precious as good.'

'You're entitled to your opinion,' sniffed Jaffer, clearly indicating by his manner that the count had it all wrong. 'Now, that'll be sixpence, if you please, and I want to see the child-queen's head on one side and a pitcher of Whistleminster Palace on the other.'

'Why?'

''Cause I've bin given a number of forin coins lately.'

Count Flistagga gave him the money and Jaffer turned away to moor the boat. In that instance his scrawny otter's neck was exposed to foreign teeth. The count automatically leaned forward, his mouth open. But then, just as suddenly, he drew back with a grimace. 'Too old and skinny,' he said. 'What am I thinking of? All right for an emergency, but not for a dining-out night.'

'Eh?' asked Jaffer, straightening.

'Oh, nothing. A very good evening to you, boatmammal.'

'If you say so,' said Jaffer, 'but I doubt it. I'm sure I'll be pullin' some mother's son or daughter out of the water before the dawn washes over the gunnels.'

Flistagga stepped ashore in the swirling mists and wrapped his black cloak around himself. Without another glance behind him he strode off into the cobbled streets, in search of a coffee house. He found one and entered. It was only partially lit inside. The waiter found him a table for one in the corner, from where he could survey the whole room, scrutinizing the other customers with a practised eye. That eye grew perceptibly brighter when a group of young stoats entered, full of merriment, talking animatedly about some play they had just seen.

Count Flistagga rose from his own table and

271

approached theirs. 'Do you mind if I join you for a moment?' he said. 'I'm waiting for a friend, and I couldn't help overhearing that you enjoyed *Of Mustelids and Moles*. I saw it in Slattland when it first went on the stage and was astonished by it. I believe it has the same cast . . .'

By now he was sitting down and ordering a hot chocolate with a wave of his claw, while the five youngsters gawked at him. He continued to ask them questions about their evening's entertainment and they responded with enthusiasm.

'Listen,' said the count, taking out his pocket watch and staring at it, 'it seems my dinner companion is not going to appear. What do you say we all go on to Strapferrets' restaurant, where I'll treat you all? What do you say? It's been so long since I've had this much fun.'

'Well – yes,' said one of the jills. 'Anyone else?'

'I think I'll call it a night,' said a jack. 'Ilkymoor, you coming back to the lodgings?'

'Yes, I think I will.'

The other two said they would go on to dinner and the young jill clapped her paws together. 'Goodie,' she said.

All six of them went outside and four parted from two. Flistagga's eyes ran over the residue of the group and his eyes settled on one young stoat, a male, who looked lusty and strong. This was a healthy young jack with fresh clean blood – you could tell by the innocent brightness of his eyes – and he had recently been to sea. There was a bloom about his pelt, which looked fine and silky in the evening light. The count began a conversation with this young blade, stopping occasionally to make a point, so that they fell a little behind the other male and the female. After a short while the mist swallowed the pair in front, and the count and his enthusiastic young companion were alone.

'I think travel broadens one's horizons,' the youthful stoat was saying. 'If one doesn't get to meet—'

He was halfway through his sentence when the count suddenly gripped him by the shoulder and forced him into an alley.

'Here, that hurts,' began the jack.

He tried to break free, but found his captor was immensely strong. A short struggle was enough to tell the jack he was no match for the count. Flistagga forced his victim's head to one side, just as the poor stripling let out a gargled scream. Then the count's head dipped, he sank his fangs into the artery in the throat, and began to siphon blood.

The young jack felt the sharp pricks of the fangs, as they punctured his throat and artery. He knew instinctively that he was not going to see another happy day. The warm blood from his body was being drained incredibly swiftly through the hollows in those two teeth, and he sensed his heart was about to collapse in on itself. Indeed, the next moment it began to flatten in his chest and he knew he was dying.

'Hel-arrgghhh-don't-pleas-errrggghhh.'

Gradually the sounds from the writhing jack grew quieter, until he finally fell limp. Flistagga hung on as long as there was a drop of blood in the youngling's body, then let him fall to the ground, where he lay flaccid and still. A final lick, to get that last scarlet liquid jewel that hung from a whisker, and it was done.

Flistagga wiped his mouth with his paw, leaving a red streak on his palm. It was good blood. Very good. Refreshing, sweet and rich with life. He could feel it coursing through his veins, giving even more strength, youth and vigour. Flistagga's heart now pulsed with a strong drum beat. His head was full of fertile images, the thoughts and dreams contained within that jack's blood. He had taken the jack's life, fully, wholly, completely. The jack's ambitions, aspirations, loves, hates, desires, needs – these were all Flistagga's now, all swirling within the red rivers of his form. He would own them for the short time it would take to burn them up like so much fuel, using them to drive his living-dead state towards the next day's night.

It was blood free of stress. Of course there had been that last shock, when his fangs pierced flesh, but not the kind of stirred and caustic blood of a victim stalked through the streets, terrified out of his or her mind because a frightful fiend did close behind them tread. Flistagga found the fluid purer when it was free from anxiety, which was why he went out of his way to befriend his victim before striking suddenly, like a snake. In the past his cup had been bitter, having been soured by worry.

Tomorrow there would be another victim,

hopefully just as young and untainted, who would supply the count with yet more energy – and so the endless cycle would go on, never satisfying the undead count. Tomorrow, and tomorrow, and tomorrow, until the end of time.

The other two young stoats were out there in the street, calling for their friend. Flistagga bared his teeth, then slipped away along the alley. At the other end he began scaling the wall to the rooftops. There he ran amongst the chimneys, danced amongst the chimneys, like a demon released from a cell, on his way back to his crypt.

CHAPTER THIRTY-TWO

The telephone jangled. Although it was just before dawn, Monty was up and dressed. He couldn't sleep. There were too many things rattling around in his head. He picked up the receiver. 'Hello, Montegu Sylver speaking.'

'Ah, what's-his-name. That you? Haukin here.'

Monty was still ragged from travelling and lack of sleep, but he rallied on hearing his friend's voice. 'Hannover? How are you?' The line was bad, as usual. It sounded as if someone were carrying a frying pan of sizzling bacon up and down a gravel path. 'What's wrong?'

'Why d'you say that?'

'Well, you usually don't ring to chat. If you

want a social talk you see me at the Jumping Jacks, or come round here.'

'Look, thingamy, I've got some mammals round here – two of my young friends. They've got a jack with them and he's in a pretty bad way ...' There was a sound of crashing glass. 'Uh, oh! There goes my cabinet full of sea shells. Get over here as quickly as you can.' The phone went dead.

Monty fetched his overcoat, scarf and gloves. Then he took his black bag from beside the sofa and went straight round to Hannover's place. When Culver the butler let him in he saw two stoats, a jack and a jill, sitting on a third, holding him down. A crack of light was just penetrating the curtains. Monty went straight to them and closed them tight.

'Why d'you do that?' asked Hannover, his monocle forgotten and dangling from its cord.

'Daylight is a destroyer,' said Monty, 'to some creatures.'

Hannover clearly didn't get it. 'See, here's the problem. This young jack keeps trying to bite us. And when he's not baring his teeth, he's thrashing around and crashing into my display cabinets. I think he's drunk something that doesn't agree with him.'

'I hope he *hasn't* managed to bite anyone,' replied Monty. 'He hasn't, has he? Don't let him get up – pin him there. You might not realize it, but he's very dangerous.'

'No, we've been taking turns to sit on him.'

'Good.' Monty opened his black vet's bag and reached inside, taking out a phial. 'This is holy water from St Pompom's font,' he said, 'taken with the permission of the human bishop, of course. I'm going to sprinkle it on his lips. It worked on Princess Sybil, and we've caught this one early, by the look of it, so it should work on him.'

He opened the lid and shook a few drops into the mouth of the pinned stoat. The creature's eyes opened wide. He thrashed for a bit, then lay perfectly still. However, the two stoats remained sitting on their friend's chest.

'You can get off him now,' Monty said.

But the jill replied, 'Ha! He went all limp like this before. Then, when we got off him, he went berserk. Look at all the broken things around the room. That was him.'

'He'll be all right now, I assure you.'

They climbed off their friend gingerly and found, to their relief, that he stayed where he was, seemingly unconscious.

'Oh, well done, whodyamaflip,' cried Hannover. 'Blasted fellah's just about wrecked me home for me.'

Monty spoke to the two young stoats. 'Do you mind telling me what happened?'

'Well,' said the jill, after a quick glance at her companion to see that he wasn't going to tell the story, 'we were in a coffee house late yesterday evening, when we met this long stoat, dressed in black. He was quite old, you could see that by his pelt, but he seemed to want to talk to us. We split

278

up when we left the coffee house and he came with the three of us. Frederik was walking behind with the gentlemammal and Steeven and me – I – were just ahead of them . . .'

The young jack took over here, his excitement getting the better of him. 'We heard a shout. A sort of strangled scream, I suppose you'd call it. When we looked for Fred, we couldn't find him anywhere. Then a groan came from an alley, and there he was, lying on the ground with blood oozing from his throat. He's got these sort of pin-pricks in his neck. It's vampire voles, isn't it? They got the old gentlemammal too, didn't they? Carried him off, I expect.'

'It wasn't quite like that,' said Monty. 'In fact, the vampire was the "old gentlemammal" him-self. He's a very dangerous creature. Now, I want you to describe him to me very carefully. Then tell me where you think he went after he left you. Don't worry, I won't blame you, if you're wrong. Finally, I want you to go over your conversation with him and tell me everything he said, no matter how unimportant it may seem. We have to find this creature, or the whole city is in grave danger.'

The two young stoats were unused to being told what to do by weasels. In any other circum-stances they might have resented it. But they took their cue from Lord Haukin, who was quite high up in the aristocracy of Welkin. If he respected this weasel, they felt they ought to as well. So each in turn gave Monty the information he required, until they had exhausted themselves. Once they had done so transport was sent for to take their friend to the infirmary.

Alone, except for Culver, who was clearing the breakfast things, Hannover and Monty discussed the situation.

'Well, Monty,' said Hannover, obviously very perturbed by the whole episode since he actually remembered his friend's name, 'what d'you make of it all? Do you really believe there's a vampire stoat in the city?'

'I'm absolutely convinced of it. We came over on the ship with the creature. He bit several sailors, then threw their bodies overboard. This is a creature with absolutely no morals or principles, seeking some kind of warped revenge. That's not his highest priority, which is survival, but he's willing to risk a little exposure to turn Muggidrear into a city of fear.'

Culver brought in two drinks. As usual there was a book of poems on the tray alongside the cups. Hannover ignored this item. Monty decided he would be kind to the rather sniffy servant. It did no harm to encourage those who dabbled in the arts.

'Is that your latest book of poems, Culver?'

The butler's eyes widened in pleasure. 'It is indeed, sir. My third, to be precise. "Good Bottom Land" is the title poem. Published privately by a little firm in Ockender Crescent. You notice the royal blue binding with the fleurs-de-lis in gold leaf? Also the paper is expensive Waldorf Street, creamy-yellow – I think they call it Kornisch Kream – ninety-millimetre. There's a rather handsome watermark – a leopard, I believe it is – authenticating the quality. This is a collector's copy, sir. There are only eight others like it in the whole world.'

'I'm very impressed. I don't have to enquire after the quality of the poems themselves. How would I obtain a volume for myself?'

'Would you be so kind as to accept this copy as a gift?'

'As a gift?' asked Monty. 'I'm overwhelmed, Culver. I know how highly sought after your little volumes of poetry are. Would you sign it for me, please? To Montegu Sylver, of 7a Breadoven Street?'

Culver's eyes narrowed slightly and he stared at the weasel detective, wondering if there was a hint of mockery here. But no! Monty meant it. Culver's heart was filled with warm gratification. 'Might I recommend that when you dip into the contents, you begin with "If Mute Swans Could Sing". I'm particularly fond of that one. It was written last summer on the banks of the Bronn, while we were out on a picnic.'

'I remember that day,' said Hannover. 'Boat race day. What, Culver – writing poetry instead of watching the boat race? That's sacrilege in this household.'

'Fortunately, my lord, we were not *in* this household, but out in the country.' Culver left the two mammals to their tea and biscuits.

'What did you do that for?' grumbled Hannover. 'He'll get all uppity and snooty on me for at least a week.'

'Oh, you know. He tries so hard.'

'He's very trying, I know that much. Now, what about this vampire thing? What are we going to do?'

Monty said, 'We have to find the creature and destroy him.'

'Really? Sounds pretty drastic.'

'I'm afraid it is—'

At that moment Culver poked his head round the door again and Hannover became a little tetchy. 'See here, Culver, we're trying to have a conference on something a bit more important than pretty verses.'

'I realize that, my lord, which is why I wish to pass on some information to the right honourable gentlemammal.'

'Yes?' said Monty.

'Well, we Culvers have always had good noses—'

Hannover interrupted with a snort: 'Your nose is no better than anyone else's. Looks a fairly common sort of nose to me.'

'I mean I have a very good sense of smell. My olfactory organs are very sensitive.'

'And?' said Monty.

'I thought you might like to know that the gentlemammal who smashed our cabinets had a tinge of human scent about him. I would say he has come into contact with someone who is living on the human side of the river. I don't think it was strong enough to say he had been handled, but there was that about him which offended the nostrils, just faintly, if you know what I mean, sir

– as if it had been passed on from someone who had direct contact with the west side.'

Monty said, 'Thank you, Culver. You've given us what we need.'

The butler looked directly at his master. 'You're very welcome, sir.'

'What's all that mean?' asked Hannover.

'Count Flistagga is hiding over on the other side of the river. That makes sense. Where better to hide than amongst those galumphing humans and their dogs and cats? It's not often any of us goes over there, precisely because it's a place where accidents can happen to mustelids very easily. He's probably hiding in one of their houses – in a shoe cupboard or wardrobe of some kind – and picking up their scent.'

'Can you track him down then?'

'I'm going to have a jolly good try,' said Monty. 'I'll take my three friends with me – Bryony, Maudlin and Scruff – and we'll see if we can't root him out. It'll be an ugly business, I'm afraid. We're really going to have to destroy him this time. No more holy water or garlic. This time we are going to have to drive a stake through his heart and cut off his head. Then, if we are able, I suggest we burn the remains.'

'Can we do all this? To a live creature?'

'You must understand, Hannover, Count Flistagga is not *alive* in the sense you mean. He's one of the undead. Well, I won't take up any more of your time. I'll be at home tonight, if you want anything, but now my friends and I will start out for the west side.'

283

CHAPTER THIRTY-THREE

Monty rounded up his gang of three and told them they were going to have to cross the river.

'To see the queen?'

'No, not this time, Maudlin. This time it's to search for a count. Our vampire is over there somewhere and we have to find him and root him out. Well, not exactly. We've got to destroy him. Bryony, how are we going on the vampire voles?'

Bryony had been out with other vets, pulling teeth, for the last two days. She reported success. 'I think we've got rid of the last of them. We had to deal with one or two of their victims too, and they've all been inoculated against vampirism. Good job too, because we've run out of holy water and I don't really want to ask the human bishop for more. He's getting a bit fed up with being dragged out at all hours to bless more water in the font.'

'Good, so now we can concentrate on Count Flistagga.'

Scruff rubbed his paws together. 'Can't wait,' he said. 'Nothin' like a vampire hunt to raise the temperature of the blood.'

'I think I've got a sore throat,' said Maudlin huskily. 'I'll probably have to miss it.'

'Open wide,' Bryony ordered, tapping his lower jaw. Maudlin reluctantly opened his mouth and let Bryony peer down his throat, using a spatula to keep his tongue flat. 'Nothing wrong there,' she murmured. 'Clean as a whistle.'

At that moment Ringing Roger struck twelve noon and they all had to hold onto something. The vibrations rattled every teacup in the cupboard and a kitchen chair went for a juddering stroll across the lino. Finally it was all over.

'I wish Spindrick would blow that clock up again,' grumbled Maudlin, hoping to divert the subject away from his throat. 'It's like waiting for a bomb to go off every quarter of an hour.'

'Right,' said Monty. 'Is everybody ready for the vampire hunt? All got your little black bags with stake and hammer? Don't worry, Maudlin, we might not have to use them. If we can find him sleeping the best thing to do is expose his body to sunlight. He'll simply crumble to dust before our eyes and no violence will be needed. Let's hope

285

for a swift and clean end to this whole horrible saga.'

'Indeed,' said Bryony.

They all set off, heading for Whistleminster Bridge. On the way there they just happened to pass Varicose railway station. And who should they meet but a very tired-looking Spindrick Sylver, wearing a dented pith helmet and khaki shorts and shirt and carrying a battered brown suitcase in his paw. His eyes looked bloodshot and jaundiced, his coat was ragged as well as sun-burnt, and there were insect bites showing through his fur. In all he looked as if he had just climbed Mount Nevertoil in the hot season.

'Spindrick! What are you up to?' asked Monty suspiciously.

His cousin glared at him before answering, 'I've been to Tarawak – don't you read the newspapers? I'm a foreign correspondent for *The Chimes*. If you *had* read my column, you would have seen that I found the two lost professors – Jyde and Spred – and have brought their story back with me. In short, cousin, I have been into the heart of darkness, and have returned alive and well.'

'Not well, surely?' said Bryony. 'You look like death warmed up. Better come and see me at my surgery tomorrow morning.'

Spindrick glowered. 'I'm fine. I've had some experiences, that's all. You don't go up the Klangalang river and return without scars of some sort. I've seen sights you would not believe.

Witchvets, driving out demons . . . Single combat between mongooses—'

'Mon*geese*, surely?' interrupted Maudlin.

Spindrick ignored him. 'Sights that would curdle your blood. Whether you like it or not, cousin,' he said, 'I'm a famous explorer now. Mammals look up to me. The Tortoise Globetrotting Society has asked me to lecture to its fellows. My name is going up on the border of their lecture hall, along with such names as Dr Deadbrick, Thus, Spake, Zarathruster and Nevertoil. I'm afraid I've left you behind in the fame stakes, cousin. You came in second.'

Monty beamed. 'Glad to hear it.'

'No you're not – you can't be.'

'But I am. I'm very proud of you, Spindrick. You've been a bit of a pain in the neck in the past, but hopefully all that's behind you. I'm very pleased to be your cousin and bask in reflected glory.'

'Poooohhh,' said Spindrick, put out. 'We'll see.'

At that moment seven weasel porters came out of the station wheeling trolleys laden with huge sacks. They stopped behind Spindrick, who hailed a cab. The cab-driver turned his yellow-necked mouse and trotted it over to the kerb. He viewed the sacks with great distaste. 'You're not takin' that lot in my cab.'

'No, no, they're following on,' said Spindrick. 'I've ordered a dray.'

'That's all right then, squire. 'Op aboard.'

'Spindrick,' said Monty, 'what's in the sacks?'

'Fertilizer. I brought it back from Tarawak. It's wonderful. It makes plants grow like magic. Not only will I be more famous than you, cousin, but I'll also be richer. You can't help being jealous, but that's the way it's going to be. We'll see who's the brains of the family then, won't we? We'll see whose name goes down in history.'

With that Spindrick climbed up into the coach and the cab-driver clicked his tongue at his mouse, who trotted away, the steel-rimmed wheels of the vehicle rattling on the cobbles.

Monty watched his cousin go with some misgiving. 'Hmm. I'm not sure about this,' he said. 'Spindrick has always wanted to be famous, but he's never wanted to be rich. He despises wealthy mustelids and tries to bomb them at every opportunity. There's something funny going on here. I wish I could get a sample of that fertilizer he's got there – if that's what it is.'

'No problem, guv'nor,' said Scruff. He opened his paw to show the others a clawful of soft, brown, peaty earth. 'I reached into one of the sacks when they wasn't lookin'.'

'Brilliant, Scruff. Bryony, will you put this in the pocket of your little black bag and analyse it for me when we return?'

'*If* we return,' muttered Maudlin gloomily.

Half an hour later they were crossing Whistleminster Bridge. On the other side of the bridge the atmosphere was not pleasant. Humans had many more and larger factories than the mustelids. The smoke that hung over their side of the city was – as Scruff had once put it – 'ap-pall-ing', and much of this factory smoke mingled with the fog from the river to produce a poison-ous mixture. The weasels were going into a hazy area where their lungs would suffer.

It was also quite dangerous on that side of the river. The chances of being accidentally trodden on were quite high. Weasels were very small. Humans had difficulty in seeing them. If one did tread on Monty or any of his friends, it was certain death. Thus they had to have their wits about them at every second of the journey, dashing this way and that, avoiding the great clumping boots and shoes of an oversized population.

'Ruddy stoats,' said a man, typical of his kind, 'can't you stay your side of the river?' He had almost trodden on Maudlin, who had at the last minute seen the foot descending and dashed out of the way. It wasn't that humans *wanted* to hurt mustelids; they were simply clumsy creatures. This particular man would have been most upset if he had trodden on Maudlin. But like many of his kind he was lumpish and short-sighted. Nor did he know the difference between weasels and stoats.

But that was humans for you. If one of the weasels had confronted the man with this accu-sation of ignorance, he would probably have replied, as they always did, 'It's all right for you – you've only got to recognize one human; we've got to learn the difference between six or seven mustelids.' Which was quite true, of course.

However, their broad ignorance remained a source of discussion amongst mustelids. Many humans thought there was only one kind of mouse and were amazed when they learned that on Welkin Island alone there were at least four kinds (not counting a dormouse), three types of vole and four different shrews.

Maudlin was annoyed with the human. 'Why can't they look where they're going?' he complained.

Monty was more generous. 'Well, it's difficult for them, especially in this foggy atmosphere.'

Scruff said, 'Let's get back to vampires, guv'nor. Where should we start lookin' for the count? He'll be somewhere dark, won't 'e? Maybe in a warehouse, or a cellar, eh?'

Bryony said, 'I think he'll also try to find somewhere which suits his kind. Graveyards, as we've seen, is a favourite haunt of vampires – or belfries. Where shall we start? At the cemetery?'

'Good idea,' replied Monty. 'The cemetery it is.'

When they got to the local graveyard, they found enormous tombstones, some ten times the height of a weasel. There were mouseholes around many of them, which a slim weasel could slip down to inspect the contents of coffins below. It was not a very pleasant task, but it was one which had to be done.

'"Kenneth Grahame,"' Bryony said, reading one gravestone, '"whose riverbank tales of Ratty, Mole, Badger and Toad delighted many children."'

'Well, there's a human who liked mammals,' Maudlin said approvingly. 'And amphibians. You don't get many of them writing about us, do you? In that author's time they mainly used to spend their days setting traps and snares and trying to wipe us out. Jolly good for him.'

They didn't investigate this particular grave, because Monty said that the count would probably choose the coffin of someone with whom he felt comfortable, like another human, Bram Stoker, author of a book entitled *Dracula*.

Maudlin found it very distasteful having to crawl down these narrow tunnels to the graves beneath. The first one he went down was long, dark and winding. It smelled musty and corpsey, and was rather warm. When he reached the coffin and was able to enter by the hole the mouse had made, he lit a candle stub and surveyed his surroundings with trepidation, hoping he wasn't going to be the one to find Count Flistagga. Indeed this time he wasn't. All he found was a human skeleton stretched out in the roomy coffin. The skull was grinning with fierce intent to remain cheerful, even though its owner had been consigned to the earth for all eternity.

'What are you smirking at?' growled Maudlin, glaring at the human skull. 'Haven't you got better things to do?'

'I wasn't smirking!'

Maudlin almost jumped out of his pelt. At first he thought he had come across the first talking human corpse, but then Scruff emerged from behind the bony structure.

'You scared me to death!' accused Maudlin. 'I nearly passed out then.'

'Sorry,' replied his friend. 'I just followed you down. No cause for alarm. No Flistagga? No vampires?'

'Not that I can see.'

'Well, let's get topside again, then. We've got a lot of coffins to search, old buddy.'

Maudlin groaned and his breath blew out the candle.

CHAPTER THIRTY-FOUR

The four weasels continued their search of the
human side of the river. It took a long time:
the graveyards were immense, bearing tombs
that could have housed a dozen stoats. They
searched parklands, big public buildings with
dark recesses, sarcophagi in museum store-
rooms, art galleries, cupboards and boxes in
stately homes, stables, cellars, churches, and the
big cathedral, St Pompom's. However, there
were so many nooks and crannies there was no
guarantee that they had covered every hiding
place. During the search of the cathedral Scruff
fell through an iron grid into an oubliette, a dry
well where the early bishops threw heretics and
forgot about them. He landed with a bump

amongst the dust, rags and bones of the unfortunates who had been cast into the pit.

'Hey, up there,' he called, shaking himself. 'I've gone an' fell down a hole!'

Maudlin's voice came floating down to him. 'I'll get a rope, or some cord. Have you got a light?'

'Got some matches, that's all.'

A moment later something hit the floor at Scruff's feet. He lit a match to find a candle stub lying amongst the bones. 'Got it!' he called. He lit the candle and waited. While he was there he inspected his prison. It was a very grim place. The grid above had been located under the table where the monks ate, and the scraps of food fell through and down to the prisoners below. They would have remained alive for a time.

Looking further Scruff saw that one of the occupants of the well had scraped away the mortar from the stones and had broken through the wall into another room beyond, creating an escape route from the oubliette! This was just as well, for a few moments later Maudlin was back.

'Can't find anything. Can't find Monty or Bryony, either. What shall I do, Scruff?'

'Look, don't worry, I can see a tunnel someone's made. I'll get out that way. Can you chuck down me bag with me hammer an' stake?'

There was silence for a while, then Maudlin's voice came down: 'Can't see it anywhere. Didn't it fall down with you?'

Scruff had another search amongst the pile of rags and bones, but could find nothing. 'Nah, never mind. I'll come up as quick as I can. You go an' find Monty and Bryony. I'll see you all outside on the cathedral steps.'

'Can't you climb out?'

Scruff tested the walls, which rose sheer and slippery from the floor of the oubliette. 'Nope. The stones are covered in wet algae. I don't want to risk a broken leg. No, don't worry, I'll find another way out.'

'All right then.'

Scruff slithered weasel-like through the man-sized hole in the wall of the oubliette. With candle in paw he found himself in a smelly cavity which he imagined must once have been the sewer serving the monks' hostelry. Here were more human bones – some of those poor fools who thought they had escaped the oubliette had died in this chamber. Yet the candle flame wavered occasionally, which made Scruff think there must be a breeze entering the old sewer. And, he reasoned, sewers have to come from somewhere and go to somewhere.

He went round all the walls, testing the bricks, to see if any were loose. It was possible that the cathedral staff had walled up the sewer at some time, once it had fallen into disuse. However, the most painstaking search of the walls did not reveal any outlet. It was possible, of course, that the breeze in question was coming from above, which meant that Scruff was in the same position in this chamber as he was in the last, and only a rope or ladder would get him out.

He turned his attention to the centre of the

wide chamber. The candle flame reached out, flickered and fell on something which made his blood run cold. There, in the centre of the floor, lay a stoat-sized coffin. There were strange symbols on the coffin, such as those Scruff had seen on marsh rat banners and flags, when he visited the battlefront. Clearly he had stumbled on the hideout of the master vampire. To make sure, Scruff tiptoed to the coffin, lifted the lid and peered inside.

There lay a long lean stoat wrapped in a black cloak. The creature's eyes were open, but staring sightlessly. His forelimbs were crossed over his chest, just like those pictures of vampires in repose which Monty had shown all three weasels. His claws were long and sharp, his eyes red-hued, his lips and complexion an ugly blue, like some old stoat with a heart condition, his teeth, bared, showing the extra-long fangs of one of the stoat undead.

'You're him all right,' murmured Scruff. 'No doubt about that.'

The vampire stirred in his coffin, like one moving in sleep, and he uttered something in a low, foul tongue.

Scruff stepped back, alarmed, but the vampire was still again. Scruff stared into the creature's eyes, fascinated by their darkness and their depth. Here was naked evil, dormant, waiting for the night to arrive, so that it could rise from its stale-earth bed and go out and hunt for mortal mustelids in the twilight. Here was horror incarnate, such as no weasel would ever wish to encounter alone, in a dark confined space, with no evident escape.

Closing the coffin lid very carefully, Scruff then scrambled back through the hole into the oubliette. 'Maudlin!' he yelled up the shaft. 'Monty? Bryony? Somebody help me! Chuck down a hammer and chisel – I mean, stake. For Gawd's sake, somebody hear me. I dunno what time it is, but I think his alarm clock's goin' to go off in a bit, an' then there'll be hell to pay.'

He listened. Nobody answered. He yelled again, fearful of waking the vampire early in this place of darkness. Still no answer. Clearly his friends had either gone or were searching in another part of the cathedral. Scruff wouldn't put it past Maudlin to forget where the oubliette was and fail to return at all. It seemed that Scruff had been thrown on his own resources, which admittedly were pretty formidable.

He went back and checked the coffin. The vampire did not seem to be awake yet. He then rechecked the chamber for escape routes, finding none. His mind began running over the possibilities of remaining out of sight of the vampire. He could go back to the oubliette – but wasn't that rather obvious? There was no way the vampire had not seen the hole in the wall and had a look in there. Flistagga would not go to sleep without making sure the whole area was secure. So the oubliette pit was out. It had to be somewhere less obvious.

Holding the candle high above his head, Scruff saw that the chamber had once had a ceiling. He could see where the stonework had broken away just a few metres above his head. It had been one of those areas where humans celebrated the animal kingdom. Around this upper room were niches which held worn and broken statues of mustelids. Scruff could see a badger in ancient dress, and several stoats, some carrying staves, some with books in their paws, others helmeted and showing their ferocious – albeit damaged – war faces. There were even one or two weasels, monks by the look, with eroded features. There were also a number of empty niches, presumably where statues had once stood.

Scruff made a decision – none too soon, for the vampire was beginning to stir prior to rising from his coffin. He saw a dangling water-pipe and shinned up it to the floor above. Grasping its tip, he managed to cling on, dangling there. With supermammal strength he managed to pull himself aloft, where he could stand on the projection. From there he managed to haul himself up to an empty niche. He blew out the candle. Once in this recessed part of the wall, he stood absolutely still, mimicking the pose of another statue opposite.

At that moment the coffin lid flew open as if propelled by a mighty force within. The vampire sat up, coughed and cleared his throat. He sat there for a few minutes in the darkness, just as an ordinary waker might do at dawn, getting used to the idea of being conscious again. Finally he climbed out of his daytime bed and sniffed. The sniff was at first an automatic testing of the air for danger. However, that first test proved positive. A faint whiff of weasel was in the air, over-powered by a more compelling scent of snuffed candle. Hot wax! He could smell hot wax. The smoke still lingered in the air – and, yes, it was true, the delicious fragrance of weasel's throat.

The vampire growled. He would root out any intruders and snap their spines like twigs. Apart from having sharp teeth, a vampire is immensely strong, and will not hesitate to use that strength on jack, jill or even tiny kitten. He began prowling the chamber, sniffing this way and that, trying to pick up the specific scent of the outsider. But he could not pin it down in this place of archaic smells. His nose told him nothing except that a weasel holding a lit candle had been there. It was possible the weasel had gone by now, leaving only the lingering fragrance of its visit.

But perhaps it was still here?

Now it was the vampire stoat who was search-ing the chamber, lifting stones, moving timbers, kicking aside human skeletons.

Scruff could hear the creature scrambling around below him, but unlike the vampire, he couldn't see in the dark. He remained absolutely still. He was well aware the vampire might be able to see *him*, even though he couldn't see *it*.

Once or twice the sounds came perilously close, the searcher stopping dead and allowing a few minutes' silence before continuing, but Scruff remained hidden. He hoped – and his hope must have been borne out by the lack of discovery – that he resembled the statues in the other niches.

To this end (bearing in mind the features of the statues were crumbling away) he screwed up his face, trying to make it look as if it had been ravaged by the centuries. For Scruff, this was not difficult.

Finally, and blessedly, the vampire gave up. Now Scruff's ears needed to be sharp, to hear how the creature escaped from the present prison. There was a scraping sound and a lot of grunting: the sound of a stoat at work. This was followed by deep silence.

Eventually Scruff felt it was safe to light a candle. He did so, looking down and around the chamber, to see that a stone had been moved. Behind the stone was a hole, presumably leading to the outside world. Sighing with relief, Scruff climbed down from his niche, and made his way to the hole. Soon he was crawling to freedom.

Chapter Thirty-five

'Scruff?' cried a delighted Maudlin, as he stepped through a doorway and into the vestry of the cathedral. 'You're all right!'

The sound of relief in that other weasel's voice did much to lift the weight of darkness and evil from within the young lamplighter. His spirit no longer felt quite as heavy. 'Good to see you, Maudlin,' he said sombrely. 'Never so good to see you as now.'

'Are you all right?' Concern in the tone now. 'You called me by my full name.'

'Yes – yes, I think so. I saw him, Maudlin. He was . . . can't describe it, exactly. A nightmare. Monty's right. I think we got to remove this creature from the face of the earth. He's like somefink that's crawled out of the deep fire-pits of the otherworld. I dunno how we're goin' to do it, but we got to do it somehow. Have you seen the others?'

'They're outside. I told 'em you'd fallen into the sewer and Monty thought the exit might be outside the cathedral. They're worried about you, so we'd better find them and tell them.'

'Worried about *me*?' said Scruff, surprised by this outside view of himself.

'Of course. I was a – a bit worried too. But I knew you'd be all right, really. You always are. You're a genius at surviving, you are. But still – you were gone a long time.' There was still a note of anxiety in Maudlin's tone. Clearly he had been frantic. Scruff imagined his friend pacing up and down, watching the doorways, hoping that any second he would appear. How *good* it was to have such friends. How lonely must be the world of the vampire, who seeks out others only to corrupt them.

'Come on, let's go and find them.'

When the pair of them descended the steps of the cathedral, Scruff saw that the city had been swallowed by the night. Soft rain was falling gently on the breezes above, sparkling in those gaslights he had once lit and snuffed. Scruff had been the bringer of light in the darkness and had extinguished that light once the greater light of the day overwhelmed it. Now not one small star was brave enough to come out tonight. It was no wonder with such a ghastly being abroad. Even the moon was hiding its beamish face above the rainclouds.

'Ah, Scruff,' cried Monty, relief in his voice too. 'Where have you been?'

'I saw him,' said Scruff. 'He was in the disused sewer underneath the cathedral. Ghas'ly thing.'

Monty nodded gravely. 'Then you know what we're up against. Did you gather any clues? Do you know where he might be heading?'

'Not at all. I was terrified, guv'nor. I couldn't even think straight. I had to make like a statue, an' he was sniffin' around in the dark, tryin' to smell me out. Like a hunt, it was, by scent. I know how them rabbits felt, in the old days, when we used to track their spoor, sniffin' them down, till we had 'em cornered. I know just how they felt.'

Bryony said, 'You've had a shocking experience, Scruff. I think we'd better all go back across the river. Flistagga won't be here now. He's running the rooftops over there somewhere. We need a new plan, Monty. I suggest we go back and you chew on that old pipe of yours for an hour or two, then come up with one of your brilliant schemes.'

'I hope I can justify your faith in me.'

'You can do it, guv'nor, if anyone can,' said Scruff.

'That's just the trouble. Perhaps no-one can stop this creature. Perhaps his genius for hiding is greater than mine for seeking. Still, we can but try.'

The four friends walked through the mizzle, finding their way by lamplight to Whistleminster

Bridge. Halfway across they were rocked by the great clanging of Ringing Roger. It shook the bridge to its very foundations. Finally the normal rattle and bustle of the evening city was allowed to return. There were many coaches and cabs out as the four walked along the bank of the river. A new steam car hissed and huffed between them as they crossed the road, its solid rubber tyres slipping on the rounded cobbles. A clockwork sedan suddenly shot sideways, down an alley, its occupant yelling that it was going the wrong way: sedan chairs had a habit of getting out of control.

Once in the flat, they were chastised by Jis McFail, one and all, as if they were two-month-old kittens: they shouldn't be out in the 'bad humours of the night without their scarves and hats', they were told. 'It'll settle on yer chests, and then where will you be?' she scolded them. 'In yer beds, that's where. And me running back and forth with gruel and what not. No thought for your old landjill's knees, you young mammals. Up and down those stairs, fifty times a day, if it's once, and never a complaint passes my lips, I'm sure.'

'We're sorry, Jis McFail,' Monty said gravely. 'It won't happen again.'

'I should think not. Now, I've made five cups of hot chocolate. What am I to do with the other four?'

'Why, Jis McFail, we'll drink 'em right down, if you please,' said Scruff. 'Hot chocolate. That's a feast after a cold walk.'

While Monty sat by the fire, sucking his chibouque, the others got on with various quiet activities, so as not to disturb him. Bryony was cutting clippings from *The Chimes* about various new medicines and draughts produced by chemists for the cure of mammal diseases. Scruff and Maudlin settled down to a game of chess. They would have preferred hollyhockers, but the rattling of the seeds in the cup, and the noise they made when scattered on a hard surface, would have disturbed the thoughts of the great weasel.

Monty lost himself in the flames of the fire. There was an era when weasels were terrified of fire, back in the old times when they lived in small holes in hollow oaks and mossy banks. Even now Monty could slip back in his dreams to a time when his fur was warmed by the summer sun as he lay on a log, basking in its life-preserving properties. In those days one had to use both eyes independently: one to watch for predators on two legs, the other to watch for the chance of prey on four. Future plans and schemes had to be hatched while the brain was alert on those two other fronts. It was not a state into which Monty could enter in these modern times, even if he wanted to.

They were not all long, hot days either. There were also days of rain, snow, sleet and hail. Storms that slapped the trees right and left. Hurricanes that tore them from their roots. On such days a weasel would be deep in a hole somewhere, fearful of the noise and violence of the weather, yet secure from other harm. The world was a tighter place then. Small holes, yes, but narrow lanes through the tall grasses too, and a clinging to familiar paths through the trees, along ditches, down dry wells, up dykes and under banks. Weasels were not above using the run ways of others: badgers, rabbits, rats. Most mammals borrowed or stole such diggings from one another. It took time to make a hole and some were better equipped to do it. Even the ducks would use old rabbit holes in times of need.

In such a vein, Monty's mind drifted back and forth, between the eras of his ancestors and the present day, with its cities and towns, its engines and devices. Like most mammals he never attacked a problem head on. He let it nestle in the bottom of his brain and thought of other things, so that any flash of inspiration might come like lightning from a cloud. He found if he worried at something too much he went stale on it. Best to let it come from his subconscious, *zap*, into the waiting snare of his conscious mind, where he could trap it and do with it as he would.

And that flash did come. It wasn't terribly brilliant. In fact it was pretty simple really – but then, the best schemes often were. His mind had wandered over the journey through Slattland and down into Transylvladia, and he recalled the masked ball in Krunchen. Clearly the Transylvladians were fond of such balls, for everyone had been there. Count Flistagga might not be amongst those who loved masquerades, but he would want to gather intelligence about his enemies, just as his enemies were trying to build up their store of knowledge about *him*.

Know your enemy. If you didn't bother to glean information, they had the upper paw.

A masked ball would tempt Flistagga to come and move amongst his enemies. It would allow him to come in disguise. He would know that Monty would be expecting him to come, would be there waiting, ready to unmask him if at all possible, but that was all part of the game to outwit the foe. What was the use of being clever if you never gave yourself the opportunity of exercising that cleverness? Monty was no different from Flistagga in this respect. He wanted to set the stage so that the pair of them would be together in the same room, manoeuvring, seeking to triumph over the adversary.

So, a masked ball! Time to go and speak with Mayor Poynt.

CHAPTER THIRTY-SIX

Spindrick unpacked all his things very carefully, while whistling the national anthem. The 'sleeping soil' had been stuffed into every crevice of his luggage: into his mug, his toothbrush holder, the pockets of his backpack – everywhere. It had been important to get as much back as possible. He needed plenty of samples in order to find out its chemical makeup. Spindrick was a good chemist. He was a lousy musician but a good chemist. As an anarchist he had to be in order to make various explosives. 'My time has come,' he murmured to himself. 'The world will know the name of Spindrick Sylver . . .'

There was a thumping on his door, followed by

the sound of the salesmammal's voice. 'You comin' down to breakfast?'

Normally such an interruption would have infuriated him, but today nothing could spoil his mood. 'Yes. Be with you in a second.' He took out of his backpack something wrapped in grease-proof paper and slipped it into his pocket. Opening the door he found the stoat sales-mammal waiting impatiently, dressed in his usual sharp suit and brown shoes with white toe-caps.

'I say,' said the traveller in jills' underwear, 'the wanderer returns. I must say you look a bit beaten up. Was it tough, out there in the jungles of Tarawak? I bet it was. We all read your columns in *The Chimes* – well, everyone except Jal Kritchit, who said his bank work did not allow him time for activities of a frivolous nature. I told him exploring was not a frivolous activity, but he said it was, compared with the world of high finance . . .'

Thankfully at that moment they were joined by the actress. 'Oooooohhhh! Spindrick!' she cried. 'How looovely to see you, dah-ling. My, what a rugged exterior. You're my hero, you know. Fancy you still being alive, after all you've been through. I felt sure your articles would stop abruptly, to be followed by an ominous silence, so I prayed and prayed and prayed, and here you are!'

'All due to your prayers,' said Spindrick drily. 'Without them I should be travelling slowly through a crocodile's gut. I brought you a present.' He reached into his pocket and gave her the article wrapped in greaseproof paper.

She squealed in such a high, penetrating voice it almost punctured the eardrums of the two jacks. They were on the third landing now and had gathered up the retired stoat colonel from outside his door, but he was nearly deaf because he had once pressed his ear to a cannon barrel to try to ascertain why the weapon had not fired, when it suddenly went off. He had never quite been the same stoat since.

'A gift for me!' shrieked the actress of unknown mammal origin. 'What is it, you sweet dah-ling, you?'

She unwrapped it feverishly as they descended the stairs, then shrieked again as she held it up by the fur. 'It – it looks like . . .'

'Yes, a shrunken head,' said Spindrick. 'I thought you'd like it. I saw it and immediately thought of you. The mongooses of Tarawak—'

'Mon*geese*, surely,' said the salesmammal.

'–cut off the heads of their enemies and use a process unknown to the civilized world in order to shrink them. They hang them from nets in the ceilings of their longhouses. A groom has to give one to his bride on their wedding day, as a token of his affection. She sleeps with it under her pillow for good luck. You might try that. Get you a good part in a play, perhaps? They don't like them to leave the country but I smuggled this one out specially. I knew it would go down well. You said you were interested in antiques.'

'Antiques, yes,' she said doubtfully, trying not to let the grisly object touch her dress.

'Well, this head is over a hundred years old – oh, there goes a maggot. Dropped onto the carpet. You have to watch that, they tend to collect parasites. Best to clean the eye-sockets, earholes and nostrils with cleaning fluid from time to time. It keeps such pests down to a minimum. I find a light solution of sulphuric acid works best.'

'Yeeeessss. Thank you, Spindrick. Thank you for thinking of me, out there in the jungle.' She continued to hold the object at forelimb's length in front of her, like a lantern lighting her path.

'Don't mention it.'

The two retired schoolteachers joined them at this point and the colonel boomed, 'Mornin', jisses. Spindrick here is back from operations in the Far East. Looks jolly battle-weary, don'tcha think? Gave the enemy hell, I understand. Got one of the beggars there. Chopped off his head. Weren't allowed to do that in my day, not in the north, but maybe things are different in the jungle. Destroy the enemy's morale, create confusion and mayhem, creep into his camp at night, find a threesome, cut off the head of the middle one, leave the other two to wake up and find the headless body between them. Blood and gore and all that. Absolutely destroys any confidence. Makes 'em puke up their guts in fear.'

Far from looking horrified, the two elderly jills

311

beamed at Spindrick. 'Nice to see you back,' said one.

'Was it a package tour?' asked the other. 'Or did you go individual?'

'Individual,' said Spindrick, always pleased to see them.

'How brave of you. And you killed lots of creatures?'

'Only mosquitoes,' replied Spindrick, 'and then only the ones who deserved to die.'

'How wonderful.'

Lob Kritchit, the bachelor badger, was at the breakfast table already, tucking into a mouse sausage. 'Back, are we? Have a good time? Sorry – couldn't read any of your articles. Too busy, I'm afraid. The general manager is very pleased with us at the moment, the way we focus on our work. Can't let that slide just for the sake of a few columns of print, can we?'

'Look what he's brought me,' cried the actress. 'A present. Isn't it – fine?' She dangled the object before his face.

The bank clerk squinted at the severed head. 'What is it? A mask?'

'No, no, it's real. It's a severed head.'

'That's disgusting!' said Kritchit, screwing up his black-and-white furry nose. 'That's revolting! What kind of a creature was it?'

Spindrick had been looking forward to this moment, ever since he had been given the head by a mongoose chieftain. 'It's a badger,' said the explorer.

Kritchit's chair went flying back as he stood up.

His eyes had gone blood-red round the edges. He roared at Spindrick, 'You're a liar!'

'Oh,' said Spindrick mildly, sitting down and tapping a hard-boiled egg on the edge of his plate, 'I don't tell lies.'

'A badger?' said the badger. 'They don't have badgers in Tarawak. They're not indigenous to that region.'

'You're quite right,' replied Spindrick. 'This was not a native. He was an explorer. Went out there in the early part of the century as a missionary. Established quite a reputation for himself at first, but then the mongooses got tired of him— Shut up,' he warned the salesmammal, who had opened his mouth to say something about the plural of mongoose – 'and they decided he was a bit of a blowhard, so they cut him off at the windpipe, so to speak. Yes, quite definitely a badger. You can see by the markings. And, I might add, I know the name of this particular badger.'

'Oooo, who is it?' chorused the elderly sisters. 'Do we know him?'

'Well, you will know *of* him. Ah, I see my bank clerk friend has gone a little pasty around the gills. That's because he has remembered something. A grandfather? By the name of Baldakesh Kritchit? Yes, Lob, this is he. This is your very own forefather, cut off in his prime, hung from the rafters with several maggoty others, in the company of mongoose heads of various tribes from many regions.'

'We – we don't believe it.'

'It's true, my friend,' sighed Spindrick, enjoying himself enormously. 'It's so very true. How grieved you must be to see how your long lost grandfather ended his life. But he died for a cause, Lob. Everyone should die for a cause. I hope to myself. I envy him that. And now he's come home, a little wasted perhaps, covered in parasites unfortunately, but home he is.'

Kritchit could hardly contain his fury, his horror, his utter consternation. He reached towards the actress, who was still dangling the offensive object by its hair. 'Give us back our grandfather!' he demanded in a choked voice.

'I will not,' said the actress, withdrawing the head. 'It was given to me as a gift.'

'He – he needs a decent burial. This is the remains of our own flesh and blood. We must have him. We must. We must see he gets the last rites. Have you no heart?'

'She has a heart,' said Spindrick, 'and also your granddaddy's head.'

This brought guffaws of merriment from the salesmammal, who shut up immediately on being glared at by the badger.

'How much?' said Kritchit to the actress. 'We're willing to pay any reasonable price.'

'A hundred guineas,' snapped Spindrick. 'Not a guinea more, not a guinea less.'

The actress, who had been about to refuse the offer, closed her mouth again. If Spindrick didn't mind her selling the foul remains of the badger, she didn't mind letting it go. A hundred guineas was not to be sniffed at!

The bank clerk stood there for quite a while, staring miserably at the table, before he finally muttered, 'All right. We'll go and get it.'

When he had left the room, Spindrick said cheerfully, 'He keeps it in a potty under the bed. A crock of gold.'

'I say,' said the colonel, frowning, 'this ain't very sportin' of you, Spindrick. A fellah's ancestor, after all. Not really the thing.'

'Oh, we'll let him get the money and then tell him,' replied Spindrick, tucking into his egg. 'That's not really his grandfather. I looked all that up, about his family, in Winterset House. That head's a fake. Well, not really a fake, because it's a rat's head. The fur's been dyed and the eyebrows made bushier. We'll tell Kritchit when he comes down that it's just a joke. Did you see his face?' Spindrick clicked his teeth and the others, still a little unsure, clicked with him. 'We really had him going there, didn't we?' Spindrick's use of the plural dragged them all in as fellow conspirators. They nodded.

While the bank badger was out of the way and when the others weren't looking, the second part of Spindrick's breakfast plan went into operation. He swiped the badger's egg from its cup and put the demon egg from Tarawak in its place. Spindrick had been saving the egg with the trapped demon inside it. The others were still chattering amongst themselves and hadn't noticed the switch.

'So,' continued Spindrick, 'what's the news on the street?'

'Well,' said the actress, 'I've heard a rumour that there's to be a masked ball at City Hall. It's not official yet, because the mayor doesn't know, but my friend Maudlin – he used to be night-watchmammal but he now works for a very important weasel called Montegu Sylver – say, isn't he your cousin, Spindrick?'

'Yes. So, Monty's behind this ball thing. Wonder what he's playing at? Doesn't sound like the sort of thing he usually gets involved in.'

'I don't know,' replied the actress, 'Maudlin wouldn't say, but I know everyone's going to be there. Everyone important.'

'Are they now?' muttered Spindrick, who could see the perfect opportunity for testing out his sleeping soil, at the same time as getting his own back on his cousin. 'Everyone important, eh? Sounds like fun.'

'I think it will be dreamy,' said the actress, looking round the table at the enthusiastic heads, all nodding away. 'Positively dreamy.'

'So do I,' replied Spindrick. 'Positively.'

The bank badger returned with his hundred guineas. The others all joshed him and told him it was just a joke. He glared at Spindrick. 'We don't consider that funny.'

'Oh, well – poor judgement on my part. I thought you might have a sense of humour. Sit down and eat your breakfast egg.'

The badger sat down. Spindrick's heart did a little pitter-patter as the bank clerk picked up his teaspoon to crack the egg. He glanced around the table, wondering if the demon would exit in a

316

great rage and start laying about it with all kinds of dark and horrible magic. However, he couldn't leave without seeing the fun so he got up quietly and went to stand just outside the doorway, ready to run. The others were still chattering away.

The badger's spoon descended.

The next moment there was a scramble as everyone vacated the breakfast room in great haste.

'Terrible!'

'Awful!'

'Disgusting!'

'Yukky!'

'Gaaaaahhhhrrrgggahh!'

These were some of the expressive words which came tumbling out of the mouths of the escapees. Once out of the room, they turned to stare back in horror. Never had they known anything like it. It was a nightmare. Still, most of them had got out unscathed. The only mammal who hadn't made it was the badger, who actually broke the egg. He had been too close. The fumes had overcome him and it had been all he could do to stagger towards the door. There he had collapsed in a badgery heap of black-and-white fur. There he remained, twitching, still breathing in the noxious gases which had struck him unconscious. No-one felt inclined to go in and get him out.

There was no demon, of course. It was simply that the egg, months old and from a tropical region, was thoroughly rotten. It stank to high heaven. It choked you with its green-grey fumes. Only when the colonel thought to go outside and smash a window with a stone, to let out the stinking fumes, were they able to rescue the badger. He said afterwards, recovering in hospital, that he considered himself lucky not to have suffered brain damage. As it was he had lost the lining to his nose and would probably never have a sense of smell again.

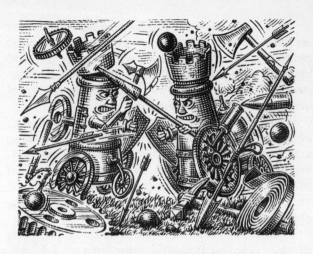

CHAPTER THIRTY-SEVEN

There was to be a mighty battle. Things had recently come to head between the century's two great inventors, Thos. Tempus Fugit and Wm. Jott. The weasel against the stoat. Clockwork against steam power. Both inventors had agreed to produce an army – a chess-set-sized army, in fact – to do battle against each other. The mayor would preside. The tourney would take place in Hide Park; bishop against bishop, knight against knight. There would be no pre-set chess moves, of course. The two inventors had simply agreed to limit the number and character of the combatants to chess-pieces. It would be a free-for-all, with one side attacking the other and trying to smash it to bits.

At this moment the mayor and his sister were in their library, surrounded by books neither of them had ever opened. It was said you could place a five-pound note in every one of those books and a suddenly impoverished Poynt would still die of starvation.

'I'm looking forward to it, Sib,' said the mayor, who had not quite got over his illness, but was confining his periods of madness to his bedroom after hours, when he would race round and round the carpet, hopping onto his bed and finally boxing his pillows into submission. 'I like things smashing other things up.'

Princess Sybil was indulgent. 'Well, you always enjoyed breaking your toys as a kitten. You have this destructive side to you, Jeremy, which our mother never understood. Fortunately, I do. Some stoats are creative. You are the balance, the counterweight to the creationists.'

'Yes, I am, aren't I?' he said proudly. Then he got annoyed. 'Where's Falshed? I told him to be here by midday. It starts at one o'clock. We'll be late.'

At that moment the butler let in the chief of police. 'Sorry, boss,' said Falshed, clearly out of breath. 'Got held up by the traffic. Hello, Princess.'

'Hello yourself. My, you're looking smart, Chief. New uniform?'

'Just had it made in Savage Row,' replied Falshed, pleased he had made an impression.

At that moment the weasel-butler admitted another mammal into the library, much to the annoyance of the Poynts. 'The Right Honourable Montegu Sylver,' he cried in satisfied tones, 'come to see the mayor.'

'What do *you* want?' snapped the mayor peevishly. 'Hurry up, we're late for an appointment already.'

'And very nice it is to see you, too, Mayor.'

'Never mind all that – what is it?'

'You are aware we have this terrible destructive force in the city?'

The mayor turned to his sister. 'I like destructive forces, don't I, Sib?'

'Not this one, Jeremy. I think he's talking about Count Flistagga. We should take him seriously.'

Some of the puff went out of the mayor. 'Oh, right. Well, what about the vampire? I thought you were dealing with it, Sylver. You said you were.'

'I need help. I want you to organize a masked ball. I need to set a trap for the vampire. He'll look on it as a great challenge and won't be able to stop himself from taking up the gauntlet.'

Falshed frowned. 'Won't he suspect a trap? I would.'

'Yes, Chief,' replied Monty patiently, 'but that's the whole point. If he did not suspect we were trying to trap him, he wouldn't bother coming. He knows that it's a trap and he knows that I know that he knows it's a trap. We are all in full and open knowledge. That's the challenge for him – to be there and to escape undetected. It's my job to unmask him and put an end to him once and for all. That's *my* challenge.'

'Oh, I don't know,' said Mayor Poynt, kicking at a scuff in the rug, 'I don't really like dances and balls and things.'

'*I* do, Jeremy.' The princess had spoken.

'Yes, well then, I dare say we can arrange something,' returned the mayor. 'A nice quiet affair, of course.'

'Maximum publicity,' replied Monty firmly. 'Fanfares, posters, street criers. A big, big affair, with lots of glitz. We can't risk him not knowing about it. After all, he lives hidden from sight amongst the dead. Unless we trumpet the thing from the rooftops the ball will come and go without him knowing about it.'

'That'll cost a lot of money,' protested the mayor. 'The city can't really afford such a grand affair.'

'The city will have to, or suffer the consequences.'

Sybil said, 'He's right, Jeremy. It has to be done. Don't you worry about it, though. I'll do all the arranging. This is a *creative* thing, quite out of your province. You know how I enjoy such things – writing little place cards and sending out invitations. I'll start now, while you go to your scrapyard battle.'

The butler entered. '*Another* visitor,' he announced smugly.

'What is this, Piccacardy Circus?' cried the mayor.

Lord Haukin walked in. 'What ho, a gathering of the clans? We all going to the dustbin bash, are we?'

322

'Everyone except Princess Sybil,' said Falshed, sounding disappointed. 'Listen, Princess, perhaps I should stay and help you with the cards and things. There's going to be a masked ball, Lord Haukin, a big grand affair. It was Princess Sybil's idea.'

'No, Chief, you go to the battle. I shall be perfectly happy in my own company. You'd only be in the way. You haven't seen me bustle. I move at a hundred miles an hour when I'm bustling and anyone who gets in my path is mown down. It's a very dangerous time.'

So the four mammals set out together, rather uneasy in each other's company. They split into two natural pairs: the mayor and the chief, Monty and Hannover. These two pairs sat on opposite sides of the mayor's coach. As he was the only weasel there, and therefore the smallest of the group, the conversation tended to go over Monty's head. But he didn't mind this: he needed time to contemplate his plans. The mayor's matching pairs of mice raced through the streets and they arrived just as the gates were closing.

'Sorry, can't come in,' said the parkmammal. 'Coach park's full up. Dangerous to let any more vehicles into the ground.'

Jeremy Poynt leaned out of the window. 'But I'm the mayor! I'm the guest of honour!'

'Not my fault, guv'nor. Told to lock it when there was no more room. More'n my job's worth to let you in now.'

'I employ you!'

'No you don't – city council does.'

'I have the city council in my pocket.'

'Whoa!' cried the weasel. 'Where's a newspaper reporter when you want one? Corruption in high places! Mayor admits coercion of council members. Good one.'

'Chief,' cried the mayor, 'arrest this moron.'

Falshed was apologetic. 'I can't arrest her for doing her job.'

Monty leaned out of the other window now. 'Is it all right if we walk in?'

'All right with me, squire. Just no vehicles,' the parkmammal said.

The mayor grumbled about 'dignity' and 'standing' and climbed down from the coach with his party. As they all filed past the jill weasel, she raised an eyebrow at a mayor who was no doubt thinking it was all so much easier when his family was royal and could chop off heads at the drop of a coin. They pushed through the crowd and eventually found their seats on a stand covered in bunting and draped with flags.

Out on the tourney field the combatants were waiting, gleaming, dazzling in the sunlight. On one side were whirring, shining brass and burnished bronze figures, wonderfully wrought, carrying a variety of weapons from maces to warhammers. On the other there were duller-looking but noisy, hissing giants of iron and steel. This set definitely looked the business, fashioned as it was from railway tracks and factory boilers. There was a lot of clanking and grinding going on amongst the steamies, but the clockies seemed unworried.

The crowd was full of excitement and pressed against the ropes which had been erected to keep them back.

The mayor stood up and made the announcement:

> *'Heavy Metal versus Tricky Tin*
> *Let the games begin*
> *And may the best clankers win!'*

He had composed this poem himself and he was very proud of it. He had agonized over 'clankers' for hours, wondering whether it was all right to make up words if one was writing poetry. He thought it was, but he hadn't been sure. Anyway, in it went, and it seemed to fit. No-one had yet told him that clankers wasn't a real word. He decided they hadn't the confidence to challenge him when it came to the crunch. *Crunchers?* There was another good made-up word. He'd use that one next time.

The clockwork warriors rushed in. The king and queen began spraying the steam-engine pawns with water, trying to douse their fires. The steam-engine knights charged straight through this water attack, and began battering the clockwork bishops with their maces. Two rooks charged at each other and collided, the clockwork castle losing half its battlements. There was steam and smoke and ash everywhere, along with flying delicate cogs, levers and rachets. For a while it was difficult to sort out iron from brass: it was an utter mêlée, with axes and hammers crashing down, and spears and arrows finding gaps between metal plates.

'Come on the heavies!'

'Go at 'em, clockies!'

The crowd cheered their particular favourites, delighting in the spectacle of two groups of machines smashing each other to bits. The mayor grew frenzied, sticking up for the heavy metal army. Lord Haukin was not to be outdone in his partisanship for the clockwork warriors. Falshed and Monty were less vocal in their support of their favourites, but the excitement of the occasion was not lost on them. They were both jacks at heart, and jacks of all ages did love a good battle, especially when no-one was getting hurt.

Finally there were only two warriors left on the field: a clockwork bishop with its formidable crook and a steam knight with its vicious warhammer. They stood off from each other, one panting, one whirring. Both were damaged. Thos. Tempus Fugit was shaking his head sadly, wondering if the spring in his wounded bishop was going to hold out. Wm. Jott was looking down at his feet, aware that the strange, squealing hiss coming from his knight's boiler meant it was about to explode.

And burst it did, just a few seconds later, spraying hot water over the park's daffodil beds.

'*Ad majorum Ticktockus gloriam!*' cried the bishop, waving a bronze paw over the remains of the knight, then translating for the ignorant masses, 'For the greater glory of clockwork!'

The heavy metal army had been defeated.

It was coming up to two o'clock and Ringing Roger chimed, making the ground tremble. This was the final straw as far as the clockwork bishop was concerned. Its spring suddenly snapped and flew out of its tummy to flash across the gardens, severing low-growing blooms as it went, leaving in its path a swathe of headless tulips.

It was over, the battle, like so many battles in history, neither won nor lost. Futility, thought Monty, thy name is war. It had all been like one gigantic firework display, satisfying in its whizz-bangs, but achieving nothing lasting.

'Well,' said the mayor, rising. 'We might as well go home.'

And home they went, leaving the two inventors to gather up the bits and try to put them together for another day.

CHAPTER THIRTY-EIGHT

If there was one thing Sybil was good at – and there wasn't because she was good at a great many things – it was arranging social gatherings. History has recorded many of her assemblies, along with famous battles for freedom, mighty inventions and discoveries, and great explorations. In a list of the top ten events which helped to found the country of Welkin, Sybil's soirées would take the first seven places. Many other nations, though few would openly admit it, cursed their animistic gods for failing to ensure that Sybil had been born in their land.

She was to be found, on the morning of the masked ball, supervising the decorations, the kitchens, the lighting and everything else in City

Hall. 'Jeremy,' she called to her brother, 'I hope you're not going to get under my paws today.'

Mayor Poynt was at that moment hoping to cross from A (his office) to B (the front door) without being seen. He had a dread of being roped in by his sister to do all sorts of menial tasks. Fortunately it was one of those days when she had remembered he was more of a hindrance than a help and had decided she would get on much better without him.

'No, no, my dear. Very important business to attend to. Urgent stuff – and things like that,' he finished lamely, and was then almost knocked over by a tropical plant. 'Hey!' he yelled. 'Watch where you're going, weasel!'

'Couldn't see you through the leaves of this thing. What about you watching where *you're* going in the first place. I expect you're looking at your paws all the time, worrying about tripping over that toilet chain hanging round your neck.'

This weasel florist, or whatever he was, seemed mighty insolent. Mayor Poynt stared at him. 'This is a chain of office. The *mayor's* chain of office.'

'And?'

'Look, who are you, anyway?' The weasel was now stuffing the tropical plant into one of Sybil's precious vases – vases the mayor had paid a fortune for: antiques shipped specially to Welkin for her from the Far East. 'What do you think you're doing?'

The insolent fellow had his hat pulled down over his ears and seemed to the mayor to be a bit of an idiot. Despite the fact that it was a warm day the weasel wore a long, thick coat which covered most of his body. Only his eyes were visible, and his whiskers, both of which the mayor could have sworn were familiar to him.

'Plants,' said the weasel. 'Princess Sybil wants plants for her ball tonight. I'm the plant mammal. I'm the one putting them into pots and watering them, ready for tonight's great event. There – can't put it any plainer than that, even for dolts.'

The mayor's eyes opened wide. 'What did you say?' he squealed.

'I said,' murmured the weasel in a voice so low only the mayor could hear him, 'hare today, gone tomorrow.'

The mayor was thrown back on his heels. He still hadn't recovered from his hare ordeal and the very mention of it sent tremors of fear down his spine. He gave the weasel one last long look, then decided to beat a retreat before he had a relapse. He raced through the doorway, leaving the weasel with a very satisfied look in his eye.

'You!' called Princess Sybil. 'The plant mammal. Is that the lot?'

'Absolutely,' said the weasel. 'I've put 'em in the pots and vases you wanted me to, but they'll need watering before tonight. I'll come back tomorrow and take them away again.'

'Thank you. What was your name again?'

'Drickspin – Drickspin Revsly.'

'Well – thank you.'

'My pleasure.'

The weasel left the plants, with their noxious soil, to the good keeping of Princess Sybil. Every one of them was in bud. With just a little watering and some hot-house warmth they would burst into bloom. The weasel had explained to Princess Sybil that it would be like a fireworks display, with all the plants blooming under the hot gaslights of the City Hall ballroom just before midnight. It would make a brilliant ball – a really memorable occasion, something mammals would talk about for decades. This, of course, pleased Sybil immensely.

When evening came Sybil was waiting just inside the great doors of City Hall, ready to greet her guests. Jeremy Poynt, wearing evening dress and looking every inch the aristocrat, stood at her shoulder. This he did not mind doing. This duty was a vote-catcher.

'Lord Haukin,' cried the major dodo, from the steps. 'In an elephant mask.'

'Evening, Hannover,' said the mayor. He was wearing a lion mask. 'Nice trunk.'

'Evening, Jem. Yes – hope I don't trip over the rotten thing. Bit silly to choose a mammal with a long snout, I suppose, but I did hope to impress others with these majestic ears. Princess Sybil, you've surpassed yourself as usual. Fine display of tropical plants,' said Hannover, peering through his monocle at the greenery.

'Thank you,' murmured Sybil graciously. She was wearing the face of a leopard. 'You're not actually supposed to give your *name* to the major dodo. He's supposed to just announce you by your disguise – by your mask.'

'Oh, sorry. But among friends and all that.

331

Royal friends too. Lions and leopards and all that big cat stuff. Nobility and royalty go paw in paw. Don't want to seem standoffish in such company, especially since there's no doubt who *you* two are.' Despite being a supporter of good causes, always working tirelessly for charities for the poor, Hannover Haukin was fiercely aristocratic. It was a contradiction his friend Monty Sylver always had difficulty coming to terms with.

Other guests began to arrive and the mayor greeted them enthusiastically. All except one fellow, wearing the mask of an orang-utan – a horrible, red-haired face with eyes that burned into the mayor's with a terrible hatred. The mayor was shocked by the intensity of that glare and if his sister had not been there to protect him, he might have done something silly, like yell for help. Yet when the mayor had recovered his composure a little and the orang-utan was lost in the crowd, he recalled that those eyes were the eyes of the weasel who had provided the plants! Infamous creature. Loathsome jack. The mayor was going to have to do something about that jumped-up flower-seller.

Monty Sylver and his three friends had arrived early. Monty was wearing the mask of a fox, Bryony was a bear and Scruff was a hyena. No-one quite knew what Maudlin was wearing – a fish of sorts, or so it seemed. When asked, he was a little put out. 'It's a shark,' he said. 'A savage creature of the ocean deep.'

'Looks like a cod,' replied Bryony.

'Or a monkfish,' said Scruff.

Maudlin went huffy on them. 'Anyone can see it's a shark by the sharp teeth. You're just jealous you didn't think of it.'

The ballroom began to fill with more and more chattering mammals. Monty stood by the doorway, watching them enter. Opposite him was a full-length mirror, partially hidden by a huge plant. Every time a guest walked past this mirror, Monty watched, hoping to spot a creature who had no reflection. The detective weasel was aware that this was a very crude device and it was doubtful Flistagga would fall for such a trap, but one never knew. Bryony, Scruff and Maudlin were on the lookout for anyone who did not cast a shadow from the bright gaslights which ran all the way around the room, and from the candles in the chandeliers.

As expected, the evening wore on, with mammals dancing and feasting and having a glorious time, without the vampire giving himself away. Monty was constantly on the move, looking for any small sign of a masked guest whose actions, however subtly, might reveal a vampire. He ran his eye over the dancers and watchers. There was a stag, a wolf, a horse, a rat, a dragon, a mongoose, a parrot, even an octopus mask with tentacles hanging down like hair. Who? What? Where? It was all a game of guess and out-guess.

The clever creature remained hidden, however, leaving Monty to guess which mask a vampire might wear. A snake? Too obvious – the twin hollow fangs and all that. A nightjar – the

333

nocturnal bird? Now, there was a possibility. The shepherd's name for a nightjar – not known by many – was the *goatsucker*. Was that subtle enough? Doubtful. Anyway, Monty could see no nightjars amongst the guests. There was a breed of domestic cat known as the *drain cat*. That was quite shrewd. To drain the arteries of victims. No. No, the drain here was a noun, referring to the fact that such cats lived in the storm drains of Far Eastern towns.

Monty's brain worked feverishly over such possibilities, scanning the crowd of guests at the same time, hoping one of the masks would give him a clue. He wondered how bold the vampire might become, if there was no unmasking; whether the creature would have the effrontery to venture a word or two, as a stranger, in Monty's ear. It was possible. Anything was possible. Monty just had to keep his brain alert, tuned to the finest pitch, ready for the slightest clue. His chance would come, he knew, so long as he was sharp enough to notice it.

'Hello, what's-his-name, how are you?'

'Hannover,' said Monty to the elephant who had come up alongside him. 'How did you know it was me?'

'Oh, I'd know that ratty-looking tail anywhere. Trouble with you peasants – you can disguise your ancestry behind a mask, but your tails give you away. Now, take my tail: you can see it belongs to a lord of the manor by the gloss of the fur, the depth and texture of its pile.'

Lord Haukin was, of course, joking. Monty was

probably the only mammal on the earth Hannover could rib in this way. Not that others would have objected, provided they recognized the chumminess in it, but Monty was the only creature to whom Hannover felt close enough to be able to open himself up in such a way.

'Hannover,' said Monty, 'how do you find the other guests? Does any one of them seem strange to you in some way? I'll tell you why. I'm looking for our vampire friend, Count Flistagga. He's here somewhere, I'm certain. I can *sense* his eyes on me now. Any ideas? I'm running out of time. The evening's wearing on and I still haven't a clue.'

'Ah. Understand. What about the orang-utan? Didn't like that fellah the moment I set eyes on him.'

'That my cousin Spindrick. Shifty, isn't he? He's probably up to no good too, but I've got enough to worry about without wondering what schemes or plans *he* has to destroy the city.'

'Oh, yes, the weasel who blew up Ringing Roger and brought the common rats out of the sewers. Nasty piece of work—'

At that moment the strident tones of the mayor's party voice rose above the general hubbub. 'Glasses everyone. Champagne toast. Come on – I mean everyone. We must celebrate my sister's triumph. I think you'll agree that Princess Sybil's masked ball has been one of the greatest successes of all time. Something to talk about to your grandkittens, those of you who expect to have 'em.'

Weasel-waiters were hurrying through the room, distributing champagne glasses, filling them from big magnum bottles, until everyone in the room had the equipment for the toast. All except the leopard, who Monty knew was Sybil herself. 'All right?' cried the mayor. 'Glasses charged? Tuppence? Ha! Ha! Ready then? To Princess Sybil Poynt, our hostess and the mostest, bestest princess in the whole world.'

Swiftly, Monty scanned the room for those who failed to drink. One or two non-drinkers raised their glasses and took the tiniest sip. A crocodile. A bull. A hippo. No-one, given the occasion, could actually *not* make the effort and at least *look* as if they were drinking. But vampires despised food and drink – could not, would not, let it near their lips. And by luck, by chance, Monty noticed a great reluctance in a guest nearby, a tall, thin creature, to allow the champagne near his mouth. A dragon. The guest had on the mask of a dragon. Of course! How stupid of Monty not to notice it before. A *dragon*. How subtle, yet how obvious!

Monty took a phial of holy water from his pocket and withdrew the cork. It was his intention to fling this onto the head of the vampire, thus rendering the creature helpless for a few moments. Holy water would act on Flistagga like scalding water on any natural creature. It would cause him to recoil in agony, perhaps even blind him for a short while, to enable his enemies to overcome him completely. Monty regretted the need to attack the blood-sucking stoat with such a distasteful weapon but, given the strength, the power of a master vampire he had little choice.

'Help, ho!' cried Monty, weaving towards the vampire. 'Over here, weasels. Hammers and stakes! Hammers and stakes!'

From the four corners of the room Bryony, Maudlin and Scruff came running, bowling through protesting guests. They had whipped their anti-vampire weapons from beneath their costumes and each bore a sharp stake and a hammer. It was a gruesome task they had to perform, and that in front of Princess Sybil's guests, but it was a necessary one.

Flistagga was even swifter than Monty had imagined. The vampire leapt high up – a magnificent standing jump – onto the minstrel's gallery. There, above the heads of the crowd, he snarled and roared, baring his fangs and claws at the weasel musicians who were softly playing a minuet. They scattered, their discarded instruments banging and clattering in their wake.

From there Flistagga flung himself outwards to grasp a chandelier, sending flaming candles down amongst the screaming guests, and swung across the room towards a window. He crashed through the small panes, showering glass and bits of wood everywhere, and onto the lawn.

Monty said to Bryony, 'I should have guessed. A dragon! The only *mythical* creature in the room.'

CHAPTER THIRTY-NINE

Monty was in time to see the count scramble up the side of a building like a tree-creeper up an oak's trunk. Foreseeing such an escape, Monty had the day before taken the time to study architects' plans of the houses around City Hall, and he knew which of them had accessible stairways to the roofs. He banged on the door of an undertaker's parlour. The elderly stoat who ran this business had a weasel who lived on the premises, an apprentice who slept amongst the empty coffins. This young stripling had earlier been made aware of Monty's plans and was ready to wrench open the door and let the detective in.

'Thank you,' cried Monty, running past the

young jack. 'Won't forget this.' He took the stairs three at a time up the four-storey building, until he came to the door to the roof. This was already open in anticipation of his coming. Out onto the flat roof ran the detective, just in time to see the count leaping from the edge of that very same roof to another, sloping one. Monty dashed for the edge, flying across the gap, and was hard on the heels of the escaping vampire.

'You fool!' yelled Flistagga, his mask, like Monty's, discarded. 'You think you can outwit me? Outrun me? Never in a thousand years. That's how long I have lived – and more! A millennium. And my paws are still as nimble as when I first walked the earth. See, I am hardly out of breath and you, though close behind, are panting hard.'

Monty made no reply to this. It was true he was breathing harder than the vampire, but he was by no means fatigued. He kept himself in good physical order with brisk walks along the river. The vampire was powerful, with supernatural strength, but Monty, too, skipped around chimney pots and leapt over parapets and gables with the athleticism and alacrity of a wild weasel. In his small body were the ancient skills of his ancestors, hunters of old, prey that fled the weapons of men.

Ahead of him the black-cloaked shape hardly seemed to touch the tiles and skylights. The count could have been a dancer, a trapeze artist, or any of those professions which required balancing talents and lightness of foot. Monty was quick and sure in his movements, but he knew he was no match for the fleeing vampire.

But the idea was not to *catch* Flistagga – for what could a mere mortal weasel do against a supernatural stoat? The count was actually enjoying the chase; otherwise he would have turned and ended it in a few moments. He was enjoying showing off his prowess. What Monty was attempting to do was to drive Flistagga unwittingly in the direction of the river. He wanted to force the creature down to ground level, where hopefully the other three weasels would be able to overpower him. They were shadowing the pair at ground level, racing for all they were worth along the streets below the rooftop runners. When Flistagga fell to earth, they would be there with their stakes and hammers, to pin him to the ground through the heart before he could recover from his long drop.

'I'll have you yet,' shouted Monty into the wind. 'You will not see the end of *this* night.'

The vampire screeched with merriment at this speech. 'You pathetic mortal! When I am ready, I will turn and rip your backbone from your body and fling it to your friends down there. You think I haven't seen them? They're as clumsy as oxen thundering over boulder-strewn plains.'

Monty's heart sank. Was there no way to get the better of this undead stoat? Even now he realized the vampire was leading him towards the tall pointed roof of Ringing Roger. The clocktower's new height could now be reached by a supernatural leap from the dome of a new museum. Up the rounded curve of this dome went the vampire, onto the peak, then with a jump he was standing on the pinnacle of Ringing Roger.

He stood there, looking down on the dome where Monty had halted, unable to make the great vault from the lower building to the higher one.

'You see? Pathetic!' called Flistagga, bending down as if to tie his shoelaces. 'What can you do but watch in wonder as a superior being leaves you to stew in your own frustration. I think I *will* leave you. It amuses me to have you in the world, trying against all odds to capture me. One day I will come to you, through your window at night, and have you join the mammals of the undead.'

Monty remained silent. He was looking at the clockface. In a moment or two Ringing Roger would strike the hour of twelve. No creature on earth, supernatural or otherwise, could cling to the top of the new Ringing Roger when it was in full peal. Flistagga would be thrown to the street below, hopefully stunned long enough for those three weasels to drive their stakes through his foul and rotten vampire's heart.

'No, no,' chided Flistagga, waving a hooked claw at Monty. 'That will not do it. That will not do it at all. I can read your mind. You should not stare so at the hands approaching the devil's hour. You expect me to be shaken like a flea from this tower's back. It will never happen. I am leaving now, on the back of this night's wind.'

So saying, he stretched out his forelimbs.

Monty saw that the count had tied the corners of his large black cloak to his ankles. Now he had the wings of a bat and could glide like a kite over the river to safety on the human side. The vampire took off, just as the clockwork inside the tower gathered itself together and the hammer struck the mighty bell. Down he glided, past the dome, heading towards the far shore, where he would surely touch down with ease. He shrieked with base joy at having defeated the weasel detective.

However, as the vampire passed below him, Monty jumped, careless of the great height, interested only in grappling with his near-immortal foe. He dropped through the darkness and snatched at Flistagga, managing to grasp the creature's right hind leg.

Immediately the vampire dipped sharply, uttering an earsplitting, terrible shriek. Monty clung on. Now they were dropping down over the river. The tide was out and the mud was gleaming in the gaslights along the promenade. Monty reached up with his free paw and gripped the flapping edge of the cloak, pulling and tearing it. The vampire's makeshift wings now ripped asunder, parting the cloak down the middle.

'You stupid fool!' Flistagga yelled at Monty. 'Now we'll both end up in the river.'

They plummeted down.

Three weasels below rushed to the river bank to watch the pair descend from the night sky. Monty hit the mud with a loud *plop*, sinking at least half a metre down into the soft ooze. From the vampire stoat came a horrible scream, a death cry, which penetrated the night with its utter despair.

When Monty had recovered his breath, he managed to struggle to his paws in the thick sludge. Looking to where the vampire had fallen, he saw an old mooring post, its top weathered to a rough point. It was covered in green weed and algae, with barnacles all down one side, and some mussels clinging to its base. Halfway down the post, pierced through the heart, was the decaying corpse of a now unrecognizable being, withered and crumbling with every second. The remains of Count Flistagga were wasting away, dropping into the rising tide of the river, leaving nothing but rags behind.

Monty was trapped in the mud up to his thighs, but an excited trio on the bank soon roused a sleeping Jaffer Silke, who rescued the detective before the water reached his chin.

'Thanks, Jaffer,' said Monty, accepting a greasy towel with which to dry himself. 'I'm in your debt.'

'Glad to be of assistance, guv'nor,' replied the otter. 'Any time.'

Maudlin broke the silence on the walk back to the ballroom at City Hall. 'That was one of the most exciting things I've ever seen,' he said. 'I thought you were a goner for sure, Monty.'

'To be truthful,' replied the weasel detective, 'so did I.'

But Bryony said confidently, 'I knew you'd come through. You always do.'

'Likewise,' added Scruff.

When they reached City Hall, Monty was expecting a hullabaloo in the wake of the vampire's dramatic escape, but everyone seemed remarkably quiet. Most of the guests were walking around as if in a dream; they looked as if at any moment they would fall down into a deep slumber. The only mammals who seemed to have any life about them at all were the hosts, Mayor Poynt and his sister Sybil, both of whom were terribly upset by the night's events.

'See here, Sylver,' said the mayor, rounding on Monty. 'This is all your fault.'

But Monty's attention was elsewhere. He was standing by a plant whose blooms were, like most of the flowers in the room, half-open.

CHAPTER FORTY

Sybil said, 'I think, dear brother, the weasel did us a service. He did destroy the vampire. That was, after all, the reason why we had the ball in the first place. I just got carried away with it, that's all. You know how excited I get when I'm entertaining.'

The mayor patted her paw. 'There, there, dear, don't fret. Look, I'm feeling rather tired. I think I might have a nap.'

Monty frowned as he began to feel sleepy himself. 'What's going on here?' he said. He glanced at one of the plant pots. There were flies and other insects all lying dead around it. Dead – or *sleeping*?

'Quick, Bryony, Scruff, Maudlin . . .' Maudlin

was already lying on the floor, preparing to doze. 'Open the windows,' cried Monty. 'Get rid of the plants. Quickly now. There's not a second to lose.'

So saying he opened the nearest window himself and tossed a potted plant through it. The pot crashed onto the pavement outside, shattering into a hundred pieces. Bryony and Scruff asked no questions. They followed by example. Soon pots were flying through the windows one after another. Fresh air began to blow into the room, removing the poisonous fumes from Spindrick's plants. Crash followed smash, as Sybil's porcelain pots hit the cobbles below the windows.

'My vases! My pots!' she cried, distraught. 'They're Mole Dynasty. Three thousand years old. Priceless.'

The weasels took no notice of her. They continued to destroy her collection of precious porcelain. With every splinter, with every tinkle and clatter of flying shard, the princess's heart broke too. She gave a little moan and sank to the floor, sobbing quietly to herself.

The mayor was not prepared to let this monstrous piece of vandalism go without a fight. He struggled with Scruff, trying to wrest a large pot from him, but Scruff was a wiry creature and, though smaller than the chubby ermine, far fitter than most city stoats. He shrugged off the mayor and threw the last pot out into the night. He heard it hit the street with a satisfying explosion of breaking china.

'What?' shrieked the mayor. 'You thugs! You weasel Luddites! You've destroyed my sister's life. Do you know how much those pots cost me? A fortune! A king's ransom. I'll have you jailed for the rest of your natural spans. Constable Debbie! Chief Falshed!'

Chief Falshed, recovering now that the night air had blown away the fumes before they could do any serious damage, stepped forward with pawcuffs at the ready. But just at that moment someone appeared in the doorway, someone who had left the party early and had returned to see how his pawdiwork had fared. It was a weasel in an orang-utan mask with a piece of treated gauze tied over his nose and mouth. He stared about him then gave a snort of disgust. 'You've done it again, haven't you, cousin Montegu? Thwarted my best-laid plans. I curse your side of the family with great venom.'

'Who's this?' snapped the mayor. 'Another weasel vandal?'

'The worst of the lot,' replied Monty. 'It's my cousin Spindrick. He's recently returned from Tarawak with some toxic soil. If we hadn't thrown those pots through the window, you and your guests would be sleeping for the next decade. Look at those flies . . .'

The mayor looked. The flies were on their backs, legs stiffly in the air.

'Those insects breathed in the fumes and I doubt they'll come out of their slumber for many years to come.'

'How did you do it this time?' snapped Spindrick. 'Come on, let's hear you brag how you foiled your cousin's plans.'

347

Monty shrugged and seemed about to demur, but Bryony spoke for him in the end. 'He won't brag,' she said, 'you know him better than that, Spindrick. However, I will. It's basic, Spindrick, basic. Monty has kept me and our two associates informed all along.'

'That's us,' murmured Maudlin to Scruff. 'Associates.'

Bryony continued, 'Spindrick, you don't think you're the only weasel who reads *The Chimes*, do you? Monty read that article too, about Professors Jyde and Spred and their discovery of the special soil. He also read your Tarawak column. He guessed you were not in the rain forest for your health. He gave us some soil to analyse – unfortunately, I've been busy, but he put two and two together. I'm afraid he's far too clever for you, Spindrick.'

'Curses!' cried Spindrick, shaking a claw. 'What did I do to deserve such a respectable cousin? Am I the last of the outlaws? The last of the freedom fighters? Curse your eyes and liver, Montegu.'

The mayor cried, 'Arrest that orang-utan, Chief!'

Falshed stepped forward. 'Come quietly, Ginger,' he said.

But before Falshed could slap on the cuffs, Spindrick was gone, into the night.

Several nights later Monty was sitting in his favourite forelimbchair at 7a Breadoven Street. Bryony was sitting at the table nearby, working through some sums to do with her vet business. Jis McFail could be heard sweeping the hallway downstairs. The two other jack weasels, Scruff and Maudlin, were out on the town somewhere. Life was pleasantly quiet for a change.

Monty ceased chewing on his pipe. 'The toothless vampire voles were rounded up today,' he said. 'Falshed put them on a ship back to Slattland.'

'Oh really? Good. Be better for them to be back in their natural environment.'

'Yes, well – they were annoying respectable mammals by slobbering over their necks in back alleys.'

'Quite. What's happened to Spindrick? Has he been arrested?'

'No – Falshed couldn't catch him. Spindrick's skipped back to Tarawak. I expect he'll stay there until all the furore blows over. He's more of a pain in the neck than any vampire.' Monty clicked his teeth when he realized he'd made a joke. 'Pain in the neck,' he repeated.

'Yes, I heard it,' murmured Bryony, adding 2 to 6 and writing the answer down as 9 in blissful ignorance of the laws of mathematics. Weasels were not good at arithmetic. Even worse than they were at reading and writing. But she tried. She tried very hard. It was a good job there were learned stoats and badger clerks in the great city of Muggidrear to correct all the weasel errors. 'Very funny. And what about poor Sybil? Has she got over the terrible trauma of seeing her Mole Dynasty pot collection destroyed before her very eyes?'

'It'll take some time for her to recover from such an ordeal.'

'I suppose it will. Look, Monty –' she turned from the table with a sheaf of papers – 'would you mind checking my figures? I think they're all right, but you never know with me.'

Monty looked doubtfully at the rows of numbers. 'Jis McFail would be better than me. She's a stoat, after all.'

'So she is. She keeps her rent books to the farthing, doesn't she? I'll ask her. Thanks anyway, Monty.'

'You're welcome,' said the weasel detective, going back to chewing on his chibouque. 'Most welcome.'

THE END

ABOUT THE AUTHOR

Garry Kilworth was born in York but, as the son of an Air Force family, was educated at more than twenty schools. He himself joined the RAF at the age of fifteen and was stationed all over the world, from Singapore to Cyprus, before leaving to continue his education and begin a career in business, which also enabled him to travel widely.

He became a full-time writer when his two children left home and has written many novels for both adults and younger readers – mostly on science fiction, fantasy and historical themes. He has won several awards for his work, including the World Fantasy Award in 1992 and the Lancashire Book Award in 1955 for *The Electric Kid*.

THE WELKIN WEASELS
Book 2: Castle Storm

by Garry Kilworth

Rats! Hundreds and thousands of rats are pouring down from the northern marshes in Welkin to seize power from the stoat rulers. Sylver – the leader of a band of outlaw weasels – has no love for the vicious stoats but, with Welkin itself under threat, must offer a helping paw.

But stoat treachery serves only to speed him on his his real quest: to find the humans who mysteriously abandoned Welkin many years ago. With his small company of jacks and jills, he journeys south, through myriad adventures, to the dreys of the squirrel knights who live beneath the shadow of an ancient castle – *Castle Storm*.

The second title in a dramatic and marvellously inventive series, *The Welkin Weasels*.

ISBN 0 552 54574 3

All Transworld titles are available by post from:

Bookpost, PO Box 29, Douglas, Isle of Man, IM99 1BQ

Credit cards accepted. Please telephone 01624 836000, fax 01624 837033, Internet http://www.bookpost.co.uk or e-mail: bookshop@enterprise.net for details

Free postage and packing in the UK. Overseas customers: allow £1 per book (paperbacks) and £3 per book (hardbacks)